Cleese's gaze fixed briefly on the scar at the corner of Laurel's mouth.

She was levelheaded, practical, independent, sure of herself, smart, funny—how the *hell* had she gotten herself into the kind of mess he suspected? Yet underneath the strength and intelligence, and behind the grin in her eyes, he detected vulnerability.

Or maybe he was seeing what he wanted to see, Cleese thought derisively. He'd realized this morning that it had been a long time since anyone had needed him....

Dear Reader,

Welcome to another month of top-notch reading from Silhouette Intimate Moments. Our American Hero title this month is called *Keeper,* and you can bet this book will be one of *your* keepers. Written by one of your favorite authors, Patricia Gardner Evans, it's a book that will involve you from the first page and refuse to let you go until you've finished every word.

Our Romantic Traditions miniseries is still going strong. This month's offering, Carla Cassidy's *Try To Remember,* is an amnesia story—but you won't forget it once you're done! The rest of the month features gems by Maura Seger, Laura Parker (back at Silhouette after a too-long absence), Rebecca Daniels and new author Laurie Walker. I think you'll enjoy them all.

And in months to come, you can expect more equally wonderful books by more equally wonderful authors— including Dallas Schulze and Rachel Lee. Here at Silhouette Intimate Moments, the loving just gets better and better every month.

Happy reading!

Leslie Wainger
Senior Editor and Editorial Coordinator

Please address questions and book requests to:
Reader Service
U.S.: P.O. Box 1325, Buffalo, NY 14269
Canadian: P.O. Box 1050, Niagara Falls, Ont. L2E 7G7

AMERICAN HERO

KEEPER

Patricia
Gardner
Evans

Silhouette®

INTIMATE MOMENTS™

Published by Silhouette Books

America's Publisher of Contemporary Romance

SILHOUETTE BOOKS

ISBN 0-373-07559-6

KEEPER

Copyright © 1994 by Patricia Gardner Evans

Printed in U.S.A.

Books by Patricia Gardner Evans

Silhouette Intimate Moments

Flashpoint #151
Whatever It Takes #228
Summer of the Wolf #243
Quinn Eisley's War #493
Keeper #559

*Eisley and Company

Silhouette Books

Silhouette Summer Sizzlers 1991
"Over the Rainbow"

PATRICIA GARDNER EVANS

has lived in New Mexico all her life, and has traveled extensively throughout the West, exploring old ghost towns, Indian ruins and abandoned homesteads. She avoids housework by spending much of her free time outdoors fishing, and raising her own fruits and vegetables. She gets inspiration for her plots and characters from the land and people around her.

With thanks to Francis Ray and Sandy Steen; the Kelly boys, Duane and Aaron, distinguished bass fishermen; and the Bass Pro Shop for producing such a wonderfully entertaining catalog.

The gods do not subtract from the allotted span of men's lives the hours spent fishing.
—20th century B.C. Assyrian tablet

Time spent fishing cannot be deducted from a woman's life.
—20th century A.D. American bumper sticker

Chapter 1

The splash warned him that he was close. Pushing through the willows clogging the bank, Cleese Starrett looked up-river. A ray of sun breaking through the cloudy gauze overhead spotlighted the figure standing about thirty yards upstream, across the river, holding up a nice bass to admire it. He had to admire it, too. The poacher eased the fish back into the water, turned and faded back into the shadows, toward a log that had washed down and jammed against the shore. He started to yell, then glanced up at the dark, wet-looking cloud that was almost on top of them and squatted down on the bank instead. Fishing was about over for the day, and now that he knew the trespasser wasn't one of the rustlers reportedly working the area, there was no harm in letting the guy enjoy himself a little longer. Besides, he thought as he heard another loud splash as another nice bass tried to shake the hook, he'd like to get a closer look at what the guy was using.

In hip boots, a fishing vest with no empty pockets and a baseball cap pulled low, the man was shortish and dumpy.

He was too far away for his age and features to be clear, but he was probably retired, Cleese decided as the poacher released the bass, since he was fishing on a weekday, when most men should long since have been at work. He glanced at the watch on his right wrist. Including himself, he thought, but he made no move to stand up. The river song of water playing over smooth rock harmonized with the fresh green smell and color of returning life, and watches and time clocks suddenly didn't seem so important.

Shafts of sunlight rainbowed the faint fog hanging over the river, creating an oddly mystical effect. The mist blurred the lone figure out in the river a little, so that it, too, seemed not quite real, almost magical somehow. Certainly the man's skill was. He was using a fly rod instead of the spinning rod most bass fisherman preferred, and using it as if it were part of the flesh and bone of his arm, not a fancy stick stuck in his hand. It was generally accepted that expert fly casters were over six feet, because height gave the extra leverage needed to get out more line, and it wouldn't be bragging for Cleese to say he was an expert. In a contest between him and the man out in the river—unhooking yet another fish now, bigger than the other two—it would be no contest, but he would win because of size, not skill. He wouldn't want to go up against the man strictly on talent, not if serious money was involved.

Following along on the bank, Cleese stopped when the fisherman paused at the edge of a quiet backwater. Dull golden sparkles flickered from expanding circles in the green-glass water where a large fish was feeding. Leaning a shoulder against a leafing cottonwood, he squinted at the fly on the end of the chartreuse line as it flew behind the man to flirt with the reaching limbs of a willow, then danced away in a flat arc to land in the center of the concentric rings. He still couldn't figure out what the guy was using. All he could make out was the color of the fly—yellow. He would have guessed a Chug Bug or a Sneaky Pete, or maybe a Canary Hair Bug, if not for the metallic flash as the fly caught the thinning sunlight on one flight. The yellow fly buzzed back and forth again, landed, and had just begun a twitchy swim when what he was fast accepting as the inevitable happened: The water boiled, the fly disappeared, the poacher jerked back on the line and white foam exploded as the bass leaped clear, trying to throw the hook. He grunted to himself. This fish was the nicest one yet.

Around a bend, the Brazos briefly widened and slowed. The water was shallower, but it still foamed close to the tops of the man's hip boots as he waded across the river. Cleese kept pace on the shore as the man continued upstream and began working likely looking water. Although he was making no attempt to conceal himself, the fisherman didn't appear to have noticed him, his concentration distilled down to the few square yards of water in front of him and the feel of the line in his hand. Cleese's own attention was hardly less focused. He was peripherally aware of occasional rustlings in the brush behind him, as if a large animal were moving around, and once he glanced back, making a note to have a couple of hands check for strays, but his only real interest was the man in the river.

The fisherman had stripped about eight feet of line off his fly reel, leaving the fly close to the tip of the rod, then flipped it so that the bit of yellow landed a fraction of an inch from a stand of reeds growing out of the water, the kind of cover bass loved. Cleese had lost more lures and flies than he cared to remember, trying to perfect the technique that this guy had just made look like nothing harder than a shrug. The man didn't make the fatal mistake of overworking the fly, either, but let it float, twitching the rod tip occasionally, just a hair, to make the artificial fly sink the way a struggling live one would, to attract some attention. The attention came, although number five wasn't as big as the last one, he decided objectively.

He followed the poacher a few dozen yards upriver, wishing for the tenth time in as many minutes for a pair of binoculars. Never had he seen anything that could charm fish like the killer fly this guy was using. Whatever it was, he was going to buy a dozen. Crouching, he watched the man study the old oak that had fallen into the river several years before. Its drowned branches provided the kind of structure bass liked, but they were also a line-snagging nightmare. He whistled soundlessly as the yellow fly landed in the middle of the nightmare without so much as a ripple; the guy had the softest touch he'd ever seen. The fly swam across the open water, then crawled over an exposed branch as the fisherman kept up a slow, steady retrieve, walking it over snags. Cleese held his breath unconsciously as the fly caught on a splintered branch, then let it out as the bug was freed with a delicate twitch. Suddenly it disappeared in a flashing swirl of water. He sat back on his heels. Hooking the fish was easy; getting it out of the tree was the hard part. Now he'd see just how good this guy really was.

He was good. The fish jerked and thrashed and tried to run, but the poacher controlled it almost as if he knew what the bass was going to do before it did. He wound in line or let it out—a foot, then a fraction of an inch, then a couple of inches—over and over, and worked the rod tip to maintain exact tension on it, enough to keep the fish from diving and wrapping the line around a branch to snap it, but not so much that the fragile monofilament overstretched and broke. The fish jumped, shaking its head furiously, and line wound in in a blur. When the fish hit the water again, it was clear of the tree, and all that was left was reeling it in.

If he had any criticism of the man's skill, Cleese thought, watching him test the knot tying that magical fly to the line after letting the bass go, it was that he didn't jerk the rod as hard as he should to set the hook. He had nearly missed two fish because of it. When Cleese's father had begun teaching him the finer points of bass fishing, the first lesson had been "yank 'em till their eyes cross." He had a suspicion that the poacher had begun his education on trout, whose soft mouths required a much gentler hand than did a bass's iron jaw.

The man waded next toward a stump sticking up about three feet out of the river. The stump was all that remained of a huge cottonwood that had drowned when the river changed course. Over the years, one big bass after another had taken up residence in the hole at the base, staying until either caught or evicted by a younger, stronger competitor. The current resident had moved in about six years ago, a huge buck bass that had so far defeated all comers. His own running battle with the bass was a draw so far: He'd hooked the fish twice; the bass had gotten loose twice, throwing the hook the first time, breaking the line the second.

The fisherman's arm moved back to cast, and, on its own, Cleese's hand picked up one of the river cobbles near his knee. The poacher's arm snapped forward, sending the fly in a line drive toward the stump. It landed, and a split second later was swamped by the wave thrown up by the heavy rock splashing down a foot away.

In the first clumsy move Cleese had seen him make, the fly rod lurched and the chartreuse line went slack, then started drifting downstream as the poacher's head jerked around. Spotting Cleese standing on the bank, the man paused long enough to retrieve his line, then began splashing through the shallow water toward him. Thumbs tucked into the pockets of his Levi's, Cleese waited, watching himself grow larger in the mirrored lenses of the sunglasses the man wore.

His thumbs came out of his pockets as he stood straighter. The *woman* wore.

Between the sunglasses and the mold-green baseball cap, he couldn't see much of her face beyond the mouth and chin. Both defined annoyance at the moment, but even tight and set, the mouth was finely, almost delicately, shaped. Definitely a woman's mouth.

She halted just out of reach, the fly rod aimed like a sword at his gut. "Do you have something against fishing?"

Definitely a woman's voice, too. The question was sca-
thingly polite; the voice was low-pitched and slightly husky,
as if she had a cold.

"Not at all, not even when it's my river and my fish."

She took off the sunglasses, hooking them in the neck of
the T-shirt she wore under a flannel shirt and the zipped
fishing vest, and the ground under his boots shifted subtly,
as if it were a little spongy. "I didn't see any No Trespass-
ing signs."

He'd never seen eyes like that. Rimmed in some darker
color, and with long, dark lashes, they were such a light blue
that they looked nearly white, with a curious, almost opal-
ine glow. "The signs are posted every hundred feet along the
road."

"Every hundred feet?" She evidently wasn't easily per-
suaded.

He nodded. He wished she would take off her hat so that
he could get a look at her hair. From the little bit showing
under the cap and the few wisps that had escaped being
tucked up, it looked red.

"How far down the river?" Doubt edged into her voice.

"Three miles, give or take a few hundred feet." He swiveled automatically, pointing out the direction, and the rod
tip tracked him, then held steady again, still *en garde,* when
he turned back around.

"Ah." She nodded to herself in understanding. "I came
into the river at Arsenic Spring. I wasn't far enough up—"

"You came in at Arsenic Spring?" The question was
sharper than he intended, but if she'd come in at Arsenic
Spring, that meant she'd walked close to three and a half
miles up the isolated—sometimes dangerously isolated—
river, alone and unprotected.

His tone earned him a wary look. "Yes. I'm sorry. I
didn't intentionally mean to poach."

Her mouth softened with the apology. Her lips, bare of
lipstick, were a natural deep-rose color. The top lip was a
little fuller than the bottom, giving her mouth a startlingly

lush look, and the desire to see her out of the hat and boots and vest was as strong as it was suddenly urgent. "Don't worry about it. In fact, why—"

He'd been taking a step toward her when something thumped him hard in the back. Puzzled, he turned around.

She wasn't alone, after all. The dog—it must be a dog, because he couldn't think what else it might be—looked like it had been put together in a laboratory somewhere in Transylvania. It had the legs of an Irish wolfhound, the body of a rottweiler on steroids, the head and ruff of a giant chow, the teeth of a grizzly bear and a rusty wire brush for fur. All the beast lacked was a bolt on either side of its neck. He wouldn't need to send any men to look for strays, he thought absently; the rustlings he had heard had been the animal stalking him. Black lips curled upward, giving him a better view of its teeth than he needed, as electric-yellow eyes dropped significantly to the front of his jeans, and he felt an involuntary shriveling.

"Frank! It's okay, boy! Come here."

Giving him a final warning leer, the huge animal lumbered toward his mistress. *Frank?* The name couldn't be a coincidence. His eyes narrowed on the woman as the dog took up guard duty in front of her. Was a slightly off-center sense of humor hiding under that god-awful hat?

"I am sorry about poaching. You can be sure it won't happen again. Now, if it's okay with you, we'll be on our way," she said, already turning away.

It wasn't okay with him. "You'll be soaked before you get back to your car," he warned casually.

Pausing, she glanced up at the black clouds overhead. Obligingly, a few fat, cold raindrops spattered down. "Come on." He started toward a faint trail leading back to the road. "I'll give you a ride back to your car."

When he didn't hear her immediately following, he glanced back to see her still eyeing the clouds, no doubt gauging her best chance—the weather or him. The weather lost. After a few seconds, he heard her clumping behind him in her hip boots.

A few minutes later, he opened the tailgate of the faded green pickup parked in a wide spot in the dirt road. "You can throw your stuff in the back." The invitation was more than routine courtesy; he hoped it would work as a subliminal suggestion, and the vest and boots would be part of the "stuff." To help the suggestion along, he reached for her fly rod—a slow, careful reach since it had to be over Frank's head. The dog kept himself between his mistress and the stranger at all times. All the way up the trail, Cleese had felt the yellow eyes on his back, as if the creature were daring him to make a move, wrong or any other kind.

"Thanks." She handed over the rod—custom-made, and costing what would be two weeks' pay for most people—and suddenly he remembered the killer fly he had been so anxious to see. He examined the tiny yellow contraption hooked on one of the eyelets on the rod. "Looks a little like a Slippery Clyde," he muttered.

"Closer to a Weedless Willard, actually. I started with that design, used fluorescent-yellow maribou instead of plain, and replaced the white hackles with a propeller. I've had pretty good luck with it."

He gave her a dry look. "I noticed."

A smile lurked in her swift sideways glance, just enough of one to whet his appetite for more. The suggestion had worked. Braced against the side of his truck, she was tugging off one hip boot. The olive neoprene slid down, revealing snug and soft faded denim, a nicely rounded hip, and what looked to be a great leg. Clearing his throat silently, he concentrated on the mutant Weedless Willard.

Spinner flies had been around for years, although he'd never seen one made up for bass before. It was one of those ideas that were so simple no one ever thought of them. The silver flash of the miniature propeller would look like a minnow to a hungry bass. If that didn't get the fish's attention, either the eye-popping color or the vibrations of the tiny rotating blade would. No wonder she had "pretty good luck" with it. As he set the rod down carefully, he saw that one boot was off and in the truck, but the other one seemed to be stuck.

"Grab the door handle." After a split second's hesitation, she wrapped both hands around the pitted chrome handle and raised her foot. As he started to reach for the boot, there was a growl and a rerun of teeth, in case his memory needed refreshing. At her murmur, the animal backed away, but not out of range. Keeping one eye on the teeth, Cleese picked up her booted foot and jerked, and the boot slid fee. Make that two great-looking legs.

"Thank you." There was more of a smile this time. Out of the boots, she was a little shorter; she would just about fit under his chin—a nice height for dancing and...other things. Her hand reached for the zipper of the vest, and he blindly dropped the boot in his hand into the truck. She shrugged out of the vest, exposing a thin open flannel shirt and the T-shirt underneath, which advertised "Phil's Live Bait and Sushi Bar." The vest had also hidden a narrow waist, surprisingly broad shoulders and high, full breasts.

Taking the vest, he busied himself with finding room for it in the forty-odd square feet of empty truck bed until his Levi's fit again. Her unconscious clothes-on striptease had had an effect, he thought in rueful consternation, that no professional had ever achieved taking hers off.

He glanced toward her as he straightened up. Now the hat, he commanded silently. "Will your dog ride in the back of the truck?" The three of them crowded into the cab, especially with Frank in the middle, didn't have much appeal.

She nodded. "He's used to that." He stood aside as she patted the tailgate. "Come on, Frank."

Abandoning his guard post with obvious reluctance, the huge dog made a short leap that was more like a long step up into the back of the pickup. Before he could grab it, she lifted the heavy tailgate with no apparent strain and slammed it shut. The rain was holding off, but the sharp breeze that had sprung up wasn't. Cleese had suspected she was cold when he saw her button the flannel shirt, and his suspicions were confirmed when the breeze gusted and a hard shiver racked her slender body. Taking the lead as they started down the side of the truck, he opened the passenger door and grabbed the blue rag sweater lying on the seat.

"Here. Put this on." For a second she looked as if she were going to argue, but another shiver settled the question. "I'm Cleese Starrett, by the way," he said as she took the sweater.

"Laurel Drew," she said with the best smile yet as she took off the baseball cap.

The sun chose that moment to make its last stand against the advancing clouds and shot down a bolt of pure light. What color had he said her hair was? *Red?* What a puny description. It was cinnamon, sorrel, copper, gold—all shimmering together as it fell over her shoulders while the ground seemed to turn to quicksand.

Finally he could see her face clearly, too. Her skin was fresh and clear, a light honey gold that contrasted with the rose of her mouth and made it even riper-looking. The only flaw was a small scar at the corner of her mouth. It was a perfect circle, and absently he wondered what had caused it. Her eyebrows were dark, like her lashes, making her odd-colored eyes even more exotic. Narrow and fine-boned, with delicate features, her face had the look of a beautiful cameo; then she smiled, and the beautiful, cold, lifeless cameo became something better—warm, and full of life and intelligence and humor.

He held out his hand for her hat so that she could put on the sweater and tossed it onto the seat of the truck. With any luck, Cleese thought, she wouldn't put it back on. She pulled the sweater over her head, tousling her hair a little more into a disorder that was somehow sexy and innocent at the same time. His sweater swallowed her, effectively shrouding her body and hanging halfway down her thighs, and he almost wished he hadn't given it to her. Shoving up the sleeves, she shook her head to shake the hair out of her eyes, then ran a hand through it, neither gesture coy or designed to attract his attention. She didn't need to, he thought wryly; she already had it, every atom.

She smiled up at him again. "Thanks. I didn't think it would be so cold today."

"You're welcome, Laurel." He said her name so that he could feel it on his tongue. *Laurel.* The letters flowed together sweetly, none of them harsh or abrasive; the name suited her exactly.

The blackening sky overhead rumbled, echoed by a spate of quarter-size raindrops. "I think we better get a move on," he said, reaching swiftly past her to pull her door open wider.

And she flinched.

Why had she done that? Laurel sat frozen on the bench seat, as astonished as she was furious with herself. On the night she had walked out of the big house in Houston, she had promised herself that she would never cringe before another man. And she hadn't—until today, for absolutely no reason. His hand hadn't come near her.

In the side mirror, she followed the progress of the man rounding the back of the pickup. Any resemblance was negligible. Both men were tall and dark-haired, but that was all. Where Paul Falco had been thin, Cleese Starrett was lean, his broad shoulders, chest, arms and long legs powerfully muscled, his size and strength clear but not obvious. He didn't have a narcissistic interest in clothes, either. Like his truck, his clothes had been chosen for practicality, not show. Her eyes cut to the other mirror to keep him in view as he came up along the driver's side. He wore old shrink-to-fits that proved there was, indeed, sometimes truth in advertising, rough-out cowboy boots and a heavy blue denim shirt, open at the neck. With the beat-up clothes and beat-up truck, he could have passed for a big, good-looking cowboy, if not for the glint of the gold watch she'd seen under his right cuff, the kind that kept perfect time for only the price of a good economy car. His face had nudged at the back of her mind, too; she knew she had seen him before, but in another context, other clothes, and when he introduced himself, she realized where.

Anyone who read the Fort Worth papers knew who Cleese Starrett was, and she wasn't illiterate. Cattle, oil, shipping, real estate and a silver mine, if she remembered right, and probably several more enterprises she didn't remember—Cleese Starrett was a big fish in the Fort Worth-Dallas business pool. Most likely pools elsewhere, too, she thought as he reached for the door handle. Underneath that Texas drawl was a tone that was used to being listened to, whether the boardroom was in Fort Worth, Dallas or New York.

He was a big fish in the social pool, too. A good half of the newspaper mentions and photographs involved a charity ball, opening night of the symphony or opera season, or one fancy fund-raiser or party or another. The word *bachelor* was usually worked into the caption, too. She couldn't blame photographers for spending film on him, though. No man had a right to be that good-looking. He wasn't storybook, handsome-prince good-looking; he was real-life, real-man good-looking, and nature had accessorized him perfectly. His thick hair was dark brown, straight, short and cut, not "styled." He wore it parted, and a few strands fell over his wide forehead. Under eyebrows as dark as his hair, and as thick and straight, his eyes were a clear golden-brown, the color of old amber. His mouth was well shaped, maybe a little hard, but he had a killer smile. With a square jaw, broad cheekbones and a strong, straight nose, his face had pure masculine planes and showed signs that, despite his wealth, his life hadn't been one of idle ease or—glancing over as he opened the door, she saw again the long, faded scar just below his hairline on his temple—entirely safe.

He slid behind the wheel and slammed the door shut, and the roomy cab of the truck became abruptly smaller, yet the closeness didn't bother her. There was something very... comforting about his size and strength.

Which did nothing to explain why she had flinched, Laurel thought uneasily. She had worked long and hard to rid herself of irrational fears, and, until ninety seconds ago, she'd been certain that she had been successful. She could only hope he hadn't noticed. She had enough to worry about without worrying about being taken for a neurotic fool.

He started the truck, but instead of putting it in gear, he turned and regarded her silently, and Laurel braced herself.

"Do you make a habit of getting into trucks with total strangers?"

His tone was casual, almost light, although he wasn't smiling. Laurel relaxed; he hadn't noticed. "Actually, you're the first," she said wryly. "And you aren't exactly a total stranger. M. J. Tinnin is one of my best friends. I believe you and her husband fish together?"

"Yeah, Jack and I do some fishing together," Cleese confirmed absently. Her eyes were as clear and direct as her answer, confirming that it hadn't been some stranger who was responsible for that disturbing flinch. He hadn't thought it was—although she'd been as wary as any woman should be, she had accepted his offer—but he had wanted to be absolutely sure. He felt relief, because the kind of attack by a stranger that would cause that kind of automatic reaction was all too easy to imagine, but the relief was minor, because her answer confirmed what he had already been certain of: The flinch was a conditioned reflex. He'd tried to convince himself that he had misjudged the distance and come closer to her than he'd intended, but he hadn't been successful, because it just wasn't true. She had cringed like a small, scared animal expecting to be hit because someone she knew intimately had taught her to expect it. He swallowed as he put the truck in gear, but the foul taste didn't leave his mouth. The impotent fury didn't moderate much, either.

"You live in Fort Worth?" he asked, shifting into second.

"Yes, in the university area."

Maybe he was living right after all, Cleese decided. "How long have you lived there?" He knew she hadn't grown up there, because of her "Anywhere, U.S.A." accent.

"I moved there about ten years ago, after college. I left for a couple of years, but I moved back six years ago." Unconsciously she settled into the sweater as if it were a favorite old quilt wrapped around her. It smelled like him, she realized absently, that same soap-and-spice scent.

"What do you do in Fort Worth?" So far she hadn't seemed to notice that he was doing all the asking and she was doing all the answering.

She really ought to ask him a few questions, just as a matter of principle. "I'm an illustrator—children's books, mostly."

He nodded while silently cursing the conscientiousness of the county road grader as he shifted into third gear. Right now he would give last quarter's profits for a few potholes and washboards. He was driving as slowly as he dared without being obvious, which meant he had at most ten minutes to find out as much about her as he could—which was about ten years too short to find out all he wanted. "Are you single? Divorced?" He was capable of finesse, Cleese thought disgustedly; he just didn't have time for it right now.

"Widowed."

Her answer startled him. Somehow, one never expected a young woman to be widowed. She didn't look to be more than twenty-five, although the comment about moving to Fort Worth after college ten years ago indicated she was in her early thirties. He sneaked another look under the guise of checking the side mirror mounted on her door. She had announced her marital status with no indication of how she felt about it. A bruise-colored shadow passed over her cheek as they passed under an overhanging tree. But maybe that told him something after all.

"I'm divorced," he said absently, feeling her curious look.

"Why didn't you ask me if I was married? Not all married women wear wedding rings."

He glanced down at her hands, narrow, graceful and bare of rings, then back up, catching her eyes and holding them. "You're not married or living with anyone because no man allows his woman to traipse around the boondocks by herself," he said flatly. That earned him a pair of raised eyebrows, which he met with a level look before turning his attention back to the road. He was a chauvinist; he admitted it, and he was working on it, but if thinking a woman had no business running around out in the wild by herself was chauvinistic, then he guessed he would stay one and be damned.

There were a few words in his statement Laurel knew she ought to take exception to. *Allows,* for starters, and certainly *his woman* deserved a comment or two, but it would be quibbling over semantics, because, as much as she didn't want to admit it, he was right—she shouldn't have been fishing by herself. There was a thump behind her, and she turned, smiling at the yellow eyes that had been looking steadily through the back window, a worried frown between them. Frank wasn't foolproof protection, good though he was; she had done something stupid, and she knew it.

As she turned back, her glance lingered for a second or two on the gun rack across the rear window. She had concluded that any pickup sold in Texas came with one as standard equipment, but this one held not a rifle but a custom-made fly rod. He had said something about "my river and my fish," which she had taken for a statement of general ownership, but maybe it was more personal than that; and then there was that rock, when a simple shout would have sufficed.

"How long have you been fishing for the bass by the stump?"

Out of the corner of his eye, Cleese had seen her study his fishing rod, then slant him a speculative look, so the innocent tone didn't fool him for a second. He should have known he would pay for that crack. "About six years."

"Have you caught him?"

He glanced over at her. "I've hooked him. Twice."

"Mmm..." She nodded thoughtfully, then slanted him another look. "That explains the rock."

He chuckled reluctantly, then, after a minute, returned to the previous topic. "Why do you go fishing alone?" He should drop it, Cleese knew, but she seemed like a sensible woman; she had to know, Frank or no Frank, how she was risking herself. Why had she done something so damned stupid? He caught himself leaning ever so slightly to the right. She was wearing some subtle scent, sweetish, elusive, something he didn't recognize, something that teased a man closer to get a better whiff.

She gave him a sardonic look. "How many women do you know who like to get up at four in the morning to stand in cold water all day?"

His wry grin conceded her point. "One, now."

"I don't really fish much anymore, but all week the weather has been perfect.... Spring is finally here." Her shrug and small smile were a little sheepish. "I couldn't resist."

He understood, because he had been similarly afflicted all week, but her problem was bigger than a simple case of spring fishing fever. It wasn't right that someone who liked to fish—and was so obviously good at it—couldn't, for want of a "companion." Even thought, the word brought a grimace. He had the solution to her problem, but it was probably, he conceded reluctantly as he glanced over to where she was keeping very carefully to the few square feet of seat by the door, too soon to present it. "Did you learn to fish when you were a little girl?"

"When I was three." Laurel relaxed into the seat as she chuckled softly. "The first time a fish bit on my line, I dropped the pole overboard in eighty feet of water. My father didn't know whether to laugh or cry."

He grinned over at her. "I was four and capsized the boat my dad and I were in." Her laugh was a little husky, too, like her voice. He caught himself leaning closer again. "Where did you learn to fish?" Somewhere up north, he bet himself, where trout, not bass, were the staple fish.

"Scotland." At his look of surprise, Laurel explained, "My father was in the navy, almost always assigned overseas, so I grew up fishing all over."

Well, Scotland was north, and there were plenty of trout there, Cleese thought with a silent laugh. She was just full of surprises. He eased off on the gas, slowing the truck another mile or two an hour. "Did you ever trout-fish in New Zealand?"

"My dad and I spent two weeks on South Island once. I caught the biggest rainbow I've ever seen—nearly ten pounds. Have you ever been there?" A yawn caught her by surprise, and she barely smothered it in time. How bizarre! Despite the pickup's bump-bounce-and-bang ride and the fact that the man was a stranger, she'd gotten so comfortable and cozy that, with no effort at all, she could go right to sleep! Hastily she forced her reluctant body to sit up straight.

"Yeah, a couple of years ago," he said, hiding a grin. Getting up at four in the morning was catching up with her. "I fished North Island and caught a few browns about the same size." It was just like talking fishing with a man, although, Cleese reflected sardonically, he couldn't recall ever wanting to pull any sleepy man over and ease his head down on his lap. A mental image came without warning, and he found himself shifting uncomfortably. "Your mother didn't like to fish?"

"She died when I was small." Laurel shook her head with a rueful smile. "I really don't remember her." She looked away, frowning a little. There were people who had known her for several years who didn't know as much about her as he did after only a few minutes.

"Mine died when I was fourteen," he said matter-of-factly. "Your dad's retired now?"

"He died eight years ago."

Her voice was soft and a little sad. Cleese caught and held her eyes. "I lost my dad six years ago."

There was the mandatory sympathy in her quiet "I'm sorry," but in her eyes he saw empathy—she was sorry for both of them.

He turned his attention back to the road. "Do you—"

She raised her hand abruptly, pointing to the dark blue vehicle parked in a turnout just ahead. "That's mine."

He shot her a surprised look as he pulled up behind her car. Instead of the station wagon or minivan he'd expected, she drove the closest a four-by-four came to being a hot rod. Half-angry, he turned off the key and stamped on the emergency brake. He still had too many unanswered questions. While she was opening up the back of her vehicle, he dropped the tailgate on his truck, standing back as Frank stepped down, then, after giving him a long assessing look, leaped into the back of hers.

The rain chose that moment to finally make good its threat, and huge, ice-cold drops began pelting down. With a startled gasp, she ran back to his truck and gathered up her rod and vest while he grabbed her boots. Carefully he reached past the dog to stow the hip boots as she threw the vest in the back, then broke the rod down rapidly and slid the pieces into a black metal case. After closing up the back, he started around to the driver's door, expecting her to be right behind him. Instead, she dashed back to his truck. By the time he caught up with her, she had opened the passenger door and was reaching for the bottom of the sweater.

"Leave it on," he said quickly. "You'll get cold. I can get it back later." Having to return it would be a reason to have to see him again.

She ignored him, and for a brief second the flannel shirt she wore pulled tight over her breasts as she dragged the sweater off. Giving him a quick smile, she tossed his sweater on the seat and grabbed her baseball cap. "That's okay. I'm all warmed up now."

So was he, Cleese thought wryly, watching her jam the disreputable hat on her head and slam the door.

The rain began falling harder. "Thanks very much for the ride," she said hurriedly, "and for being such a good sport about the poaching."

Her sprint for her car caught him flat-footed. "Wait!" He started after her. "I didn't get your phone number." He'd already memorized her license plate, but if she trusted him enough to give him her phone number, it would make his next move easier. And there was definitely, he promised himself, going to be a next move, and a next, and several more after that.

"I'm in the phone book—L. J. Drew, on Wabash!" she yelled back as she jumped into her car. The door slammed, the engine roared, and it seemed like no more than a couple of seconds before the four-by-four was disappearing down the road, a hand appearing in a hasty wave through the window.

He watched the patch of dark blue against the wet gray road grow smaller. With the vagaries of the spring weather, the sun was out again, and the falling raindrops caught the light as they fell through the air, looking like tiny strobe flashes against the dark cloud background. The effect was strangely surreal, and long after the dark blue vanished through the flashing curtain of water and light, he stood in the cold rain, not entirely convinced she had been real.

Closing the back door behind her, Laurel dropped the flannel shirt she had been wearing on the washing machine before crossing the small utility room into the kitchen. She no longer needed the house to be the sanctuary it once had been, but she still felt a distinct pleasure and peace every time she entered it. Perhaps because it was the first *home* she had ever had. She dropped her purse on the square oak table, then continued through the kitchen to a small alcove off the hall. The message light on her answering machine was blinking, and she pressed the replay button. She listened to the first, jotted a return number down on a pad during the second message, then waited for the beep and the start of the third. She listened briefly, and then, with a hiss of annoyance, jabbed the skip button and went on to the fourth.

Hours later, she made a last trip through the house, checking doors. As she passed the alcove on her way to bed, the cordless phone beside the answering machine rang, the sudden sound in the midnight silence making her jump. She stared at the phone as it warbled again, Frank watching her with a puzzled frown, as if wondering why she didn't pick it up. In the midst of the third ring, she did, and pressed the button to answer.

"Hello."

After a few seconds, she pressed the off button, set the handset down gently, then, with a vicious yank, jerked the plug out of the phone jack.

Chapter 2

"Well, excuuuse me!"

"Your behavior is inexcusable. Stop it!"

You know you're too dumb to do that.

"I'm not interested in your opinion. Stop it!"

"It's your fault! If you wouldn't make me so mad..."

"I'm not responsible for your behavior. Stop it!

"You're overreacting. You always blow everything out of proportion."

"No, I'm not. You're treating me badly. Stop it!"

"What's the matter with you? Can't you take a joke?"

"You're not funny. Stop it!"

"Shut up! You never say anything worth listening to."

"S-stop it. I will not tol— I— I will— I'm sorry."

Laurel smiled at the young blond woman, who looked like the all-American cheerleader, except for the fading bruises. "You have nothing to be sorry for, Cindy, nothing to apologize for. Just try it again. Olivia, will you repeat your line?"

Olivia Jaxon, as dark as Cindy Thomas was blond, said her line again. Cindy opened her mouth to reply, but nothing came out, and she shook her head helplessly. This was only the group's fourth meeting, and ingrained behavior wasn't changed in a few hours, Laurel reminded herself.

The gray-haired woman across the table spoke. "How do you feel when your husband tells you to shut up, Cindy?"

"I feel—" Cindy's pretty face wrinkled into a hurt scowl "—angry, because I'm not stupid. I do have things to say that are worth listening to."

"That's right, you do. You should feel angry. You're not stupid," Hattie Sparks said briskly. "Use the energy from that anger to let him know how you feel."

Like all the therapists working at the center, Hattie Sparks was a volunteer, donating a dozen of her hundred-and-ten-dollar hours each week. She tolerated no self-pity, cut through self-deception like a blunt chain saw, and was, under the no-nonsense brusqueness, completely kind. She was happily married—something preferred, but not mandatory, for a counselor—to a man as short and chubby as she was tall and lanky. Yet Laurel had long suspected that at some point in her life Hattie had had firsthand experience with the same kind of abuse the center's clients did. A very private person, she had never even hinted at it, and no one else who worked at the center had ever voiced similar suspicions, but Laurel was certain. Maybe it takes one to recognize another, she thought ironically. Did Hattie ever feel dishonest, too, as she sat around the table, listening to others recount the intimate, painful details of their lives, something she was unable to bring herself to do? Laurel frowned suddenly, remembering a conversation in a beat-up pickup yesterday, an uncharacteristically revealing—for her—conversation. What was there about him that had drawn her out so extraordinarily?

Olivia repeated her lines once more, and Cindy responded, this time easily and with conviction. "Stop it! I will not tolerate being spoken to that way."

"Attagirl, Cindy! That's telling him," Olivia said with a broad grin. There was general, laughing agreement from the others, relaxing the stomach-crawling tension that always built up during these sessions.

The role-playing continued around the table, each woman taking her turn as the recipient, then the dispenser, of the verbal abuse. All of the women were married to men who regularly beat them up without laying a hand on them, using words as weapons, although two of them, Laurel thought starkly, *had* had hands—and feet—laid on them. Hattie used the role-playing in almost every group session, and the first time Laurel had seen it, she'd had serious doubts about it. Turning the victim into the victimizer, even for a few minutes, would seem to run the risk of giving the women a taste of the power their abusers enjoyed over them, with the likelihood that they would, to alleviate their sense of powerlessness, become abusers themselves—of their children—perpetuating the sickening cycle. Hattie had asked her to suspend judgment for a month, and, when the end of the month came, she had realized that her fears had been groundless.

"Oh, come on! You get upset over every little thing. It isn't that bad," Mary Cruz, the short, cute, dark-haired woman next to Laurel, told her in a trivializing tone. Hattie included cues for tone and body language in her scripts, but the women didn't really need them. They knew them all already, by heart.

"Yes, it *is* bad. Stop it!" Laurel answered. Hattie wrote a new script for each session, using the very insults the women reported had been used against them. It kept the scripts fresh, so that they didn't become meaningless and rote, but, more importantly, it helped the women to hear the ugly words for what they were—lies. The whole exercise was aimed at reconditioning their responses so that instead of feeling ashamed, worthless or hopeless, accepting disrespect or undeserved blame, the women would respond to the lies by firmly refusing to believe them, telling their abusers emphatically and confidently to stop it.

Laurel looked at the middle-aged woman next to her, Allene Watts. "You always screw everything up," she said witheringly. Allene had reported last session that it was one of her husband's favorite insults.

"I've heard all I want to from you. Stop it!" Allene didn't wither, and she didn't have to consult her script for the response, either, Laurel noted with approval.

Instead of switching roles and delivering her next lines to the woman on her right, Allene glanced at Hattie. Hattie nodded slightly. Laurel understood Allene's hesitation. Lina Renko, tall and thin, with dull brown hair and duller brown eyes, was the newest member of the group, and the most emotionally fragile woman Laurel had ever seen. The first time around, she had been unable to read her lines, and Hattie had skipped over her without comment. Lina really wasn't ready for group therapy yet. She needed more one-on-one counseling to build up her confidence before she had to cope with a half-dozen strangers, and Hattie wouldn't have accepted her ordinarily, but Lina's husband was contesting her divorce suit. What promised to be a very ugly trial was scheduled to begin in a few weeks, and both Lina's lawyer and the therapist who worked with her privately agreed that she would never hold up on the witness stand as she was now. She would break down, proving Charles Renko's claim that his wife was mentally incompetent and couldn't possibly leave the man who took such loving, self-less care of her.

Allene leaned toward Lina, putting them almost nose to nose, crossing the invisible physical boundary everyone maintained around themselves. It was part of the abuser's standard repertoire to invade his victim's physical space, just as he invaded her psychological and emotional space. Lina didn't pull back in a normal reaction, but just sat, as motionless and spiritless as a broken doll. "You stupid bitch, you'd lose your head if it wasn't attached," Allene said in a tone of extreme disgust. Lina's private therapist had given Hattie a list of Charles Renko's favorites; that was one of the milder ones.

Laurel knew they were all holding their breath, waiting to see if Lina would respond this time. She looked down at her script, and then, after several long seconds, read in a dead monotone, "You're insulting me. Stop it." She looked at Hattie anxiously, like a small puppy that hoped it had done whatever it was supposed to well enough that it wouldn't be kicked again. It was the first expression to cross her face since the tiny, painful smile when she had been introduced. "I'm sorry."

"You have nothing to be sorry for," Hattie said forcefully, repeating the center's unofficial mantra. "I'm sorry" was the most common phrase in the vocabularies of practically every woman who walked through the center's front door, insidiously ingrained from the constant, undeserved blame they heard in the relentless streams of verbal abuse that poured over them until they thought they were responsible for everything from the weather to the price of cigarettes. One of the things Hattie and the other counselors worked hardest on was the removal of those *I'm sorry*s, striving to make the women see that they were *not* to blame for the way they were treated, they *didn't* deserve the insults, the threats, the accusations, the belittlings, the black eyes, the broken arms and ribs. Those two words were, Laurel knew, very hard to expunge; it had taken her nearly two years.

Hattie pursued the subject. "What do you think you did or didn't do that you should be sorry for, Lina?"

Lina Renko stared at her with a slight, bewildered frown. "I... don't know. Nothing, I guess."

Hattie nodded her head vigorously. "That's right! Nothing! Not one thing," she repeated deliberately. "Now, you say the next line to Olivia."

Lina turned to Olivia Jaxon. "Nag, nag, nag. All you do is bitch, Bitch." The lines were original with Mary Cruz's husband, who thought himself quite a wit.

"You may not talk to me like that," Olivia answered with calm authority. "Stop it!"

Laurel, watching Lina Renko instead of Olivia, saw another puzzled frown. The role-playing portion of the session over, Hattie started to ask for reports on how things had progressed at home since the last session. "Do you have a question, Lina?" Lina had learned it was safer not to ask questions, Laurel was sure.

"Well, it—just sounds like she's talking to a child!" Lina blurted out, then covered her mouth with her hand, appalled at her own audacity.

"She *is* talking to a child. You all—" Laurel's sweeping glance encompassed the table "—talk to a child because you are married to one." She focused again on Lina. "It may say your husband is forty-three on his driver's license—" silently she thanked Hattie for that bit of information on Charles Renko "—but that's his physical age. Emotionally, he's a two- or three-year-old, behaving the way a two- or three-year-old behaves—irrationally. That's why you use authority, not rational explanations, to make him stop. Two- and three-year-olds don't respond to rational explanations, but they do respond to authority—a calm, firm voice telling them to stop doing whatever they're doing that's wrong. That's why Hattie writes 'Stop it!' in the scripts, why you'll practice saying it—" she smiled at Lina "—until you say it in your sleep."

She saw the clear doubt in Lina's eyes and, as she looked around the table, in more eyes, as well. "Mary, you teach three-year-olds at your preschool," she said, addressing Mary Cruz. "What do you do if one of them starts throwing blocks at you when you tell her it's time to pick up?"

"I tell her to stop it," Mary Cruz said, without having to think about it.

"Do you explain why she shouldn't throw blocks at you?"

Mary shook her head. "She knows why not—because they can hurt me, but three-year-olds don't care about anybody else. At that age, it's still 'Me, me, me.'"

"That's right. All three-year-olds care about is themselves." Laurel emphasized her words with another look around the table.

Hattie joined in. "Cindy, does your little girl ever call you 'dummy' or 'stupid' when she's mad at you?"

"Sometimes. I tell her to stop it. She knows she's not supposed to—to call me that." The brief break came, Laurel knew, when Cindy realized that she was allowing her husband to do what she wouldn't allow her daughter to do: call her names.

"So you use 'Stop it!' when your husband starts talking ugly, the same way you're supposed to say 'No!' to a rapist?" Olivia asked slowly.

"Yes," Laurel said, knowing what was coming next.

"But 'No' doesn't always work with rapists," Allene pointed out.

"No, it doesn't," Hattie agreed, "and 'Stop it' may not work with your husband."

"Then what do you do?" There was an underlying note of abject resignation in Cindy's question.

"Then you say 'goodbye,'" Hattie said flatly. "You make sure that you always have some money tucked away, and car keys where you can get at them."

Laurel saw from the stunned expressions around the table that Hattie's blunt practicality was not the answer they had expected or could accept—yet.

"Men!" someone muttered.

"Not all men," she said with quiet conviction.

The session ended a long thirty minutes later, and, after a few minutes of comparing notes with Hattie, Laurel started down the hall.

"Laurel! Wait up. I'll walk out with you."

Laurel turned to see M. J. Tinnin hurrying toward her. Fourteen years before, in a rare serendipitous matching, they had been assigned as roommates their freshman year of college. It was the first time she had met a woman known by initials rather than a full name, and when she asked why, M.J. had explained that, while "Mandolyn" might do very well for a Playmate of the Month, it wasn't the name of a psychologist. Laurel had then asked about M.J.'s middle name, and had had to agree that Jeribeth didn't quite convey the sense of sober maturity one looked for in a psychologist, either. M.J. had stuck to her goal and her initials, adding "Dr." to them seven years ago. The only deviation from the career road map she had laid out the first day of college had been Jack Tinnin, ten years before.

M.J. caught up with Laurel, and they both began walking toward the front door. "How did it go with Lina Renko?"

"Can her lawyer get a continuance?"

"That bad, huh?" Grimacing, M.J. brushed a strand of blue-black hair off her cheek. Tall and slender to the point of thinness, she had straight hair cut in a china-doll style, creamy olive skin and subtly slanted green eyes that combined to give her a somewhat exotic look.

Laurel glanced down at the sheaf of childish drawings in M.J.'s hand. "How did things go with her children?" To make Lina Renko's situation more desperate, she had a seven-year-old son and five-year-old daughter. Not only did she have to prove she was capable of taking care of herself, but she also had to prove she was competent to care for them just to get visitation rights, much less the full custody she was suing for. M.J. was doing a court-ordered evaluation of Randy and Amy Renko to determine what effect their father's abuse of their mother had had on them.

M.J. made another face. "Children learn best by example, and Randy is a *very* fast learner. In the session with his sister today he was bullying, ordering, demeaning—a perfect imitation of his father. And Amy just sat there and took it."

"Amy's a fast learner, too. That's what she's seen her mother do—sit there and take it," Laurel pointed out mildly.

"Yeah, well, I wouldn't take it for nine minutes, much less nine years," M.J. muttered darkly.

Laurel looked at her. "You still don't understand, do you?"

"Here—" M.J. jabbed a finger at her head "—I do. I know all the reasons, intellectually. But here?" Closed into a fist, her hand stuck the vicinity of her heart. "No, I don't. I don't understand why any reasonably intelligent woman would put up with that kind of garbage for ten seconds, much less year after year after year."

Laurel saw M.J.'s sudden, stricken look. No one at the center knew that she had experienced that "garbage" herself, and for more than ten seconds, but she was certain M.J. had suspected it, even though she had never broached the subject directly, for which Laurel had always been grateful. She counted it as one of the signs of how far she had come that M.J. sometimes forgot. "That's why it's good you only work with children," she said lightly, then changed the subject. "Did you get a chance to see the boy and Lina together?"

"He's Charles, Jr., with her, too—disrespectful, insulting, disobedient." M.J. shuffled through the drawings in her hand, pulling one to the top. In addition to her doctorate in psychology, she was also a certified art therapist. "You can see it here."

Laurel saw a large, powerful and mean-looking male figure with a big mouth at one side of the white drawing paper, a much smaller male figure in the middle, and a tiny, hunched-looking female figure almost off the edge of the paper on the other side.

"I asked him to draw a picture of himself, his mother and his father," M.J. explained. "The fact that he positioned himself in the middle rather than beside his father is a hopeful sign, though.''

"It's almost as if he's trying to protect her," Laurel murmured. There was something oddly valiant in the pose of the crayon-drawn figure.

Nodding, M.J. reached to open the front door. "I think so. At least he doesn't completely identify with his father yet. I don't think it will take that much therapy to turn him or his sister around—if Lina gets custody."

"A big *if.*" Shaking her head, Laurel looked back at the door shutting behind them. "I feel like such a fraud in there sometimes—especially when someone like Lina comes into the group. They need a trained therapist, not an amateur."

"You're hardly an amateur, Laurel." M.J. paused in the shade cast by the awning overhead to put on her sunglasses. "You have much more experience working with women who've suffered verbal abuse than most 'professionals,' me included. Besides, you balance Hattie. She can be a trifle…assertive at times. You're strong, confident, but not overwhelmingly so. The women don't feel threatened by you."

Laurel gave her a dubious look. "Thanks—I think."

They started walking toward the downtown garage where both of them usually parked. "Have you seen the public service announcements yet?" M.J. asked.

"No." After glancing at the building they were passing on the next block, Laurel looked back, for longer this time. Engraved on the plain, square brass plaque on either side of the entrance was Starrett, Inc. She hadn't realized his offices were so close. None of the captions under all those newspaper pictures had ever mentioned his business address, as she recalled. She frowned slightly. And she recalled them rather surprisingly well. Involuntarily she glanced up at the rows of tinted glass overlooking the park. Which one…? "Hmm?" she murmured absently to M.J.'s comment.

"I said I think it's a good idea we also used a woman's voice on those PSAs. Some people don't realize that there are battered men, too."

"Hmm . . ." Probably on the top row . . . in the middle?

"Laurel? What are we looking at?"

Suddenly she realized that she was standing in the middle of the sidewalk, staring up at the building. M.J. stood beside her, staring up, too, a puzzled look on her face. "Nothing," she said gruffly, starting to walk rapidly.

A red light slowed her pace half a block later. "I thought the announcements weren't due to start running until next week."

"Several of the stations liked them so much, they decided to start early." M.J. sounded a little out of breath. "It was probably your graphics."

Laurel gave the other woman a dry look as they stepped off the curb. "My 'graphics' were a glorified stop sign. My guess is it was the black screen with the voice-overs." With the help of the news department at one of the local television stations, several organizations had worked together to produce a series of public service announcements to kick off a month-long campaign in the Dallas–Fort Worth area to heighten awareness of domestic violence. Hattie's trademark "Stop it!" had been adopted as the campaign slogan, and she had jazzed up a standard stop sign to serve as the campaign symbol. For their particular thirty-second spot, Hattie and Edie had recruited their husbands, the male news director and one of the camerawomen for the roles of verbal abusers. The spot began with a black screen, the audio portion the lines the four had recorded. After each line of abuse came Hattie's authoritative "Stop it!" With no visual distractions, attention was focused on the audio, and the ugly words had the impact of a fist, letting viewers experience them the way a victim would. The blank screen went to her "stop sign" graphic, then she and Hattie appeared to briefly explain the Stop It! campaign and give out the necessary phone numbers.

M.J. got her car keys out of her purse as they reached the garage. "Edie said the phone started ringing right after the first announcement ran yesterday."

Laurel followed her out of warm spring sunshine into dankish shade. "Potential clients?" The women who came to the center were not "victims"—they were clients. "Victim" was an identity that could become too comfortable all too easily, and some women might never progress beyond it. "Victim" carried an unconscious connotation of helplessness, and frequently shame, as well. The goal was to help the women see that they were not helpless, that they could take control of their lives and take pride in themselves for doing it.

"Mostly clients. Some contributions—"

"Our anorectic budget can use them."

"And a few cranks."

Laurel ignored a brief, sharp chill. "They're unavoidable, I guess."

Making a sound of disgusted agreement, M.J. took the stairs to the second level. Stopping beside a silver Mercedes, she glanced at her watch. "Want to get some lunch? My first appointment isn't until two."

Laurel checked her watch. "I'm not very hungry, and I really should go home, anyway. I didn't get much work done yesterday. I may have to see what other good robot junk Jack has in your garage, by the way." Mentioning Jack's name called up a face, but instead of Jack's smooth blond handsomeness, she got an unexpected mental image of a harder, darker man. Startled, she blinked the image away immediately.

"Sure," M.J. said brightly after a brief hesitation. "What did you do yesterday?"

"I went poaching."

M.J. paused in the act of unlocking her car door. "Poaching?"

"That's what the owner of the river called it after he got my attention by throwing a rock at me. Well, not at me," she amended scrupulously. "Close to me."

M.J.'s look of astonishment changed rapidly to exasperation. "You were fishing alone? How many times—?" She took a deep breath before she wasted any more air. "Whose river was it?"

"Cleese Starrett's."

M.J. looked at her with something akin to blank shock. "Oh."

"You know, M.J.," Laurel added thoughtfully, "I got the impression he wasn't a nice safe man." For a while now, M.J. had been chiding her for her "nice safe men," as M.J. called them, meaning that the men she went out with were nice and safe to the point of being dull, boring and juiceless. Nice safe men. Once she had repeated it like a litany to herself.

M.J. about-faced. "He's not, Laurel! He's too big a leap from nice and safe. You need to work up to a Cleese Starrett gradually."

"I'll start exercising right away," Laurel promised gravely, then suddenly remembered something. "Oh! I almost forgot." She dug in her purse for a pen and a scrap of paper. "I need to give you my new phone number." She scribbled it on the back of an old gas credit card receipt.

M.J. gave the paper a scant glance as she took it. "What happened to your old one?"

"One of those crank callers—a very persistent one."

M.J. looked immediately concerned. "How many times did he call?"

"About half a dozen. He left a message on my machine, called a few more times yesterday after I got home and once this morning, after I plugged the phone in again. That's when I called the phone company and got my number changed and unlisted." She dismissed the caller with a shrug. "I won't hear from him again."

* * *

Lowering her arm a few minutes later as the silver Mercedes disappeared down the ramp, Laurel looked with little enthusiasm toward the stairs to the third level and her car. Her gaze was drawn back to the rusty iron rails at the edge of the garage and, visible between them, the treetops several blocks away. The light breeze blowing through the garage carried a perfume of water and fresh grass under the usual car exhaust and stale city smells, and she started for the stairs down to street level.

A soft trickle grew to the roar of a waterfall as Laurel crossed the last street and entered the Water Gardens, an oasis of live water and growing green in the midst of downtown Fort Worth's concrete-glass-and-asphalt desert. She walked along the rim of a man-made canyon where water cascaded three stories to a caldron of green and white foam. A class of preschoolers scampered, shrieking and laughing, down the steps to the pool, dashing through the rainbows of mist thrown back by the seething water. On the far side of the canyon, she climbed down through a cleft between high, steep walls, flowing with slow, cool water. At the bottom the narrow chasm opened unexpectedly onto a quiet pool surrounded by tall cypresses. Pink-and-white water lilies floated on the surface, while occasional orange glinted just below it as giant koi cruised lazily. Water ran silently down the surrounding walls, adding to the serenity and soothing quiet that she sometimes needed after a particularly intensive session. There were a few people from the surrounding office buildings brown-bagging it, but the pool area was large enough that an illusion of seclusion remained. She sat on the edge of the pool in the sun, content to do nothing more than watch the giant dragonflies buzzing the water lilies and dogfighting above them.

Cleese leaned back in his chair and propped his feet on his desk, toppling the pile of pink message slips that had built up during the board meeting. He probably ought to do something about lunch, he thought, but made no move toward the phone to order some in. Locking his fingers behind his neck, he stared up at the white ceiling. The unformed dissatisfaction he'd been feeling lately had finally coalesced an hour and a half ago, during the comptroller's report. He'd handled his share of challenges the past ten years or so—a bad marriage and worse divorce, his father's illness, the oil bust. Bitterness had faded, and he'd come to appreciate that the marriage had lasted no longer; he still missed his father and always would, but the pain had settled into a kind of bittersweet acceptance; and Starrett, Inc. was back, bigger and better than ever. While Del Boyer had been explaining that profits were up nineteen percent this quarter, he'd suddenly realized what was wrong: he needed another challenge. Now, swinging his feet to the floor, he stood up. He had known immediately just what the challenge would be.

Leaning against the glass wall of his top-floor office, he looked down on the urban forest below. He was "smitten," as his granddad would have said. And the challenge wasn't going to be easy. Her straightforwardness and self-assurance conflicted with the subtle touch-me-not air about her, and then there had been that flinch and his suspicions. The traditional dinner dates, parties and such wouldn't meet the challenge of Laurel Drew, he was certain. He would need a more novel approach: he would go after her with a fishing pole, not flowers, in hand.

Unwittingly, she herself had suggested the lure that would attract her when she admitted it was hard for a woman to fish alone. First, he would do some chumming to get her interested in taking the bait—him. The "chum" would be a few invitations to go fishing. There would be no "dates," just simple, casual, unpressured fishing trips with a "fishing buddy," until she took the bait.

His gaze wandered absently over the park. There were five reasons fish bit on any bait: because it irritated them, reflex—grabbing whatever passed by; competition—to keep other fish away; curiosity; and hunger. He sure as hell didn't want to irritate her, and she wasn't the kind to grab whatever man was passing out of reflex, or just to keep some other woman from getting him. He wouldn't be interested in her if she was. No, he would use curiosity first, entice her closer until she was so hungry that she couldn't resist taking him. Yet even then, when he had her hooked, he would have to play her carefully. Try to land her too soon, and she'd fight and throw the hook; give her too much slack, and she'd slip free and be forever the one that got away. But once he set the hook deep, she was his; he had already decided he wouldn't be letting her go. This one was a keeper.

His eyes focused suddenly on a touch of autumn color in the midst of the fresh spring green below. The hardest part, he knew, straightening away from the window, would be waiting until her hunger matched his.

"I think they're a little small."

It was odd how she already recognized his voice. "They're bigger than the last trout I caught," Laurel said, looking up from the big goldfish she'd been watching to him. Her small wry grin widened unconsciously into a full smile; she wasn't unaware of the strong purl of pleasure that eddied through her at seeing him.

He laughed. "My last one, too." The ground in the park was a little boggy, too, Cleese noted abstractedly.

Her smile took on a faint puzzlement. "I'm surprised to see you here." His shadow as he stood over her completely engulfed her, reminding her again how big he was.

"My office is right across the street." Cleese indicated which street with a nod. "I chose it because of the park, so I would have something to look at besides buildings and blacktop." He smiled slightly. "I saw you from the window." Seeing her in the mist yesterday, with her otherworldly eyes and her mythic beast-protector, he could have believed that he had stumbled into some enchantment. A little of it must remain, he thought with a silent laugh, because he had felt no surprise at seeing her in the park to-day. That was exactly where she was supposed to be, waiting for him. "I was just on my way to lunch. Are you hungry?"

The hunger that hadn't been there when M.J. asked about lunch suddenly was. "Yes." Laurel smiled up at him. "I am hungry."

He stepped back so that she could stand up. He really should offer a hand to help her to her feet, but, Cleese thought with sardonic self-disgust, he couldn't be sure his hair wouldn't stand straight up on end if he touched her, among other— She had seduced him, without laying a hand on him.

She was wearing a shirt today made of some kind of soft blue fabric that looked like silk and lent more color to her eyes. It fit a little loosely for his taste. Her skirt was a darker blue, made out of the same silky lightweight material. He had never appreciated before now, he reflected, how fascinating a long, full skirt could be. It wasn't glamorous, and it hid most of her legs from view, a masterpiece of innocence that was sexier than any short and slinky or thigh-high slit number could ever be. Instead of revealing, it suggested—the long, slow motion of her legs and hips, the shape of a thigh under the soft, silky fabric, hinted at but gone before being fully exposed, then almost back again, making sure a man couldn't take his eyes off it.

Laurel paid little more than cursory attention to their route through the park, past the convention center and down Houston to a side street. His grin in answer to a comment flashed strong, even white teeth against darkly tanned skin, not acquired in a tanning booth, she already knew, although from his clothes today one might expect it. He wore a charcoal business suit, which must have been custom-tailored to fit his shoulders, a white shirt, a conservative tie and wing tips. But even without his Levi's and boots, he was proof that the "real" West still began at Fort Worth, she thought with a secret smile. The differences between Fort

Worth and its cousin down the road might be blurring, the stockyards might be closed and Filthy McNasty's and Billy Bob's in danger of becoming caricatures of their rowdy, honky-tonk selves, but there were still men—one, at least—with the Teflon-hipped, just-moseying-along walk of the true cowboy.

Reaching around her carefully, Cleese pushed open the door of a cubbyhole delicatessen, and the aromas and voice immediately transported them cross-country to the Bronx. "Be witcha in a sec," someone yelled from the back.

Studying the menu painted on the wall, she murmured, "I wonder what he'll bewitch us with? A magic wand of bologna?"

Stifling a laugh, Cleese made a pretext of looking at the menu, too. A fishing rod had worked; why not bologna? "As long as it isn't liverwurst. I hate liverwurst," he murmured back, and was rewarded with a grin.

She told the counterman the orders were separate, and he didn't contradict her, because "fishing buddies" paid for their own food. They carried their trays to one of the small tables outside, and, as she set hers down, a stray breeze caught the napkins she'd picked up. They started to scatter, and, before he could stop himself, he lunged across the table toward her to grab them.

Cleese swore ripely under his breath. He'd been so damned careful how he moved, and now . . .

She didn't flinch; she didn't so much as blink. "Thanks," she said, anchoring the napkins with her sandwich basket when he released them.

Laurel breathed a small silent sign of relief as she sat down. That cringe yesterday had just been some peculiar aberration.

"What are you doing downtown?" He was curious about how she spent her time . . . and who she spent it with.

"I was at Maxwell's," Laurel answered automatically as she tried to figure out how she was ever going to fit the oversize sandwich in her mouth.

"Maxwell's? The old music store?" A faint frown appeared between his eyebrows. "I thought that had closed a few years ago and the building had been renovated into offices."

Laurel turned her sandwich into two open-faced halves. He wasn't having any trouble with his sandwich, she noticed; more than a half of it was already gone. "It was. We just kept the name for our center."

"What kind of center?"

She swallowed a bite of sandwich. "A counseling center for battered women. I help out with some of the group counseling, do a little fund-raising." Her small shrug was self-deprecatory.

The frown grew stronger. "Then why not call it a center for battered women or victims of domestic violence?"

"Because some women get into a 'battered' or 'victim' mode and never get out of it and get on with their lives. Those identities can be very hard to give up, because they unconsciously perpetuate a sense of helplessness, and that gives a woman an excuse not to take charge of her life, not to make decisions that take a lot of courage to make. That's why we call the women clients, not victims. 'Shelter' can have the same negative effect, so the shelter we run uptown is called 'Maxwell House.' And," she warned with a wry look, "I've heard all the jokes."

Good, Cleese thought, because he didn't feel like making any, about regular, decaf or anything else. In telling him the rationale behind the naming of the center and shelter, she was telling him a great deal about herself, too, answering a few of the questions he had. The tip of her tongue, daintily sneaking a crumb at the corner of her mouth, touched the edge of the small circular scar. She knew the truth of what she said firsthand. "How long do women usually stay at the shelter?" He glanced down at her tray. "Are you going to eat your chips?"

Her mouth full, Laurel shook her head, motioning for him to take the unopened bag. "They rarely stay more than two weeks," she answered after swallowing. "The accommodations are pretty Spartan and cramped, especially if a woman brings her children. And everybody has to pitch in with the cooking and cleaning, the yard work, painting, whatever needs doing. It's the only way we can keep it going."

"Not exactly a vacation resort," he said dryly.

"No," she agreed with a drier laugh. "But it has some advantages, besides the obvious one that nobody wants to stay any longer than they have to. A little thing like changing the oil in the lawn mower or refinishing a door can give a woman who thought she couldn't possibly make it on her own enough self-confidence to begin to think that, just maybe, she can. Most women have talents and strengths they don't know they have." Now that he'd finished off her chips, he was covertly eyeing the half sandwich she was too full to eat. Wordlessly she picked it up and handed it across the table.

He took it with a grin and no hesitation. "I'll buy lunch next time, since I've eaten most of yours."

His certainty that "next time" was a sure thing had her, uncharacteristically, accepting that it was.

"How do you handle security, make the women feel safe enough that they don't worry their husbands are going to show up and drag them back home?"

It wasn't every man who understood that a battered woman's first concern wasn't comfort or the plushness of her surroundings; it was safety. "There's an eight-foot wall around the place, and a locked entry gate. The address isn't in the phone book, either. People have to call to find out what it is, and if the caller is male, we just don't give it out. The only real problem we have is—"

"Phone calls," he finished for her when she stopped to take a drink of her soda.

She probably didn't hide her surprise as well this time. "Yes, we get a few we'd rather we didn't," Laurel said neutrally. The coincidence of meeting him yesterday and the start of the phone calls wasn't lost on her. Neither was their unexpected meeting today. He could be following her, stalking her. Abusive behavior was an equal-opportunity malevolence; handsome, charming, rich men practiced it, as well as poor, homely, cloddish ones—as she well knew. But coincidence was all it was; Cleese Starrett wasn't following her, and he wasn't calling her. If she had accomplished nothing else in the six years since Paul Falco, she had improved her instincts where men were concerned. She'd worked hard at it, because she had known she had to reach the point where she could trust them or she would never be able to trust herself again. She did trust her instincts now, and herself. Cleese Starrett was many things—forceful, physical, compelling, maybe even a little dangerous, given the right circumstances. Certainly he was a man who would challenge any woman to hold her own against him, but one thing he wasn't, she knew beyond all doubt, was a man who would ever mistreat a woman.

"Where do the women go when they leave Maxwell House?"

With the interesting sun squints at the corners of his eyes, the question registered a little slowly. Laurel blinked. "Some go back home. A couple of our volunteers are lawyers who are—" she smiled slightly "—very good at getting removal orders. Those who don't want to go home or don't really have one, move in with family or get their own place. The lawyers are also very good at garnisheeing paychecks, opening up bank accounts." She answered the question before he asked it. "Some of the women have no access to the family checking account. Everything is in the husband's name. If there's no money at all, we help them get public assistance temporarily and work on job counseling or further education.

When she moved her head, the sun picked out the individual strands of copper and gold in her hair. "How did you get interested in the center?" Had she gone as a "client," he wondered.

"About five years ago, when Maxwell's was just getting started, I was thinking of making a donation, so I stopped in to look it over." She caught his glance at her plate. "I *am* going to eat my pickle." Picking it up, she continued over his low chuckle.

"When I walked in, everyone was crowded around the front desk, trying to come up with some kind of cover design for their brochure, and the next thing I knew—" she laughed ruefully "—I had a pencil in my hand."

"I caught the tail end of something on the news this morning about a campaign against domestic violence." She put the fat kosher dill in her mouth and took a bite, and the direction of his thoughts took a sudden, startling turn. Muttering explicitly under his breath, he reined in the fantasy before it got completely away from him. "The artwork was clever. Was it yours?"

She accepted the compliment with a nod and an amused smile. "Soon to be on a billboard near you."

"You said you work as a counselor, too?" She took another bite, and he shifted in his chair.

She shook her head sharply. "I'm strictly an amateur. The therapists think the groups work better with two counselors, but there aren't enough to go around, so they gave a few of us a little training. Mostly we're sidekicks and straight men."

He already recognized that quick, cheerful grin as one of her trademarks, like her eyes and the sunset hair. His gaze fixed briefly on the scar at the corner of her mouth. She was levelheaded and practical, independent, sure of herself, smart, funny— How the *hell* had she gotten herself into the kind of mess he suspected? Yet, underneath the strength and intelligence, behind the grin and depth in her eyes, he detected vulnerability. Or maybe he was seeing what he wanted to see, he thought derisively. He'd realized something else this morning, during the pie charts and profit graphs. He was needed, on an impersonal basis, as the head of any company was needed, but how long had it been since anyone had needed *him*, Cleese Starrett, personally?

Looking at him after placing the pickle stem on her paper plate, Laurel stilled, as if caught unexpectedly in the beam of a powerful spotlight. She had thought, fancifully, of him as having the eyes of a well-fed, lazy, sleepy big cat, but there was nothing lazy or sleepy about them now. The dark amber color glowed with all the power of the sun burning through it, and the full intensity of the beam was focused on her. Thick, stubby lashes shielded her for a moment, then they lifted, and the intense beam had been shut off, as if it had never been there at all.

Pushing back his chair, Cleese stood up and began gathering their lunch trash. "Do you have any plans for Saturday?"

"No." Standing, also, Laurel was distracted by trying to snatch back her paper plate from the littering breeze.

He threw out his first handful of chum. "A few of us are going to run down to Corpus for the day, go fishing for bonito. Why don't you come, too?"

Snagging the plate, Laurel frowned at him absently. Corpus Christi was five hundred miles away; one didn't just "run down" there for the—

"I have a plane," he added.

Of course he did, she thought wryly; what tycoon didn't? If she hadn't met him first wearing patched boots and driving a beat-up truck, she wouldn't have such a hard time remembering what he was. "Who's going?" she asked, tempted past the knowledge that he was really out of her league.

"Jack Tinnin, for one," he said, mentally crossing his fingers as he dumped his tray into the trash can, then reached for hers. Jack rarely passed up a chance to go fishing, even on short notice. "Maybe M.J. will come when she knows you're coming, too."

Again there was that absolute assurance that she would do as he wanted, as if it was a foregone conclusion. "Not unless the fish bait the hook, throw out the line, reel themselves in and take themselves off the hook," she said with an ironic laugh. Temptation warred with good sense again. She really shouldn't go, if for no other reason than that his healthy ego needed to hear "no" once in a while, but it had been years since she'd been deep-sea fishing . . . and she would just be one of a crowd. . . .

"Other women are coming along." None of the wives of his friends were avid fishermen, but there were several who would be agreeable to a day on the ocean.

"Everyone chips in for fuel for the plane?"

From her custom-made fly rod and the new four-wheel drive she drove, he knew she could easily afford her share, but Cleese still felt his teeth go on edge. This "fishing buddy" crap was already getting old. "Of course."

"I don't have any saltwater tackle anymore," she began.

"We can scrounge up a rod and reel." He congratulated himself on maintaining a straight face as he thought of the virtual tackle shop stored in the gear wells of his boat.

Good sense lost. "I'd love to go," she said with a big smile.

He limited himself to "Good," then looked at his watch. "I've got a meeting five minutes ago. I'll call you with where and when."

"I'll give you my phone number." Ripping a page out of her pocket calendar, Laurel printed her new phone number and handed it over, then reached to take it back. "I should write my name on it."

He smiled faintly. "I'll remember whose it is." Glancing at the paper as he folded it over, he noted that he already had the first three numbers memorized from checking the phone book the night before. "I'll call you Friday."

Chapter 3

The sky was not yet even pink when he pressed the doorbell. He hadn't done anything so juvenile as coming early in hopes of catching her in bed, Cleese told himself; it just hadn't taken as long as he'd thought it would to drive to her house. After about half a minute, the door opened.

"Oh—I didn't realize I was running late."

"You aren't," he said quickly. "I'm early." She had been running, literally, unless she wore gym shorts, a T-shirt and running shoes to bed. A faint sheen of moisture showed on her forehead, and a few strands of hair that had escaped from her ponytail clung to her neck. She was still breathing a little hard, her damp T-shirt rising and falling rapidly. Just in time, he caught himself starting to reach for her. The idea of kissing her good-morning seemed so natural, that, even knowing how wrong it would be, he still had trouble stopping. He shoved his hands in his pockets. He was going to be spending a lot of time with his hands in his pockets, he thought sardonically.

He walked into the house and came to a stop a few feet inside the door. Frank had, as usual, planted himself between them.

"Does Frank go running with you?" he asked casually. She sure as hell better not be out on the streets, alone, so early in the morning.

"He won't stand for being left at home. Be nice, Frank. You know Cleese," she added to the dog, patting his massive head as she smiled up at Cleese. He was back in the shrink-to-fit Levi's today, although he had traded the boots for deck shoes and the denim shirt for a navy pullover. She sighed unconsciously. "I'll be ready in a few minutes. Just make yourself at home."

"There's no rush. We've got plenty of time," he called after her as she started down the hallway. He had seen legs before, he reminded himself.

A door closed a few seconds later, and he heard the dim sound of a shower shortly after that. He and the dog regarded each other. The problem was, Frank did know him, and likely suspected exactly what he was up to, even if his mistress didn't. "You and I are going to have to come to an understanding, dog," he muttered. He eased down onto his haunches until he and the dog were at eye level, then slowly extended his hand. Yellow eyes narrowed, the dog stretched forward until his wet nose touched Cleese's fingers. Cleese held still while Frank lowered his head until it was under his hand, and, accepting the overture, he scratched around the dog's ears. Frank tolerated it for a few seconds before pulling back, and Cleese laughed softly to himself as he stood up. They weren't friends, but Frank was willing to give him the benefit of the doubt.

The dog followed him as he crossed the small entry into the living room. Her house was located in a neighborhood of well-tended lawns, huge elms and live oaks, and homes styled along the lines of English cottages. Built in the first half of the century, the brick houses had the fine detailing lacking in new ones. The windows across the front, including the ones in the door and the tallest gable, were stained glass, which, together with the milled wood trim and intricately patterned brickwork, gave the outside a touch of old-world elegance. The inside reflected the same fine craftsmanship, and the furnishings told him more about the owner. She loved beautiful old things, but her practical, thrifty side wouldn't allow her to simply enjoy useless beauty. A piece had to be functional, too.

There was a fine collection of antique fishing gear—brass reels, handcarved and painted bass plugs, wicker creels and split bamboo rods—on one wall, but it was the collection of photographs above the marble fireplace that he was most interested in. The oldest, yellowed and faded, were in the center, with newer ones radiating out. There was an early-1950s wedding photo of a slender, dark-haired woman and a tall, husky man with coppery hair. Laurel didn't particularly resemble either of them. She had two brothers, about ten or twelve years older, each with two children and a blond wife. She hadn't said how old she had been when her mother died, but, from the photographs, he could guess. He traced her childhood from a baby dressed in a red sleeper with an elf hat in a family Christmas photo through several more years of snapshots, then, after a photo of her blowing out the seven candles on a birthday cake with her father's help, the photos abruptly declined. Clearly her mother had been the family photographer. There was one picture of her and M. J. Tinnin, taken on their college graduation day, judging from their caps and gowns, and one other of Laurel standing with her arm around and obviously supporting a much older, emaciated version of the man in the wedding photo. Missing were any photos of her own wedding, but then, he hadn't expected to see any.

After pausing in front of a bookcase that held an eclectic mix of adult books and an impressive number of children's volumes with her name on the spine, he passed through the dining room toward the back of the house. Off the modernized kitchen was what had probably once been a sleeping porch but had been expanded into a glass-walled studio overlooking the backyard. Lawn stretched away from the studio to an enclosing thicket of hibiscus and azaleas gone a little wild, while off to one side was the glint of water from a tiny pond. With only the almost invisible barrier of glass between the studio and yard, there was the illusion of standing at the edge of a forest glade, an illusion that was deliberate, he was sure.

The shower shut off, and he concentrated on an image of her sitting, fully clothed, on the high stool at the waist-high worktable, drawing. The worktable ran along the back and one side wall, with papers, paints and drawing pencils scattered over the entire surface. Sneakers, slippers and a pair of huaraches were abandoned underneath. On closer inspection, he saw that the seeming mess was actually well organized; she was apparently working on several projects at once. His mouth turned up in an unconscious smile. As far as the sneakers, slippers and huaraches went, he guessed she couldn't work with her shoes on.

One of the sets of papers spread out on the tabletop was a story about a ghost who haunted an empty, dreary house until he worked up the courage to go outside one day. Told in simple words, it was obviously designed for a beginning reader or a young child just learning colors. Laurel had drawn the classic haunted house in drab gray with black shadows, while the small ghost was a white paper cutout. Once the ghost ventured outside, however, the pages exploded with vivid, intense color. He picked up a tube of acrylic paint idly, then set it back down beside a glass square with two dozen shades of purple dried on it. Each color was illustrated with at least fifteen or twenty objects, so that the child not only saw the color and a palette of shades within it, but a vocabulary-expanding visual dictionary, as well. The ghost was the same size and shape on each page, as if she'd cut them all out with a cookie cutter, yet, with a few extra snips of the scissors, she had managed to convey fearfulness, increasing wonder and, finally, by cutting the eyes as tiny hearts, with another in the chest, mad passion for the new colors he'd discovered.

Moving down the table, he glanced at the bulletin board above the table, which was covered with sketches, some on regular drawing sheets, some on whatever had been handy at the time—store receipts, napkins, part of a brown paper grocery sack, a bank deposit slip. She also had a yearlong calendar tacked up, with the deadlines for a startling amount of work penciled in, and, in the lower left-hand corner, an excellent charcoal drawing of Frank. The dog's name was, as he'd suspected, no accident; she'd added a bolt on each side of his neck and a collar of stitches.

Below the bulletin board was a stack of blank paper with a half-finished pen-and-ink drawing on top. Frowning, he picked up the drawing, of a lopsided tent with the start of a forest in the background, and studied it. Something about it seemed familiar, but just what eluded him. Setting it back down, he turned his attention to the series of pastels spread out on the tabletop. The text, consisting of one sentence of dialogue per page, was frankly extraneous; the story was told in the illustrations. Some kids had found an empty cardboard box about the size of a file cabinet and were turning it into a robot with junk they found in one kid's garage. Laurel drew the junk-filled garage as the background for each page, subtly drawing attention to a certain object that would become part of the robot on the next and luring the reader into taking an active part in the making of the robot by making him or her guess what would be used next and how. He knew, because she had *him* guessing. On one page, a taped-up vacuum-cleaner hose crawled like a snake out from between two boxes. On the next page, it became, like an elephant's trunk, the robot's nose. On that same page, two leftover pieces of white clothes-dryer duct waved out of a box at the back of the garage. On the following page, the robot had arms. A few pages later, it had hands, a worn-out catcher's mitt and a rusty pair of barbecue tongs, and feet, a pair of holey football cleats riding a cracked skateboard.

As interesting as the robot construction was, what was happening between the kids was even better. To the author's simple story, Laurel had added her own sly send-up of the Dick and Jane readers he remembered from elementary school. This time it was the girls who were doing all the interesting things, while the boys looked on, their arms folded across their chests. The boys had happened by, stopped to watch with skeptical faces that, within a couple of pages, became frankly envious. One finally broke ranks and picked up two old glass doorknobs that had been winking out of a box. On the next page, the boy had joined the girls, and the robot had eyes. She hadn't done the rest of the illustrations yet, but he was sure that by the end of the book, when the robot magically came alive, all the boys would have joined in to work together with the girls. Obviously, Laurel didn't confine her "counseling" to Maxwell's.

He was poking through a box of junk sitting on the worktable when he heard the door that had closed a few minutes before open, and Frank immediately left the studio. No doubt to tattle, Cleese thought with a rueful laugh. He'd felt so immediately comfortable in her house that he hadn't thought anything about making himself right at home.

The dog returned with his mistress seconds later. She had pulled her hair back into a braid except for a fringe of bangs. He liked her hair better loose, he decided, but the style did highlight the beautiful bones of her face. "I'm afraid I made myself at home."

"That's what I told you to do." Smiling, Laurel crossed the studio, ignoring a vague uneasiness at seeing how well he and her house seemed to fit together.

"Is this going to be an antenna?" Cleese held up the top section of an ancient bamboo fly rod that he had pulled out of the box of junk.

She considered the object in the middle of the floor. "I haven't decided. I might run line through it to bend it into a hook to hold the trunk out of the way when it's not in use."

She said it with perfect seriousness, so Cleese, nodding solemnly, joined her in studying the robot that was obviously the model for the one in the story. "Where did you get all the junk?" Out of the corner of his eye, he saw her surreptitiously slip the drawing of the tent under the stack of blank paper.

"From the Tinnins' garage." She laughed. "I don't think Jack ever throws anything away. I don't usually do models, but I wanted to use things kids might find lying around their own houses so maybe they would try making a robot of their own, and—" she grinned sheepishly "—I got a little carried away with the idea."

She'd redressed in a loose, lightweight sweater and looser pants, but he remembered what her legs looked like. He eased his hands into his back pockets. Very well. "The illustrations are great."

"Thank you." Laurel saw him glance toward the stack of paper where she'd hidden the drawing of the tent. "Well, we probably ought to get going," she said brightly, moving away from the table and the drawing in further encouragement.

His eyes came back to her after a moment. "Yeah, we should."

Leading the way back through the house, Laurel detoured into the kitchen. "I just need to give Frank a pill before we go."

· "A pill for what?" He couldn't imagine a healthier-looking dog.

"Hay fever. He always gets it this time of year," she answered distractedly, not seeing his look of disbelief and choked-back laugh as she tried to work off the childproof lid on the pill bottle. "I should have remembered to ask for a regular lid this morning," she muttered.

Taking the bottle, he caught a whiff of the illusory scent that haunted his dreams. "Your vet is open this early?"

She shook her head as he handed back the opened bottle. "I stopped by the twenty-four-hour pharmacy a few blocks away while we were out running. It's human medication, actually. The vet says he's never prescribed it for a dog before."

"I don't imagine so," he murmured, stifling another laugh. As soon as she shook a pill out onto her palm, Frank sat down. She touched the side of his jaw, the dog opened wide, and Cleese couldn't help a slight wince as her hand disappeared in the maw of teeth. As soon as her hand withdrew, the dog closed his mouth and swallowed.

"Good boy." She backed up the praise with a pat on the dog's rough head, then rinsed her hands at the sink before opening the back door, and Frank trotted obediently outside.

Looking past her shoulder, Cleese saw the large bones scattered under the tulip tree growing between the house and the detached garage. "The meter reader?" he asked conversationally.

"The cable man," she answered in kind, without missing a beat, and he grinned at her back as she closed the door and locked it.

She went to the pine table and grabbed a small cooler and gym bag, which he immediately took out of her hands. He would have carried them for her anyway, but he wasn't passing up any opportunities to be close to her, if only for a second or two. Fishing was not without its subtleties.

He held easily in one hand what she needed two for, another reminder—and an unnecessary one, Laurel thought, as she preceded him out of the kitchen—of how much bigger he was than she. Not that long ago, his size would have made her very uneasy; now, it felt . . . good.

They were passing the bookcase on the way to the front door when Cleese suddenly remembered something he had meant to ask her about. From beside a rare copy of *The Art of the Trout Fly,* he pulled a plain-covered book with only the title, author's name and publishing house printed on the spine. "I didn't think this was out yet," he said, holding the book up.

"It's an advance copy." Providentially, the clock in the living room began to chime the hour. "Goodness! We better go. We don't want to be late." She grabbed the book out of his hands just as he was starting to open it. It was rude, but rudeness beat the alternative. She shoved the book back in place, making a mental note to remove it permanently from the case as soon as possible. At least she had thought to remove the well-illustrated dust jacket before putting it on the shelf.

He gave her a questioning look that she pretended not to see, and Laurel breathed a silent sigh of relief outside as she waited while he opened the trunk of his car to stow her bag and cooler. The car was considered a luxury model, although it was several times less expensive than what she might have expected him to drive. Room for his long legs and head and broad shoulders, she suspected, had been more important considerations than price and prestige.

Moving to unlock her door, he paused with his hand on the door handle to glance back at her home. "I like your house."

"Thanks." She smiled her thanks again as he opened the door, but he made no move to help her into the car. This was not a "date," after all, she reminded herself.

When he was behind the wheel, she picked up the conversation again. "Do you have a house in town?" She couldn't imagine that he commuted from his ranch every day.

"A condo downtown, near my office." He glanced past her toward her house again as he turned the key and the engine started with a muted roar. "The lease is coming up for renewal, and I've got to decide whether I'm going to renew it or find someplace else." Something in the way he said it made her think the decision had already been made.

* * *

Laurel had gathered that everyone met at a coffee shop near the airfield for breakfast before the flight, and she was glad of the chance to meet the others someplace other than an airplane cabin, where the seating made introductions and conversation awkward. It lessened the sense of being an "outsider," although, after a few minutes, the others had absorbed her into the group so easily and gracefully that she might have known them all for years.

She *had* known Jack Tinnin for years, of course, and, it turned out, had met Marcia Hunt and Deane Avery at a fundraiser—one never forgot the names of generous contributors. Jack and T. C. Hunt had grown up with Cleese, while he and Aaron Avery, who was about ten years older, apparently had a business association that had evolved into friendship.

Beyond introducing her, Cleese paid no particular attention to her, certainly none that would give anyone the mistaken impression that they were a couple. There were no speculative looks, either when they came in together or, she thought wryly, when she sat between Marcia and Deane in the middle of the semicircular booth while he took one of the chairs on the other side of the table, like a quarreling couple trying to put as much distance between themselves as possible.

She would have decided that it was because he routinely brought a woman with him, if not for Marcia Hunt's teasing comment. "Well, Jack, looks like you and Cleese aren't a couple anymore." Everyone had laughed, especially Cleese. The only one who had looked the least discomfited, in fact, was Jack.

Less than an hour later they were pulling up beside a row of parked planes. The red-and-white turboprop puddle jumper met her expectations, which she had to quickly revise upward when T.C. and Jack started releasing the tie-downs on the small white jet beside it. Inside, though, it might have been the puddle jumper, she discovered a few minutes later. There were no pretensions to luxury; the plane was fast, efficient transportation, and no more. She took a seat in the cabin, while Jack Tinnin took what seemed to be his customary place, the copilot's chair beside Cleese.

Cleese checked the small mirror that gave him a view of the cabin behind him. "Everyone got their seat belts on?" he called. After the various nods and murmurs of assent, he put on a set of headphones and began taxiing toward the runway.

Once they were out of the air traffic around Fort Worth and Dallas and had reached cruising speed, Jack spoke up. "When did you meet Laurel Drew?"

"A few days ago." With a small sense of shock, he realized it *had* been only a few days ago; it just seemed like he'd known her much longer. He looked over at the man beside him. "I've been wondering why I hadn't met her sooner."

Jack shook his head with a dry laugh. "I swore off introducing her to men after the last one."

Cleese frowned at him. "Who was the last one?"

"Her husband."

Cleese gave the instruments an automatic check. "I've been wondering about him."

Jack laughed sourly. "Join the club. She's never said one word about her husband or her marriage, not even to M.J."

Cleese glanced over at him. "Maybe she did, and M.J. never told you?"

"No, M.J. still talks about it every once in a while. I'm sure she doesn't know, but it's not too hard to guess that the marriage was lousy."

He suspected that was an understatement. Checking the mirror, Cleese saw that Laurel was involved in a conversation with Marcia Hunt. "How did you happen to introduce them?"

Jack grimaced. "It was a fluke, really. Paul Falco and I had stopped for lunch, and Laurel and M.J. walked into the restaurant about two minutes behind us. It was just about a month after Doc died, and M.J. was trying to get Laurel out as much as possible. The four of us had lunch together, and less than a month later she married him and took off for Houston. Two years later, she came back, a widow."

"She didn't keep his name," Cleese murmured. Not that he would have expected her to, but at least he knew the bastard's name now.

"Or his money."

Cleese looked at him sharply. "How much money?"

"Enough to buy that shelter she and M.J. are always raising money for, pay for the major renovations and set up a trust fund to pay for the women's legal expenses, and any job training they might need to get them on their feet." He grinned at Cleese's silent whistle.

Poetic justice, Cleese thought with a grim laugh. A stream of chatter came through the earphones, and he pulled them on impatiently. He made the necessary course correction, then jerked them off again. "Doc was her father?"

"Yeah. Everybody called him Doc or Captain. He wasn't the easiest man to get to know," Jack added wryly. "He was a physicist, I think, some kind of troubleshooter for the nuclear reactors on subs, and wherever else the navy uses them. Laurel's mother died when she was pretty young, and her brothers were already in college, so it was just Laurel and her father after that. Apparently they moved around quite a bit. Wherever the navy sent him, even if it was some no-name atoll out in the middle of the Pacific, he found a way to take her with him. The four years she spent in Denton at Texas Woman's University was the longest she'd ever lived anywhere up to then." He said it in the wondering tone of someone who had spent his entire life in the same place.

Cleese smiled to himself. "Doc" was further evidence for another suspicion he had. "She said her dad died eight years ago."

Covering a yawn, Jack nodded. "He was in and out of the hospital for two years. He became ill right after Laurel graduated from college. When he felt well enough, they went fishing. The rest of the time—" He gestured futilely. "She pretty much put her life on hold for those two years."

"And since she came back from Houston, what's she been up to, besides her work and Maxwell's?" As long as Jack was in a chatty mood, he had no compunctions about taking advantage of it.

"I hear she goes out a fair amount," Jack answered, translating standard male code. "One of the guys I know said she's got a defense as good as the Cowboys, and there's about as much chance of sacking her." The brief look from the man beside him had him clearing his throat; then he suddenly remembered something. "You know, you probably met Falco, Cleese. The family owns a shipping business—that's why he was up here, looking over possible expansion sites. They ship a lot of livestock. I bet you used them before you started up your own business."

Cleese shook his head decisively. "We did a little business with Falco Shipping, but I never met him." I'd remember, he thought grimly. They were entering the airspace over Corpus Christi, and he started to put the headset back in place, pausing when Jack spoke again.

"So, how long is the 'fishing buddy' routine going to go on?"

He met Jack's sly look with a sardonic one of his own. "As long as it takes—and not one second longer."

After the jet, Laurel didn't know what kind of boat to expect; a fifty-foot sailing yacht wouldn't have surprised her. It turned out to be a cabin cruiser, well maintained but, like his car and plane, not the latest model with the newest bells and whistles. As they left the dock and he opened the throttle, Laurel closed her eyes and turned her face into the warm, rushing salt air. Once in a very rare while, she thought with a smile, you just knew a day was going to be perfect.

A wheeling flock of seabirds gave away the location of a school of feeding bonito. Lines were quickly rigged, and they spent the next hour and a half hauling the tuna out of the water, then throwing them back so that they could catch them again. By the time the white-gold sun was high in the cloudless blue sky, Laurel's arms and shoulders were aching and her throat was sore from contributing her share to the general noise level of laughing and giggling and whooping.

"Having fun?" Cleese asked as they both ducked to avoid the tuna sailing over their heads.

Fishy water from the flying bonito splashed her check. "Yeah," she said with a laugh.

The school of bonito moved on without them. Breakfast had long since worn off, and Cleese listened to the three women discuss lunch as he headed the boat at a leisurely speed toward the long, low line of Padre Island, a few miles away. While Marcia Hunt and Deane Avery went below to lay out the contents of the coolers everyone had brought, creating an impromptu buffet, he watched Laurel lay the two fish they'd kept on the cleaning board on the stern. With brisk efficiency she began to reduce the tuna to fillets, tossing scraps to the vapor trail of birds who followed them, diving and squabbling over every morsel. One by one, T.C., Jack and Aaron drifted back to help, but he noticed that mostly they rinsed and bagged, leaving the skilled work to her.

Too far away to hear more than the occasional word and laughter, he had to content himself with watching, standing sideways in the cockpit to keep an occasional eye on what was happening ahead of them. It wasn't, he decided, a bad second-best. As the day had gotten warmer, she had stripped off the baggy pants and sweater to the shorts and T-shirt hidden underneath. This shirt didn't advertise anything but her. She'd taken off her sunglasses, as well, hooking them in the neck of her T-shirt, and the weight sagged the soft tan fabric between her breasts. The worn-out pond-sludge baseball cap was still in place, however.

Without words to focus on, he paid more attention to movements and gestures, noticing that she always looked at whichever man she was talking or listening to, her gaze direct and straightforward, her manner easy. Like a man's, he realized; a legacy, no doubt, from all the time she'd spent with her father. Younger men might find it disconcerting or slightly intimidating; older, more experienced ones might see it as a challenge—a sexual challenge. A challenge that was, he was becoming more and more certain, entirely unconscious and unintentional—which only made it that much harder to resist.

The last half of the second fish was about to disappear under the thin, flashing fillet knife. "Put about five pounds of that in a bag for me," he called down. Her response was a significant look from the fish to the knife to the mess on the board and back up to him. "The captain doesn't clean fish," he told her kindly.

The wet fishtail missed his head, more because her aim was a little off than due to any great agility on his part. Ignoring the raucous laughter from the interested bystanders, he answered her sugarcoated smirk with a smug grin.

After lunch, everyone followed their own inclinations. The Averys and Marcia Hunt lolled under the awning they'd rigged, talking, sipping something cool and drowsing to the gentle rocking of the boat as it tugged against the anchor. T.C. and Jack threw lines off the stern to see what they could scare up. Laurel had found a light freshwater spinning rod and was jigging off the bow with the last of the bonito scraps. Setting aside the reel he was playing at fixing, Cleese picked up the can of beer beside it and moved out of the shade cast by the cockpit awning. Grinning to himself, he raised the can and drained the last few ounces. She'd attracted a school of hungry triggerfish, and half the local pelican population, who floated a few yards from the boat in hopes of catching the next fish she threw back.

"I think you fish just to feed the birds."

Laurel turned at the deep, lazy drawl above her. She'd known he was up there in the shadows, working on a fishing reel, watching. Her smile faded as she watched the subtle ripple and shift of muscle as he peeled off the white T-shirt he'd had on under the pullover he'd taken off earlier, leaving him in the low-slung Levi's and deck shoes.

The spinning rod was almost jerked out of her hands, and by the time she'd reeled in the fish, he was squatting beside her.

"You've attracted quite a crowd."

"I know," she murmured, glancing sideways behind her sunglasses. A dense wedge of dark hair covered his chest, tapering down to a thin, silky-looking stripe that disappeared underneath the faded denim.... There was certainly no fat on him. Objective observations only, to be sure.

One pelican, braver than the rest, glided in and landed on the railing a few feet away, and as a reward, Laurel flipped it the fish. Immediately, two more found courage and perched beside the first one. She picked up the empty hook, and he handed her a scrap of bait, their fingers brushing as she took it. A shock tingled her hand and up her arm, very similar to the shock she had felt a few days ago when he'd grabbed her foot to pull off her hip boot. She had come up with a theory to explain that shock, involving the electrical charge in the air from the impending storm, the metal door handle and the damp ground. The theory, conveniently, hadn't included the fact that she had been wearing rubber boots. She glanced up at the sky. Not a cloud in sight. She would have to come up with a new theory.

Tossing the line overboard, she let it free-fall for a dozen feet or so. She jigged the rod slowly up, a fish jigged it down, and a minute later another fat triggerfish dangled at the end of the pole. Seeing the fish, the short chorus line of big, ungainly birds on the rail began doing the pelican version of slam dancing, sliding and hopping while trying to shoulder each other out of the way. Deeper laughter harmonized with hers as Laurel worked to unhook the fish.

"Hurry up, they're getting ugly," he said through his laughter.

Glancing up, she saw the three pelicans on the rail stretching their long necks and longer open mouths hungrily toward her, and those congregated out on the water closing in as if they were about to swarm over the side, and she felt a ridiculously silly thrill of panic that made her laugh again. Finally the hook came free, and seconds later there was a furious flurry of wings and beaks and squawks.

While the birds were settling back down for the next course, he silently passed her the small pail with the tuna scraps. Placing her hand a good six inches from his along the handle, she took it and saw that it was empty. "That's it, guys. No more free lunch," she called to the birds as she stood up. He stood up close beside her, and the silly thrill of panic returned, though without the accompanying urge to laugh this time. She had forgotten, Laurel thought, frowning around her, how...constricting a boat could be.

When she finished rinsing the bait bucket and the deck, she found that he had taken care of putting away the rod she'd used. Now he stood idle, his hands in his pockets, which pulled the faded denim lower on his hips, extending the dark, silky stripe another inch or so. "Is it safe to swim here?" she asked abruptly.

"Sure. Do you—?" Her hands went to the bottom of her T-shirt, and before his mouth had a chance to go dry, she had skinned down to a blue swimsuit and dived over the side of the boat.

As she was kicking toward the sun-glazed surface, Laurel heard and felt the impact of another body in the water, but the peculiar momentary claustrophobia she'd experienced on the boat had vanished the moment the liquid coolness closed over her head. She surfaced and wasn't surprised to see a dark head, sleek and shiny as an otter's, appear a few yards away seconds later. Pointing to the island about a hundred yards away, he asked a silent question, and she answered with a nod.

Padre Island was usually overrun by hikers and beach-combers on weekends, but this Saturday they might have been the last two people on earth. For a while they wandered along the sun-washed shore, drying in the soft, warm breeze as they poked through the trove of shells the Gulf current washed up, holding up a perfect scallop or pink-throated murex for the other one to admire before replacing it for someone else to find and enjoy. Laurel, stopping to investigate one of the small tide pools, nudged a white anemone that responded with an irritated squirt. Carefully avoiding the wagging spines of a purple sea urchin, she picked up a small lightning whelk on the bottom of the pool, then dropped it with a startled laugh when the red hermit crab who had established squatter's rights stuck his head out to see who was making off with his home. Laughing again, she watched the crab and his house scuttle furiously away from her prying fingers, then watched Cleese's big, blunt hands delicately detach a brittle star from a piece of driftwood. Wordlessly he offered it to her, and she held it briefly in her palm, while the delicate legs waved at her, before she placed it back on the weathered wood.

Cleese listened to her laugh as a bigger crab tried to carry off his little toe. He'd thought the slight huskiness of her voice was the temporary effect of a cold, but it was natural, and sexy as hell. Standing up, she looked around as if trying to decide where to go next, then headed toward the slick bank of clamshells behind them. Her swimsuit was made out of some shimmery blue stuff and cut very conservatively, and it was sexy as hell, too.

Behind the bank was a dune carpeted in long grass and morning glories. Laurel climbed it, then turned to see him following her, his long, powerful legs turning the steep climb into little more than a few easy steps. He wore red trunks, not a bikini, although he was one of the few men who could actually do one justice. It was probably just as well he didn't, she thought with a secret grin; riot police were rarely stationed at the beach.

A freshwater pond lay on the other side of the dune where a great blue heron moved through the shallows with slow majesty, stalking dinner. By unspoken agreement, they sat down a few feet below the crest of the dune and for long minutes did no more than watch. Cleese felt no urge to talk, and neither, apparently, did she. While she watched the bird and the pond, he watched her. Jack had told him enough that, with what she had told him and what he had guessed, he had a pretty good idea what she had faced when she returned to Fort Worth six years ago. She had only lived in Fort Worth before during her father's illness, and, with the demands of his care, she must have had little chance to make friends. Then she had moved to Houston. When she moved back, she had not only had to recover from her hellish marriage, she'd had to build a completely new life for herself with new friends in a new house in virtually a new city. He'd had to make a recovery, too, but nothing like hers; he'd had the advantage of living in the same house he'd lived in all his life and the company of friends he'd had since childhood. He was only just beginning to appreciate what she had accomplished in six short years.

The warm fingers of the lazy breeze playing over them lifted the wisps that had escaped from her braid, and her hand rose to tuck them back. She turned suddenly and smiled at him, a soft smile of simple happiness and quiet joy. She had the rare, rare gift of finding pleasure in the simplest things, Cleese thought, smiling back.

Glancing up at the sun, she pushed herself to her feet with obvious reluctance. "I guess we should go back to the boat. Marcia said they had a dinner party to go to tonight."

Right then, he decided that the rest of his "chumming" would include just the two of them. "Yeah, we should."

As they waded back out into the sea, the incoming tide washed up a bottle at their feet, and Laurel stooped to pick it up. It was an empty wine bottle, long and thin, with the cork jammed tight in the neck. From the barnacles growing on it, the bottle had been a long time at sea, and she felt a foolish disappointment that there was no note inside. "I wonder how far it's come," she murmured to the man beside her.

She was expecting a sober, rational guess from him, but all he was wondering about was if her nipples were the same beautiful deep pink as the inside of the shell she'd found. "Probably as far as Corpus," he said, taking the bottle just to give his hands something to do. She made a face at him for his lack of imagination. Oh, darlin', he laughed helplessly inside, if only you knew.

Piloting the boat back in, Cleese watched as, her shorts and T-shirt on again, Laurel settled cross-legged on a cushion on the deck below and began to undo her French braid to brush out her hair. Soon, long, silky flames drifted back on the strong breeze as she worked out the tangles, and he turned to the man lounging next to him. "Take the wheel, T.C."

Laurel was muttering under her breath as she struggled to free a particularly mean snarl when she felt the brush being taken out of her hand. Turning around, she saw Cleese dropping onto the cushion behind her.

"You're going to end up pulling half of it out," he said in a tone of mild exasperation.

After a slight hesitation, she turned back around, and Cleese began working the brush through her hair. Fishing buddies did not brush each other's hair, he thought dryly, but a man had only so much willpower. He brushed her hair out in waves from her head, and the sun shot gold and copper through the silken skeins as they slipped through his fingers. Feeling a tickling on his chest, he glanced down. He'd pulled his Levi's back on, but not his shirt, and now threads of sunset gold mingled with the dark hair on his chest. One strand flicked over a nipple, and he felt it in the soles of his feet.

Laurel set her shoulders and straightened her spine, but, with each stroke, a peaceful languor seemed to seep deeper into her. The pull-and-release motion of the brush was strangely hypnotic, and unconsciously she began to relax, leaning farther and farther, until, totally relaxed, she was lying back against him, her head resting on his bare chest. She was aware of what she was doing and that he was only half-dressed, but it was just some unimportant detail, too insignificant to worry about.

Carefully Cleese set down the brush; her hair had been freed of tangles five minutes ago. His throat tight, he flexed his hands as he forced back the almost overwhelming urge to crush her against him. Finally he crossed his arms lightly across her throat and shoulders. She nestled closer, her dark lashes fluttering, then dropping for good as a small smile curved her mouth. He rested his head against the cabin wall behind them, thinking... savoring... planning....

She was wide-awake again by the time they boarded the jet for the flight home. Evicting Jack Tinnin from the co-pilot's seat with a look, Cleese turned to Laurel, subtly blocking her access to the cabin. "Want to ride up front? It gives you a whole different perspective on flying."

"Sure." Settling into the copilot's seat, she found the seat belt, fastened it, then sat quietly while he went through the preflight procedures with the plane and the control tower. The jet taxied to the end of the runway and stopped while the engine wound up to a high-pitched scream, then started rolling again, faster and faster and faster, until it suddenly rocketed off the ground and headed seemingly straight up into the air.

He looked over at her as the plane leveled off. "You're right," she said with a shaky laugh. "The perspective *is* different."

Grinning, he responded to something that came through the headphones, then slid them down around his neck.

"When did you learn to fly?" She was truly interested in the answer, and it might even stop the mental chasing around she was doing, trying to explain that hair-brushing interlude.

"When I was fifteen. My dad thought it would keep me from chasing girls and breaking my neck rodeoing."

She fell into the role of straight woman perfectly. "And did it?"

"Well—" he reflected a moment while he scratched his jaw "—I never broke my neck."

"Do you fly anything else?" she asked when she stopped laughing.

"I flew helicopters in the army," he said briefly.

Suddenly the mood wasn't quite so light. He must have been in the army years ago, and back then there had only been one place with a lot of helicopters flying. "You were in Vietnam?"

"Just at the end." He looked over at her with a wry expression. "I was young enough and stupid enough to think it would be just a big adventure. I wanted to join the army as soon as I graduated from high school, and my dad was dead set against it. We fought about it my whole senior year. The day after I graduated I enlisted, and my dad was so angry, he didn't come to see me off." He paused to listen to something on the earphones. "Because of my flying experience, I was offered helicopter pilot training. You only had to be eighteen and a half, and you didn't have to go through officer candidate school, so naturally I jumped at it, and before long, I was in Saigon, a brand-new warrant officer with my very own helicopter."

"How long did it take you to get older and smarter?" she asked quietly.

His faint smile was self-mocking. "The first mission. We were just supposed to be picking up a few wounded, but the North Vietnamese had set up an ambush. We got all the wounded, but the rotor got hit, and my door gunner took a round." His left hand unconsciously touched the long white scar just under his hairline. "A couple more of us got nicked. I managed to limp back to base, one hand on my door gunner to keep him from rolling out and the other on the stick." He grinned over at her ruefully. "I was at least a hundred years old when we landed. The war ended about the same time my tour did, and the army suddenly had a surplus of helicopter pilots. They offered early outs, and I took one."

"Was there still a rift between you and your father?" How sad, Laurel thought, if his father had died with the rift still between them.

He laughed. It was the first real laugh since he'd started on the subject. "He was so glad to see me back in one piece, and I was so glad to be back in one piece, that we couldn't remember what the fight was about."

His honesty, rather than the battle scar, was the true sign of heroism, Laurel thought. He'd done his duty, saved no doubt dozens of lives, but he'd had no illusions about the "glory" of war, and he'd been grateful to be out of it. "Do you own a helicopter, too?" She could see that one might be useful on his ranch.

"I used to," he confirmed, "along with a couple motor-cycles and a half-dozen boats, back when I thought I got easily bored." He gave her an ironic look. "That was before the oil bust, when I learned real quick that bigger and fancier and more isn't better."

The oil bust had occurred about ten years before, when the bottom had dropped out of the oil industry and thrown Texas's oil-based economy into a tailspin that some businesses still hadn't pulled out of. Clearly, Starrett, Inc. had, but his comment hinted that it hadn't been easy. There was more sensation of speed in the small jet than in a commercial airliner, and suddenly Laurel found herself resenting the swift passage of the miles. There was so much more she wanted to know about him; those newspaper captions hadn't been nearly as informative as she'd thought.

She was trying to think of a subtle way to be nosy when he pulled the headphones back on and began speaking, and she knew she would have to save her nosiness for the next time. Laurel sat up a little straighter when she realized with a small start that now she was the one automatically assuming that there would be a next time.

"Where is your house key?"

Laurel pulled out the key, although she didn't know why Cleese would want to see it, and he took it out of her hand. After unlocking her front door, he preceded her into the house, then continued on through the house to the kitchen. Making sure the house was safe, she realized. He took the chivalrous notion that a man should see a woman safely home farther than necessary. She was perfectly capable of seeing to her own safety, but, instead of finding his action overbearing or foolish, she discovered she thought it was rather nice. It had been a long time since a man had been concerned with her welfare.

"You should put in a dog door for Frank so he can stay in the house when you're gone," he said, setting her cooler and bag on the table.

"I've thought about it, but, unfortunately, they don't make one big enough." She looked at the time on the microwave. It was early; perhaps he would like to stay for dinner. She hadn't had anything special planned, but she could—

"Well—" Cleese slapped his hands together "—I need to get going." The chumming had gone very well; it was time to leave before he did something stupid and spoiled it.

He already had dinner plans, of course. The level of disappointment she felt astonished Laurel. "The day was perfect. Thanks for asking me along."

The flash of regret he'd seen when he announced he was leaving had been gratifying. "We'll do it again soon," he said easily, returning her smile. As soon as possible.

The cordless phone began to warble wherever she'd last left it. Deciding to let the machine answer, she ignored it, but he didn't.

"There's your phone—I'll see myself out."

After lifting her hand in a little wave as he headed for the front door, Laurel went in search of the phone.

Chapter 4

"What is this?" M.J. looked down at the slip of paper Laurel had handed her as they passed in the hallway at Maxwell's.

"My new phone number."

"You already gave me your new phone number. Last week, remember?" M.J. started to crumple up the slip to throw it away.

Glancing at her watch, Laurel tried to edge past M.J. to reach the closed door just beyond the other woman. "This is a newer number."

M.J. put her hand on Laurel's arm to stop her. "Another new number? What's going on, Laurel?"

She laughed shortly. "My crank caller is what's going on, and on and on."

Wordlessly M.J. pulled her down the hall into an empty counseling room. "How did he get your number again?" she asked after shutting the door behind them.

Turning away, Laurel dragged a hand through her hair. "I probably gave it to him," she said on an annoyed sigh, then looked back at M.J. "You know how they always ask you when you write a check if all the information on it is current? Well, before I thought about it, I said no at the grocery store, and I automatically wrote it on the charge slip at the gas station and probably gave it out several more places I don't remember."

"The grocery store? Maybe it's one of the sack boys, with a surplus of teenage jerkiness?"

Laurel shook her head with a small humorless smile. "He isn't a boy."

M.J.'s worried frown deepened. "What is he saying?"

Laurel glanced at her, then away with another small shake of her head. "Let's just say that he makes Hattie's scripts sound like Valentine cards." M.J.'s face took on a sick look. "I called the phone company first thing this morning, and they sent someone over right away with one of those caller ID attachments for my phone. The woman said that it's usually someone you know in cases like these, but the good thing is that once he's confronted, he stops—for good." She stared sightlessly at the blank white wall. "I don't even want to think about it being someone I know," she added softly.

"Have you told Cleese?"

Laurel's head snapped around. "It's not Cleese, M.J.!"

M.J. waved away the misunderstanding impatiently. "Of course it isn't Cleese. I meant you should tell him because he would want to know. You *are* seeing each other."

"Why would he want to know?" Laurel asked in honest bewilderment. "I only went fishing with him, just one of the group." Now it was her turn to be impatient. "You know that. Jack went, too."

M.J. gave her an unreadable look. "You should tell him, Laurel," she repeated.

Shaking her head at the other woman in exasperation, Laurel moved to the door. "I've really got to go. I'll call you," she added quickly to forestall further argument when she saw M.J.'s mouth starting to open.

* * *

Hattie was collecting scripts when Laurel slipped into her chair. "Sorry I'm late," she murmured. She wasn't, though, Laurel thought with only a trace of guilt. After yesterday, she wasn't really up for a session of role-playing.

"How are things going, Cindy?" Hattie asked as she arranged the scripts in a neat pile in front of her.

Cindy's bruises had faded to nothing, but now an unhappy grimace marred her pretty face. "Well, since I filed the charges, he's stopped hitting and slapping, because he knows he'll go to jail if he doesn't, but in some ways he's gotten scarier. He'll go for hours without speaking to me, even when I ask him a direct question. He looks through me like I'm not even there. Other times, he's laughing, talking, like we've never had a problem. Then sometimes he starts in with the verbal abuse the minute he walks in the door. It's so spooky, like he's playing some mind game with me." Cindy rubbed a hand across her eyes. "Sometimes I wish he'd just hit me instead," she said tiredly.

"Have you mentioned this to his monitor?" Laurel asked. Cindy was still trying to save her marriage, so she and her husband were participating in an abuse-prevention program instead of facing each other across a courtroom. In exchange for avoiding jail time for assault, her husband had to attend counseling and, of course, stop his physical abuse of his wife. The program also included weekly meetings between Cindy and a monitor, who functioned much like a parole officer, overseeing the abuser's compliance with whatever conditions the family court judge had set and what progress—or lack of it—there was.

Cindy nodded.

"What did the monitor say?"

"He told me to tape-record Don every time he's abusive out loud and to keep a log of the times when he gives me the silent treatment."

"What did you think of that idea?" Laurel suspected she knew what Cindy thought by the uncertainty in her voice when she'd repeated the monitor's suggestion.

"I think if Don sees a tape recorder or even me writing down anything, I'm going to have another black eye—or worse. I realize the monitor wants evidence, but..."

Cindy's helpless shrug was more eloquent than any words could have been. Evidence—or, more precisely, the lack of it—was the problem in verbal abuse cases. The victim had no bruises or broken bones to show, so, all too often, it became, as with Lina Renko, just one person's word against the other's. Even when the victim was believed, she frequently had another problem, because too many people still didn't understand that psychological battery was as bad as physical battery—after all, it was just *words. Words* couldn't really hurt you. Discounting the verbal battery made it even worse, because the woman herself could begin to doubt that she was being abused and lose all faith and trust in herself. Don Thomas understood both problems very well and used them to his advantage. Like many physical abusers threatened with the prospect of jail, he simply switched weapons, from his fists to his mouth, knowing he was safe from prosecution. "'But' is right, Cindy," she said. "Evidence is okay, but your first priority is to protect yourself. Don's keeping his hands to himself for now, but if at any time you sense the situation is getting dangerous, that he's about to respond physically to the way you're handling his verbal abuse, get out."

Hattie jumped in with reinforcement. "Cindy, you're fighting for your emotional, psychological and, very possibly, your physical life here. Use your common sense. If Don was a stranger on the street, looking like he was about to attack you, what would you do?"

"Run," Cindy said unhesitatingly.

"Like hell," Olivia added.

Hattie's brief smile was grim. "Right. You'd run like hell. The situation with Don is just like any other dangerous situation. You don't think about it, you just run. That's using your common sense."

Laurel met Hattie's brief glance and saw the worry that both of them felt for Cindy. The problem was that common sense was in short supply with almost all abuse victims when it came to seeing their relationships with their abuser realistically, and even after several weeks of counseling, Cindy's supply was still shorter than most. Hattie didn't lose many clients, but she felt each loss very personally, almost like a death in her own family. "Of every three women's bodies in the Fort Worth morgue, one of them is there because of a husband or boyfriend. That's where 'used, abused and dead' comes from." Nothing like shock value, Laurel thought mordantly as she watched the women, except Lina, absorb that bit of news with varying degrees of sickness. "Four times as many women are injured because of domestic violence than traffic accidents. One-third of the women coming in wounded to emergency rooms aren't there because of an accident—" she caught and held Cindy's bloodshot blue eyes "—no matter what they tell the doctor." Cindy had made an emergency room visit because of an "accidentally" broken nose. It was the ER doctor who had given her one of Maxwell's cards, which Edie kept stocked in every emergency room and urgent-care facility in town.

Cindy looked from her to Hattie in bewilderment. "I don't understand why Don's doing this. Doesn't he want to save our marriage?"

Laurel almost groaned aloud, but, fortunately, Hattie handled frustration better. "No, he probably doesn't," she said matter-of-factly, "not if it means he has to change his behavior. You can set limits, as you've done, Cindy, call him on every offense, make it absolutely clear you won't tolerate any abuse, but remember—" Hattie spaced out her words to make sure they sank in "—the only one who can change his behavior is Don. You can't."

From the mulish look on Cindy's face, it seemed that Hattie's words hadn't sunk in very far. Laurel looked around the table. Mary Cruz's expression reflected the same stubbornness, although not quite to the same degree, while Allene Watts's was thoughtful, and Olivia Jaxon just looked sad. Lina Renko looked as if she were a thousand miles away.

Hattie was only speaking the truth—verbally abusive behavior was the hardest in the world to modify unless the abuser was motivated to save the marriage, and the sad truth was that very, very few were. But Mary and Cindy had to reach that conclusion on their own. She hastened to change topics when she saw Hattie's mouth opening again. Sometimes Hattie tried a little too hard to get her point across. "How did your weekend go, Allene?"

"All right, I guess. My daughter and her husband took me out for breakfast Sunday morning. I spent most of Saturday making curtains for my apartment. It's a nice apartment—" Laurel heard Allene's effort at enthusiasm "—but it's ... lonely," she finished softly.

"Doing better, but feeling worse?" Olivia asked her. Allene nodded, and the two women exchanged smiles of rueful commiseration. After spending nearly thirty years as a verbal punching bag, Allene had decided one day that she wasn't going to take one more hit. She had moved out of the house she had spent most of her adult life in and was on her own for the first time in her entire life. She had filed for divorce, but Laurel knew she still held out hope that her husband would undergo a miraculous transformation before the final decree.

"There is stress with any change, even a good one," Hattie said, including all four women in her glance. "And change doesn't happen overnight. In a way, it's like recuperating from a bad accident and major surgery all at the same time. The accident is the abuse, and the surgery is the removal of the abuse. Your recovery involves taking responsibility for yourself and your own happiness, and even though your injuries and surgery were emotional, it takes just as much energy, and it's just as hard on your body, as if you were healing from physical wounds and incisions. You have to give yourself time, be patient with yourself and be good to yourself—give yourself little treats."

"My treat would be no more men," Allene muttered, and three of the women laughed their agreement. Lina still seemed to be oblivious.

"You have every reason to feel that way right now, Allene," Hattie assured her dryly. "Just keep in mind for the future that men are the opposite, not the opposing, sex."

There was another smattering of laughter, but Laurel knew Hattie hadn't said it for laughs. One of Hattie's greatest concerns was that women would leave Maxwell's hating—or at the very least distrusting—men in general. Emotionally crippled like that, they would never have a chance at a normal, healthy loving relationship. Maybe she should work up a poster with a picture of Cleese Starrett and that slogan to hang in every counseling room, she thought whimsically, then felt a little surprised at herself for the idea.

"Mary, how's everything going with you?" From the hearty cheer in her voice, Hattie was hoping, finally, for an upbeat success story, but, from the down look on Mary Cruz's face, she wasn't going to get it.

"Not so good. Life is just so hard right now." She attempted a wan smile. "Sometimes I'm not sure it's worth it." It was no coincidence that many of the emotional symptoms of battered women were the same as the symptoms of depression, and, unfortunately, when the women made the decision to end the battering and began putting it into action, the depression almost invariably got worse.

"Well, Mary, the upside of being depressed is that when something else bad happens you don't feel any worse than usual," Olivia told her. Olivia's one-liners had the makings of a good stand-up comedy routine, but Olivia wasn't doing much laughing lately, either. Her divorce final and back in the work force as a surgical nurse after a refresher course, it would seem Olivia's recovery was complete, but there was one last stage that didn't get as much mention as the others. It was grief—grief at the loss of all the hopes and dreams she'd had on her wedding day, all that she had missed, all the love she hadn't had. Eventually the grief passed, leaving the determination to do better next time, but it could take, Laurel knew only too well, a very long time.

Mary managed a laugh along with the others before she spoke again abruptly. "You know, I *swore* to myself that I wouldn't end up like my mother, and damned if I didn't." She shook her head in self-disgust, then looked at Hattie. "Why?" she demanded.

"Because, unfortunately, unconscious conditioning, especially at an early age, can be a lot stronger than conscious will sometimes. That's why—" Hattie aimed her next words at the top of Lina's head as she stared at the tabletop "—staying together 'for the sake of the children' can be so wrong, and why it's so important that your children get counseling right along with you. Without it, sixty percent of boys whose fathers are batterers will grow up to be batterers themselves, and fifty percent of the girls whose mothers were battered will be battered women, too. Even if a woman doesn't want help for herself, she owes it to her children to get help for them."

"My mother was a battered woman, too," Cindy said suddenly, her voice and face angry. Condemnation was clear.

Hattie leaned her chin on her steepled fingers as she regarded the younger woman. "Will it do you any good to blame your mother for your abuse, Cindy?" she asked conversationally.

Cindy started to nod her head emphatically yes, then stopped in mid-motion to look uncertainly at Hattie. "No," she said finally with a rueful grimace, "it won't do me any good at all. It would just be a waste of time and energy, and make us both feel bad."

Hattie nodded, her smile gently knowing. "It's the in thing right now to blame your parents for everything that's wrong in your adult life, and," she conceded with a wry grin, "I know sometimes the best thing parents do for their children is to serve as bad examples, but they aren't living your life, so they aren't responsible for what's wrong. *You* are, and because you *are* an adult and not a child, you can change it. And that's what you're doing, Cindy, and you're giving your daughters a good example to follow at the same time, by showing them that they don't have to stand for being treated like a dog."

"Why didn't you go back to your family when your husband started treating you so badly, Mary?" Allene asked. It was something Laurel had wondered about, too, as Mary had talked about her mother and father and several siblings with obvious love and affection.

"Because my mother had warned me not to marry him, and," she said with a sigh, "I didn't want to hear 'I told you so.' I finally figured out last week that I could have just beaten her to the punch and said 'You told me so' first and saved myself five years of aggravation," she added disgustedly.

Everyone laughed, and Mary smiled sheepishly.

Hattie grinned at her sympathetically. "Any particular aggravations the past few days?"

"Yeah." Mary's face screwed up, like an embarrassed six-year old's. "Sex. Leo seems to think that should be his reward for being 'good,' and I can't get it across to him that it's hard to feel warm and loving toward someone who just the day before was constantly putting you down and screaming at you."

The other women—except, of course, Lina—nodded in agreement. Being on the receiving end of abusive behavior destroyed all desire for sex, giving the abuser another weapon to use against—and on—his victim.

"Sex is an important part of a good marriage, a good relationship," Hattie said with her usual straightforwardness. "It can be fun, romantic, inspirational. How good it is depends on how deeply and how often two people share themselves with each other."

An image, definitely warm and loving, flashed into Laurel's mind from out of nowhere, and she choked back a startled laugh. Hattie stopped in midsentence to look at her, and, feeling her face burning, Laurel gestured for her to go on.

A rather lively discussion ensued until it was interrupted by a soft, lifeless voice.

"My husband has never hit me."

Olivia recovered quicker than the rest of them. "Don't worry, girl," she told Lina. "The broken noses and bruises will come." Olivia had never gone into details, but on her first visit to Maxwell's she had been wearing a neck brace and a cast on her left wrist.

"He's never hit me," Lina repeated, with about as much expression as the robot in her studio, Laurel thought. Lina was apparently still telling herself that if it wasn't physical, it wasn't abuse. "He doesn't do drugs or drink or run around with other women. He provides well for me and the children. We have a nice home. Everyone who knows him thinks he's a really nice guy."

Lina sounded as if she were repeating the words by rote, as if she repeated the list often to convince herself of her husband's fine qualities. The last item on the list had Laurel suspecting that, at least once, Lina had tried to tell someone about his less admirable traits and hadn't been believed, because, as with most batterers, Charles Renko's public face was pleasant and charming, not the ugly, hateful one he showed his wife. "Not everyone thinks he's a nice guy, Lina. We don't. Do you think he's a nice guy when he calls you stupid and crazy, when he tells you you're ugly and too dumb to talk to, when he tells you to shut up?"

One thin shoulder twitched in a slight shrug as Lina's eyes dropped to the table in front of her.

"Your husband can say anything he wants, Lina. Do you think somebody's going to put a halo around your head for listening to it?" Olivia asked her, her tone rich in scorn, and Laurel started to frown a warning at her, but Hattie shook her head no sharply. Maybe Lina did need to be shaken up a bit; the gentle approach seemed to be having little effect. "Saints and martyrs went out of style centuries ago."

"Lina," Allene said, more gently, and waited until the other woman finally raised her deadened eyes. "You have to ask yourself the Ann Landers question." At Lina's look of incomprehension, she elaborated. "Are you better off with him or without him?"

Laurel saw reflected in Hattie's eyes her own fear that Lina would come up with the wrong answer.

An hour later, Laurel stood in the middle of the sidewalk, staring down at the card in her hand. It was her card, with her old phone number scratched out and the newest one written beneath. She glanced up to the top row of windows in the building in front of her. Should she presume he would want to know her new number? Should she go on in and tell him in person? Should she call him instead? Should she stay out here on the sidewalk so that she could dither a while longer over something completely juvenile and ridiculous? With a disgusted laugh, she tucked the card back in her purse.

"Fed Ex just brought these, Cleese. I think they're the stuff you ordered Monday."

Cleese looked up from the papers in front of him as his secretary laid two of the familiar purple-white-and-orange envelopes on the corner of his desk. "Thanks, Elena." His glance sharpened on the return address on the top envelope. "And thanks for getting the orders out so fast." Shoving the papers out of the way, he pulled the envelopes closer.

"I forgot to give you this when you came in this morning." Cleese looked up again to see Elena holding out a business card. "Miss Drew came by Monday morning, after you'd left for Houston."

"Thanks," he said absently as he took the card, seeing the printed number lined out, the new one underneath, and the terse message "My new number" in neat draftsman's lettering underneath that. This explained the recorded message he'd gotten when he tried to call her Monday night, Cleese thought, but not why the phone company had refused to give out her new number, telling him it was now unlisted. He tucked the card into the pocket of his white shirt, then ripped open the flap on the top envelope.

She'd led an active social life her two years in Houston, he could see, thumbing through the inch-thick file from the newspaper clipping service Starrett, Inc. used. He went back to the first clipping, a photocopy of the original, like the rest. It was four columns wide and nearly half a page long, and it described a reception celebrating the recent marriage of Paul Lee Falco of Houston to Laurel Jane Drew of Fort Worth. Studying the accompanying photograph, he finally shook his head slightly. No, he had never met him. "Not exactly homely, was he?" Cleese muttered to himself.

He flipped through shots of an extremely photogenic and attractive couple at the opera, the symphony, one fundraiser after another, parties, political gatherings, horse and cattle shows, pausing now and then to read the copy. Was it his imagination that her smile dimmed as he progressed through the stack? A quarter of the way through, he stopped and backtracked to the preceding one, squinted at it, then searched impatiently through the middle drawer of his desk before finally hitting the intercom switch. "Elena, do you have a magnifying glass?"

A few minutes later, he focused it on the hand on Laurel's bare shoulder. Seconds later, he'd solved another mystery, but it brought him no satisfaction, only a tightening in his gut. Falco had worn a heavy-looking ring on his right hand, some sort of signet ring with a round raised center. It showed up often enough that the ring must have been

something he wore regularly. He hadn't, Cleese noted, worn
a wedding ring. He used the magnifying glass several times
more, but he never saw the scar in any of the photos, although he had no doubt now what had caused it and when.
By the last few photos, she had stopped smiling altogether.
The next-to-last clipping had two photos, one of a sports car
too mangled to identify the make, much less the model, and
a file photo of Falco. There was no picture of the "secretary" who had died with him in the wreck. The last clipping was Falco's obituary. For being the deceased's wife,
Laurel had had unusually scant mention in either, but he
suspected that by then she had been taking steps to remove
herself from the position. Death had just beaten the divorce court to it. He closed the file and dropped it in the
trash. It was irrational, he knew, as his hands closed involuntarily into fists, to wish that the son of a bitch could be
brought back from the dead for just five minutes.

He opened the second envelope, and his mood lightened
considerably as he drew out the book. The front of the dust
jacket confirmed his suspicion even before he flipped it over
for the author's picture that he knew wouldn't be there.
There wasn't one on either of the end flaps, either, but then
he suspected the readers would have a hard time understanding why the publisher had used a photo of a young,
beautiful redhead for L. J. Matlock, who "had roamed the
world for over forty years with a fishing pole in his hand,"
according to the author bio.

About five years before, he had opened a hunting and
fishing magazine he bought occasionally to find a hysterical reminiscence of a fishing trip that began with pitching
the tent in solid rock and went downhill from there—including the tent, in a flash flood. The story was told in the
first person by L.J., who had been accompanied by his
childhood cohorts Doc and Flea—or Flee, depending on
which description was more apt at the moment—a dog of
"various and dubious ancestry" who bore a remarkable resemblance to Frank—though only physically, fortunately.

The fish tale had been written in the same sly, deadpan manner he now knew in person, as well as in print, and illustrated with clever pen-and-ink sketches, also in a dry and deadpan style that he had recognized immediately in the half-finished drawing lying on her worktable five days ago. The byline had mentioned that the author was a first-time contributor, so, as soon as he had finished the story, he had ripped out the subscription form and mailed it off, just on the off chance that there would be more stories from L. J. Matlock. There was, one every other month or so, always with L.J., Doc and Flea/Flee, with other semiregulars making occasional appearances. When the announcement appeared in the magazine that an anthology of the best would be published in May, he had reserved a copy the next day at the bookstore around the corner. He had already read them all, he knew, but he didn't care, because he would enjoy them just as much the second time. He and his father had enjoyed—or suffered—many similar fishing trips, and her stories brought back a lot of good memories. She wrote them for the same reason he read them, he was certain: to keep those good memories alive.

As he closed the book, his glance slid across the file folder in the trash basket, and the unconscious half smile curving his mouth tightened to a thin line. As long as he was making irrational wishes, make that ten minutes he'd like to have Falco back.

Chapter 5

"My dad and I built this the summer I turned fifteen."

"This" was a weathered, sturdy one-room log cabin set back about thirty feet from the tree-lined shore of a large lake. As Laurel looked on, Cleese lifted up a section of the windowsill and removed a key ring with two keys. "We leave the keys to the boat and the cabin here so anyone from the ranch can use it," he explained.

"You don't worry about break-ins?" She admitted, to herself only, that she had been looking forward to today with a kind of adolescent excitement ever since he had called. She glanced up at the cloudless sky, then from the sparkling blue-green water to the man a few feet away. Was it possible to have two perfect days of fishing in a row? Three, she amended, adding the rainy day she'd met him.

He stepped down off the porch and picked up her rod case and tackle box along with his. "We haven't had any problems. About a mile of the shoreline on this side is ranch property. It's posted, and most people are pretty good about observing the signs." His grin accented "most," which she ignored pointedly.

He started toward the boathouse and, with that deceptive ground-eating mosey of his, was halfway there before she caught up with him. He was in Levi's again, and an old pearl-snapped cowboy shirt with the sleeves rolled up, the "tycoon" nowhere in sight. Except for a few minutes ago, when she'd glanced over and seen a look on his face more appropriate to a boardroom and the announcement of his takeover of another company. But, like last week, when his tawny eyes had taken on that peculiar and very momentary intensity, the look had been gone before she could swear with complete certainty that she had seen it.

Like all his other "vehicles" she'd seen, there was nothing fancy about his bass boat. It was plain aluminum instead of the glitter-embedded neon fiberglass that always reminded her somehow of Las Vegas and usually cost more than the truck towing it. Obeying his gestured invitation to join him, Laurel stepped down off the catwalk that ran along the sides of the boathouse and into the boat.

As she stepped down, one of the loose, warped boards that he was always meaning to fix tilted under her foot, throwing her off balance, and Cleese grabbed her arm to steady her. It was the first time he'd really touched her—his fingers had become intimately familiar with the lint in the bottom of his pockets—and he was startled when they overlapped around her bare forearm. Watching her, he had the impression of graceful, athletic strength, but that strength was in a fragile framework.

Laurel took the seat in the stern as he took his place behind the wheel in the middle and started the outboard engine. Absently she rubbed her forearm. Static electricity was everywhere, she remembered reading once. The engine settling down to a steady throb, he backed out of the boathouse. Hadn't she?

Turning the boat in a tight arc, Cleese opened up the throttle and headed across the lake. He looked in the direc-

tion Laurel was pointing, then grinned back at her, enjoying her pleasure in nothing more than the sight of so many
snowy egrets congregated on the small island they were
passing that the island was white instead of green. He gestured toward a point jutting out into the lake ahead on their
right and yelled over the roar of the boat engine, "How does
that look?" She nodded, her ponytail streaming out behind her, a hand clamped, unfortunately, on her baseball
cap to keep it from flying off.

Cutting the engine, Cleese let the boat drift into position. Taking a fishing rod and his tackle box out of a stor-
age well, he moved to the prow. Quickly he tied on a
Tornado, shaking out the purple-and-black skirt as he
craned his neck slightly to see what she was going to use.
Taking off her sunglasses, she leaned over the side of the
boat to study the water for a minute, then reached into her
tackle box. He'd breathed a sigh of relief when he'd seen it
when he picked her up. He'd wondered if she was one of
those purists who thought using anything but a fly was
committing major sacrilege. All his worries about any serious incompatibility were laid to rest when she pulled out a
glittery orange Uncle Buck jig and proceeded to dress it with
a bit of pork rind. Incompatibility? He wiped a hand down
his face. Cleese, ol' boy, you've got it bad, he thought ruefully.

"I thought you might use your Weedless Willard."

Laurel looked up from snapping on the jig to see him
standing on the prow of the boat, already casting. "It works
best for river fishing."

Nodding, he started his retrieve. "It was working pretty
well the day I met you. You caught six while I was there."

"I think I caught seventeen in all, but I wasn't keeping
track," she said offhandedly.

Like hell you weren't, he thought with a grin as something tapped the spinner and he yanked back.

"Nice," Laurel commented when he held the bass up a
few minutes later. She slanted him a look as he put the fish

into one of the boat's two livewells instead of releasing it back into the lake. So, they were going to have their own private tournament, were they? Then she'd better get busy. She abandoned her study of his rotating shoulders and hips as he cast out his line again and snapped back her arm to follow suit. Especially when he was already one fish up on her.

Cleese kept the boat in position with the electric trolling motor mounted on the prow, and for the next half hour or so the fish came fast enough that there was little conversation beyond the occasional comment on size, weight or leaping ability. When ten minutes finally passed without either of them having a strike, he looked back at her. "I think we've fished out this hole. Where do you want to try next?"

Laurel looked around as she wound in her line. "I don't know. Over there by those reeds, maybe?" She pointed her rod across the small bay.

The powerful outboard moved the boat across the bay in what seemed like little more than seconds. Before they started fishing again, they paused to admire their catch. "Yours are nicer than mine," Laurel conceded pleasantly, eyeing the contents of his livewell. He had at least two more pounds of fish than she did.

"You caught more," Cleese allowed graciously. Three more, to be precise.

They gave each other false smiles of congratulation, then grabbed their rods with discreet haste.

The fishing was slower, which gave him time to take another lesson in dippin' and flippin', Cleese thought wryly, watching her skip a ghost Rat-Lur like a small flat stone under the overhanging reeds without getting it hung up even once. "You never did tell me why you have a new phone number."

"Oh, there was some trouble on the line," Laurel said vaguely, then swore under her breath as she jerked at a strike and missed hooking the fish. That was what you got for shading the truth.

Cleese gave her a close look. That was the first fish she'd missed all morning. She wasn't telling him everything, like what kind of "trouble" had caused her number to be suddenly unlisted, but he hadn't penetrated far enough yet through that thick barrier of privacy she maintained about herself to press her any harder. So he would press in another direction. "I saw the pictures of your brothers in your house the other day. Do they fish?"

"They used to, before they decided girls were more interesting than flies and worms." After his laugh, she added with a small shrug, "Robb and Jim are so much older than I am, they've always seemed more like uncles than brothers."

He heard the wishfulness under her words. Her uncle-brothers seemed to be the only family she had. He thought of the reunion at the ranch last year, which had drawn more Starretts than anyone had been able to count, and the family photograph albums dating back to the middle of the last century. She might have aunts and real uncles and cousins and albums, but, from the way she displayed what photos he'd seen as rare and precious art, he very much doubted it. She was virtually alone in the world.

And that helped explain what had been eating at him ever since that flinch. How had she ever gotten mixed up with Falco, and, once she realized what he was—and he knew with a sick certainty that she had realized it almost immediately after saying "I do"—why hadn't she gotten the hell out right away? He'd examined his motives for wanting to know, half dreading that he might discover it was because he felt he had to come up with a mitigating excuse for the shameful thing she'd done, but his conscience was clear. On that point, at least, he thought satirically, as he gave a moment's consideration to how devious he was being in another direction. She had done nothing for which either one of them had the slightest reason to be ashamed. He just wanted to know, the way he wanted to know if her eyes were darker when she first opened them in the morning, what her favorite food and color were, how big the first fish she'd ever caught had been, what she listened to on the radio, whether she preferred baths or showers . . . in short, everything about her.

"Pass me the net, will you?"

Since his line was in, he manned the net, then, while she unhooked the three-pound smallmouth bass and added it to her livewell, he dug around in his tackle box until he found something close to the gold Cat'R'Crawler she was now using. He'd had a few nasty suspicions about her father although they hadn't lasted long. From what Jack Tinnin had told him, bits and pieces from Laurel and educated guessing, he had a pretty good idea what kind of father "Doc" Drew had been. He hadn't been a bad one, just rather selfish. Drowning in pain and loneliness when his wife died, his sons already gone away to college, his daughter had been the only person he could cling to to save himself. And so Laurel had become his best—and maybe only real—friend. Wherever he'd gone, Laurel had gone with him, learning about dry flies and crank baits and—she'd mentioned casually—bars and pool halls, becoming a pinball wizard at the age of eleven. Because of their frequent moves, she'd never had the chance to form firm friendships or put down roots; all either of them had had was each other. Her departure for college must have been hard for both of them, but it had been worse for her father, he was sure, and he had to admire the courage it must have taken to let her go. She turned to grin at him as a mallard hen and her seven ducklings chugged by. More courage than he would have had.

He yanked back automatically at the nudge on his line and began reeling in. She'd lived in a male-dominated world until college, but he suspected she hadn't had much experience with any men her own age, and going to a women's college probably hadn't given her much more. Afterward, when she ought to have been making up for lost time, circumstances had conspired against her again. She'd spent the next two years in virtual isolation; then, hardly days after

losing her father, she'd met Falco and—lost, lonely, grieving—fallen prey to him. Having had no chance to witness a
normal relationship between a man and a woman after the
early loss of her mother, and still staggered by the death of
her father, Laurel had had no ready defenses against Falco.
She had them now, though, in spades, for which he was
glad, even though it meant things were going to take longer
than he'd have liked. Fishing, he reminded himself as he
boated a respectable smallmouth, was a sport that rewarded patience.

"Do you have any brothers or sisters?" Laurel managed
a covert snoop into his livewell when he dropped in his latest fish. She was still ahead by two, but that last one gave
him the edge in total weight again.

"Two younger sisters. One's in Austin. Her husband is in
politics. They have two kids. The other one defected to
California. She and her husband have a law practice together and three kids. They both think fishing is only
slightly more fun than a root canal." He looked around as
he reeled in after another strikeless cast. "We'll move over
to the bluffs," he decided.

Settling into the rear seat as he shoved the throttle forward, she smiled at his back. She would have known his
sisters were younger; he was too bossy for them to be older.
Twenty yards from the sandstone bluff that formed most of
the eastern shoreline, he killed the outboard and moved
forward to study the water, using the trolling motor occasionally to move the boat a few yards. She'd noticed he
didn't have any of the gadgets a lot of fishermen used to lo-
cate and catch fish—no water-temperature meter, no color
selector to see which color lure would show up best in the
water, no pH meter, not even a fish finder. He fished by the
seat of his pants. She hadn't meant "seat of the pants" literally, she told her interested eyes, and directed them toward the bluff.

"Did your husband like to fish?"

"No," Laurel said briefly. "Did your wife?" The word stuck in her throat slightly, probably because she couldn't imagine him ever marrying anyone stupid enough to divorce him in the first place.

He laughed shortly. "No. She and my sisters had the same opinion of fishing. That was about the only thing they had in common."

"Then why did you marry her?" Laurel couldn't believe the question had come out of her mouth. *Because you want to know the answer,* a small voice told her dryly.

"Because I was dazzled," he said readily. *The way I'm dazzled now,* he added silently, *except my eyes are wide open this time.* "I'd known a lot of women, thought I was pretty experienced, but I'd never met one like Helene."

Laurel experienced a sudden, odd low feeling. He would have known a lot of women.

"She was a year older than I was, glamorous, sophisticated, gorgeous."

The feeling went down another few notches.

"For the first couple of years, everything was okay—not great, but okay." Noting the bubbles on the surface, Cleese sorted through the top tray in his tackle box for a topwater lure. "Helene liked to spend money, and I was making plenty of it. I knew my dad and sisters didn't much care for her, although they never said anything, but I figured they'd come around in time. Then the oil bust hit."

As he cast and began a walk-the-dog action with the Zara Mouse he was using, Laurel realized her line was still lureless. More to give the impression that she was only mildly interested in what he was saying than anything else, she snatched up a Thundertoad, tied it on and made a hurried cast.

"We had made the same mistakes everybody else had, expanded too fast, so we were overextended, owed too much money, but my dad and I were determined we wouldn't end up like everybody else. We'd taken the company public three years before, and a lot of our stockholders were retirees who couldn't afford to get only the thirty or forty cents on the dollar they'd get if we went into bankruptcy. We had a lot of employees depending on us for a paycheck, too, so we liquidated every possible asset, including personal property. The only thing we kept was the ranch.''

He paused for a few seconds while he unhooked the fish he'd caught and added it to the livewell, then continued in the same matter-of-fact tone. "Helene wasn't too happy about having to sell the big, fancy house in town and move into an apartment. The money dried up, of course, which didn't make her any happier, but I was so busy fighting to keep the company alive, I didn't really notice. We asked our employees to take pay cuts, which—'' he shook his head with a disbelieving laugh "—they did, taking on faith our promise that we'd make up the money as soon as the company was back on its feet. Then, just as we hit bottom, my dad had a heart attack. It wasn't serious, but he had to have a double bypass, which left me running everything. The morning of his surgery, I was served with divorce papers.''

Laurel had been casting and retrieving by rote, going slower and slower, until finally she had stopped altogether and sat down on the rear seat. "What a bitch,'' she breathed.

He looked over at her with a crooked grin as he threw out his line again. "Yeah, but she did me a big favor. She wanted a million dollars, or she threatened to sue for her share of my half of the company. I told her to go ahead—I'd take the company into bankruptcy, and she could line up with the rest of the creditors and maybe, in five years or so, she might get ten cents on the dollar. Her lawyer must have convinced her I wasn't bluffing, because she settled for a hundred thousand.'' He laughed wryly. "I didn't have it. Hell, I would have had trouble scraping up a hundred dollars at that point, so I mortgaged my share of the ranch, paid her off and considered myself lucky to have gotten out so cheap. Right after that, things started to turn around. Three years later we were able to pay everyone their back wages, and I paid off the mortgage on the ranch a year after that.''

His wife couldn't have bothered to get to know him at all, or she would have known right away that he was stubborn enough to do just what he'd said he would do, Laurel thought. She would have offered sympathy, but he clearly neither wanted nor needed it. "What happened to her?"

"She got married about six months later, to a rich widower twice her age, and a hell of a lot smarter than I was." His chuckle was surprisingly good-natured. "He had her sign a prenuptial agreement.''

To her surprise, Laurel found herself laughing with him, the low feeling gone as suddenly as it had come. He set his rod aside and closed up his tackle box, and she remembered her line and hurriedly wound it in, finding a fish on the end of it.

Seeing her surprise, he grinned. "Want to go get some lunch?''

Lunch was the blue whale of hamburgers and the greasiest french fries Laurel had ever seen, at the small marina across the lake. Cleese paid because, as he said, he owed her a lunch. Without wasting time, she handed over her fries, which he ate with obvious relish while she shook her head at him pityingly. Cutting her hamburger in two, she picked up one half, along with the train of thought that had begun on the run across the lake. She'd spent little time rehashing the story of his marriage. It hadn't been pretty, but she heard much uglier ones on a thrice-weekly basis. All that was important was that he'd survived it, and obviously very well. What intrigued her was how he had handled economic, not marital, disaster. Having lived in Texas the past decade and a half, she was all too familiar with stories of financial ruin, but his had had the rare happy ending. The same sense of responsibility that had made him risk his own life to save his door gunner's had been at work ten years later, when he'd risked his financial life to save those of his

stockholders and employees. From what she had seen, it
would have been much easier just to declare bankruptcy and
walk away, but he hadn't done that; he'd fought as hard as
he knew how to keep his company going, sacrificing his own
personal assets to do it. Older, more experienced men had
tried to do the same thing and failed, but he hadn't. Maybe,
she thought with an unconscious smile, because of sheer
stubbornness. It would sound corny, said out loud, but he
was just as much a hero as those who wore uniforms and
collected medals. He was one of the unsung ones who did
nothing more than keep people working and pay back in-
vestors. That took as much guts and courage as running into
a burning building to save a child; maybe more, because he
had to do it day after day, year after year. And if for no
other reason, she thought with a silent laugh, because he
looked so good in Levi's.

She looked up to see the hero studying her paper plate.
"You don't want the other half of your hamburger, do
you?"

As they were gathering up their lunch trash a few minutes later, he reached across the table suddenly, and Laurel
felt her hat being lifted off. To her amazement, he added it
to the pile on his paper plate and started for the trash con-
tainer. After a few blank moments of disbelief, she scram-
bled after him.

"Cleese, what are you doing with my hat?" she whispered furiously, mindful of the big-eared crowd in the café.

He paused, the plate poised over the open trash can. "Do
you have any particular sentimental attachment to it?"

"No, but I've had it since high school."

"It looks like it," he said, and dropped the plate in the
trash. She peered down into the mess of cups and plates and
napkins, still unable to believe he'd really done it, then
slowly looked back to him.

He pulled out the baseball cap she'd noticed in his back
pocket, wondering why he didn't wear it, and settled it
firmly on her head. She just caught a glimpse of the em-

blem embroidered in yellow on the brown hat—an *S* inside a square, the same symbol she'd seen on the door of his pickup. An odd sensation went through her. She was wearing his...brand?

"There," he said with obvious satisfaction, then took her elbow and calmly steered her toward the door.

Now he was going to find out just how broad-minded she was. After killing the engine, Cleese walked forward, squatted down beside his tackle box, opened it and lifted out the top tray to reveal a mass of worms, leeches, water dogs and crawdads in every color of the rainbow—all made out of plastic. Using a Texas-rig, he slid on a couple of red beads for the rattle effect, then embedded the hook in the plastic head of a june-bug-colored and silver-glitter-sparkled Mogambo Grub. Holding his rod upright, he paused for a minute to decide where to cast first.

"Hmm...Idiot bait."

He turned to see her delicate sneer. "Idiot bait" was the term for any plastic bait and meant the obvious: Any idiot could catch fish with it. "What're you going to use?"

Straight-faced, she held up a skinny plastic worm in Christmas colors with a bristling row of squid-like hot-pink legs grafted down each side.

"Make that, too?"

Nodding, she attached the monstrosity to her line in a Carolina-rig. She cast and proceeded to give him another lesson. The mechanics were simple: The sliding sinker tied above the worm dragged it down through the weedy cover, where the sinker sank to the lake bottom, settling into the weeds while the worm floated above them. Then the fisherman dragged or hopped the sinker over the lake bottom, and the sinker transmitted the action to the worm—in theory. In actuality, nine times out of ten, the sinker got hung up because the fisherman dragged it too fast. Laurel was the tenth time. She crawled the sinker and attached worm slowly over the lake bottom and grass as if it were a night crawler inching its way along. He was starting to count off the third minute using the second hand on his watch when suddenly she pointed the rod tip down low over the water, quickly took up the slack and yanked up, giving it all the muscle she had. A four-pounder joined his cousins in her livewell a few minutes later.

An hour later they were, by Cleese's estimation, dead even in number and weight. It was time for more drastic action. Pulling a bottle of garlic oil out of his tackle box, he held it up. "Would you like some?" he offered politely, fully expecting her to say no.

She looked down her nose with equal politeness. "Thank you, I have my own." She rummaged around in her tackle box and came up with a small white plastic bottle. The trade name was Stink, because that was what it did. Fish loved it, and he would use it himself, except he couldn't stomach the smell. Apparently she could—barely. Holding her rod at arm's length out over the water, she doused the lure liberally, then extended the bottle toward him, pointing to the long yellow worm on his line, salted with large white crystals. "Want some for your French Fry?"

"No, thanks." His eyes narrowed as she tilted her head up a little and he got a good look at her nose.

Laurel was just getting ready to cast when he came back toward her with something in his extended right hand. She held out her hand automatically, and he slapped a small tube of sunscreen into it.

"Your nose is getting a little pink."

While she was rubbing the sunscreen over her nose, cheeks and chin, he pointed to his mouth. "Do your lips, too." Dutifully, she did, hiding a smile as she rubbed her fingers over her mouth. Could a bossy big brother have had anything to do with his sisters' aversion to fishing?

"Do you want to try another spot or head in?" Secretly Cleese hoped she would choose the latter. The past forty-five minutes she and her little white bottle had outfished him to the point where he was considering holding his nose and taking her up on her offer.

Instead of choosing either of his alternatives, she pointed toward the back of the bay they were fishing. "What's going on over there?"

He looked in the direction she was pointing and saw the sparkle of flying water as something big splashed in the shallows. "I don't know. Let's go see."

Going in at low speed so that they wouldn't scare whatever it was, Cleese soon realized that he could have gone in with the engine roaring and it wouldn't have disturbed the splashers at all. "It's a school of carp, spawning."

What most people considered trash fish were an ugly dull brown out of the water but a beautiful golden bronze in it, the sun flashing off their large iridescent scales, turning them into flat prisms shining with every shade in the rainbow. "I don't think I've ever seen any that big before. Some of them must weigh fifteen pounds," Laurel murmured.

Her opal eyes were glowing when she turned to him, giving her the look of a little girl entranced by some new wonder.

"Wanna catch 'em?"

She shook her head uncertainly. "How? I'm sure they wouldn't bite on anything right now."

For an answer, he held up his hands, waggling his fingers. Her uncertain look was immediately replaced by a wide grin as she laughed. "Yeah. Let's!"

Without bothering to take off their sneakers or roll up their jeans, they jumped in, and what followed was the most uninhibited, plain stupid fun Cleese had ever had. The water was only knee-deep, and the carp largely ignored the two-legged creatures splashing after them, but the big, slippery fish still weren't easy to catch until they hit upon the trick of grabbing at the base of the tail with one hand and then, before the fish started trying to get away in earnest, slipping a hand underneath a gill cover. It didn't hurt the fish, although it probably annoyed them some, he conceded. Because they were, technically, fishing, it quickly became a contest to see who could catch the biggest. Laurel held up a lunker with a smug grin until the fish suddenly thrashed and its tail smacked her on the cheek. With a shriek, she dropped it, and he was starting toward her, concerned, until he realized the gasping sounds coming out of her were giggles and not sobs.

One fish, who looked like the granddaddy of all the rest, had succeeded in eluding both of them, so they joined forces. They moved in slowly from either side, herding the giant carp toward the shallows until they had him corraled. On Cleese's silent signal, they both lunged—and came up empty-handed.

"The one that got away," Laurel intoned gravely, staring after the fleeing fish. Still weak with laughter, she groped automatically for something to hold her up.

"No trophy today," he agreed. For a moment Cleese froze at the feel of her arm sliding around his waist, then his body thawed as a slow heat rose and radiated through him. Glancing down, he saw that the big wave they had made trying to nab the fish had dampened her T-shirt interestingly. "There's a lot to be said for pure dumb fun once in a while," he murmured, casually draping an arm around her shoulders.

Laurel laughed. "Yes, there is." Silly, I-don't-care-if-anybody's-looking, laugh-till-you're-sore fun had been in pretty short supply the past few years.

Tilting her head back against his arm, she smiled up at him, her ripe mouth curved sweetly, her eyes bright with laughter, the wisps that had escaped from her ponytail clinging to her pink cheeks. His eyes focused on her mouth. Sometimes temptation shouldn't be resisted, he decided.

He felt her startled reaction in her stiff lips, then they softened, and he pressed harder. Her mouth was as lush as he had imagined, and as sweet. Tightening the arm around her shoulder, he curled his free hand behind her neck to pull her to him. She stiffened, like a wary wild creature, but made no move to draw back. If he'd thought about it, he probably would have tried to ease her closer, but his instincts were smarter. He did close the distance between them, but he went to her instead of pulling her to him, and that small difference made all the difference. As he stepped closer, the tight muscles under his hands relaxed, and her body seemed to find all the hollows and concavities in his and fill them. The arm around his waist flexed, drawing him even closer as her other arm stole around him, her hand sliding small sparks up his backbone.

Dimly Laurel was aware of his big hand winding in her hair, changing the angle of their mouths, taking her by degrees into a deep slow kiss like nothing else she'd ever experienced. Heat spilled through her, which, paradoxically, made her shiver, and she sought more of his hard, warm body. His mouth turned from request to demand, and she met it, her lips parting, making demands of their own. His tongue explored her bottom lip, the top, the corners of her mouth, then took a deeper taste inside, and she moaned softly as her hands tightened in his shirt.

Her soft moan was the warning alarm he needed. Another sixty seconds and he probably would have ignored it, Cleese thought sardonically. Gradually he pulled out of the kiss, her arms and mouth releasing him with a reluctance that indicated she hadn't been satisfied any more than he had. Her eyes opened slowly, with a heavy, dreamy look, and he risked another kiss, shorter and harder. Her eyes widened, something that looked close to shock replacing the drowsiness, and he released her a fraction of a second before her arms dropped abruptly and she stepped back. "Mmm..." He licked his lips reflectively. "Carp and Coppertone. A unique taste."

Confusion edged into the shock, and he saw her struggle to treat the kiss as casually as he had, when both of them damned well knew it had been anything but. "As good as french fries?"

He had to admire her fast recovery; she matched his light tone note for note. "Different." Infinitely better. He saw her glance follow his around them, seeing that the school of carp had moved off. "Looks like fun's over for the day." In more ways than one. He dropped a loose arm over her shoulders, ready to remove it immediately if there was a flinch or any attempt to pull away. There wasn't. He gave her an easy smile. "We probably should head in."

After a few seconds' hesitation, she returned a smile of equal easiness. "Y-yes, we should."

After declaring a draw, they released the bass, and then Laurel took her seat at the back of the boat and began derigging her fishing rod, giving the job far more attention than it called for. He hadn't found the kiss so unremarkable, either, despite his careless attitude. His heart had been hammering against hers, his eyes glittering, his face flushed. And then there was the other sign a man couldn't hide—not that he'd tried to.

Having stowed his rod and tackle box, he took the seat behind the wheel and turned the ignition key. The engine turned over, then sputtered and died. After it happened again, he went back to the stern with a pair of pliers in his hand and removed the cover on the outboard. He fiddled with something, then glanced at her. "Turn the key when I tell you, will you, please, Laurel?"

She moved to the middle seat and waited, her hand on the ignition key. He tinkered for a minute, then said, "Now." She turned the key, and the engine caught, but then died again.

"The gas doesn't seem to be getting through the filter," he muttered, whether to her or to himself, she wasn't sure.

"Is that a variation on the old 'Gosh, I think we're out of gas!' line?" she asked interestedly.

He looked over his shoulder at her. "It might be, if this was a date," he said blandly.

"Oh! Well, no, of course." Laurel managed a credible laugh. "This isn't a date. We're just—" she gestured broadly "—fishing."

"Right." Cleese bent over the engine again, hiding a satisfied smile. He had thrown, he was sure, his last handful of chum. Removing the fuel filter, he blew through it, then reconnected it. "Now," he said.

She turned the key, the engine caught, fluttered a few times, then settled down to a steady idle, and her smile toasted his success. Now, he repeated silently.

Laurel followed as once again he did a security check through her house. It was only the second time, she reminded herself; it shouldn't feel like habit. Pausing at the front door, they both turned at the sound of a loud, wet sneeze behind them. Frank was no longer insisting on being between them, she noted absently.

"Frank's hay fever seems to be worse."

Laurel leaned down to rub his ears. "The medication he had wasn't working anymore. I picked up a new prescription at the pharmacy last night, but I don't think he's doing any better."

As she straightened up, she saw that Cleese was holding out her key. Laurel took it, surprised that she had forgotten he still had it. "Thanks." Suddenly she felt ridiculously shy. "I had a great time today."

Cleese smiled slightly. "So did I." He'd made a casual offer of dinner, which she'd declined, saying she already had "plans." He wondered who "plans" was. The sooner he got her tagged, the better. He glanced up at the new cap on her head. But then, he already had, in a way. She was wearing his brand. "I'll call you Monday."

"Okay. I—"

His mouth on hers slammed the rest of the words back down her throat. The kiss was hard and brief, and she barely suppressed a groan of frustration when he pulled away. Seconds later he was gone, and for several long moments she stood staring blindly at the key in her hand, until the phone jarred her back to reality.

Cleese unlocked the car door, then paused, looking across the roof of the car toward the house he'd just left. A light came on in the living room, making the colors in the stained glass panels glow softly against the dusk. Her mouth had been hungry on his; she'd taken the bait, and he had her hooked. He reached for the handle and swung the door open. And he could take his hands out of his pockets.

Chapter 6

Cleese turned away from the door. It had been a bitch of a week; why should it change now? What was supposed to have been a quick day trip to Mexico City on Monday to negotiate oil leases had become three days in the Yucatán jungle to look over a just-discovered oil field. A hurried call on Monday morning had only gotten him a recording telling him that her number had been changed and he couldn't have the new one. When he got back to his office this afternoon, the new number had been waiting for him, but he had decided to find out in person just what the hell kind of "trouble" on the line she was having. And just because he wanted her to be home was no reason to expect that she would be, he thought sourly. As he stepped off the porch, a congested-sounding woof came from the side yard, and he laughed softly in spite of himself. Maybe he and Frank could sit in the backyard and console each other until she came home, if the dog didn't add him to his bone collection.

He was starting around the house when he saw a familiar figure coming around the corner down the street, on foot and lugging what looked like two full grocery sacks.

"Where's your hot rod?"

With a grateful murmur, Laurel let him take the grocery bags out of her arms. "Cooling its wheels in the pharmacy parking lot."

She was wearing a dress—a very nice dress, he saw, covertly eyeing the way the slim skirt fit her hips and bottom. "Did it break down?"

"Oh, no, I leave it there the fourth Thursday of every month and carry home twenty pounds of groceries for the exercise."

He hefted the bags. More like twenty-five. The annoyance prissing her soft mouth controlled his urge to laugh. "What's the matter with it?"

As they started up the front walk, she started digging around in her purse for her key. "The sum total of my knowledge of auto repair is how to change a flat tire." She looked at him as she handed over her key. "The tires aren't flat."

She handed the key over automatically now, he noted with approval. "It just wouldn't run?" Unlocking the door, he shepherded her through it, then led the way into the kitchen.

She sighed tiredly. "It started up okay, went about twenty feet, then just died in the middle of the parking lot. Fortunately, a couple of guys drove by and were willing to push it out of the way into a parking space for me." She peered glumly into one of the sacks he had set on the kitchen table. "I bet my ice cream's melted."

The soft fabric of her skirt pulled tight as she bent over. He would just bet they'd been willing. Reaching over her shoulder, he took the ice cream out of the sack. "Almost." Sticking it in the freezer compartment of her refrigerator, he asked evenly, "Why didn't you call me?"

She paused in unloading the grocery bag to give him a surprised look. "Cleese, I wouldn't disturb you at work for something like that."

Would she "disturb" him for anything? he wondered, then shook off a sudden bleakness. Patience, he reminded himself. "Then why didn't you call a cab?"

Shaking her head, she went back to the grocery sack. "It's only a mile or so, although, the last block, it did seem closer to two." She looked up at him with a wide smile as he started to empty the second sack, setting the items on the table for her to put away. "I sure was glad to see you."

That made up, some, for not calling him. "I'll take a look at it. Unless you have plans?"

Laurel wondered briefly why his deep voice had hardened on the last word. "No, I don't have any plans, but you have good clothes on." When, Laurel wondered, looking at his charcoal wool-and-silk suit, had she begun to think of men's clothes as "beautiful"? "You don't want to get grease all over yourself."

His gesture said that wasn't worth discussing. "We'll go as soon as the groceries are put away." To speed the process along, he held up a box of shredded wheat. "Where does this go?"

"Next to the stove, the top cupboard."

The cupboard was neat, but not neurotically so. When Cleese turned around, she was tearing open a small white stapled bag. "Another prescription for Frank?"

"Yes. I hope this one finally works. He's pretty miserable."

"I hope so, too," Cleese said gravely.

Laurel shook out a capsule, then opened the back door. "Frank! Come here, boy," she called. Frank shambled to his feet, then started across the yard, head down, paws dragging, the very picture of canine suffering. "You big faker," she told him with exasperated affection, meeting him halfway. "If you were feeling half as bad as you're pretending to, you'd be unconscious." She was just putting the pill in his mouth when she heard the faint warble of her phone. Putting the warning prickle down to paranoia, she rubbed his head as he swallowed. "Good dog."

One look at Cleese's face as she stepped back into the kitchen and she knew she hadn't been being paranoid after all.

"One of the reasons I came over was to find out why you have yet another phone number. I guess now I know, don't I?"

Laurel slumped against the kitchen table in sudden exhaustion. "What did he say?"

She wouldn't have thought it possible, but his mouth thinned to an even narrower slash. "Nothing you probably haven't heard already, but I won't repeat it. How long has this been going on, Laurel?"

"Oddly enough, the calls started the day I met you," she said with a ghost of a smile. "Almost every time I've seen you since, there have been more."

"You must have suspected me," he said expressionlessly.

Laurel held his eyes. "Not even for an instant."

"Then why haven't you told me?" he asked with deceptive softness, approaching her.

Laurel looked up at him, puzzled by the question. "Because it doesn't concern you, Cleese," she said reasonably.

"It doesn't concern me?" Cleese said even more softly. "Damn it, Laurel!" he exploded. "Everything that has anything to do with you concerns me!"

He moved so fast that his big hands had her shoulders in a firm grip before she realized that he had moved. Shrugging off her startled fascination at the reignition of his eyes, she shot back, "I can't be running to you, Cleese!"

"The hell you can't, and you'd damned well bet—" Suddenly Cleese saw where his hands were and turned sick. Jerking his hands off her shoulders, he turned away and tried to swallow the rotten taste in his mouth. God, she was going to think he was no better than Falco. He would never hurt her, no matter how angry he was, but she didn't know that—yet. Steeling himself for the fear he might see, he faced her. "I want you to tell me when you're upset or worried or scared or just need help, Laurel," he said quietly.

Laurel folded her arms across her chest. "Why?"

"Because I l-like to know what's going on in my friends' lives." What he had almost said shocked him nearly as much as it would have shocked her, Cleese thought dryly.

"Well, you certainly know how to defuse an argument," Laurel said, giving him an exasperated look. That the unknown caller had somehow, once again, gotten her new phone number was frankly enough to make her panic if she wasn't careful, yet what she wanted to do right now was laugh with sheer joy. She had just had a fight with a big, strong, forceful man, and the only thing she had felt was *mad!* It was wonderful! For six years she had worried that she wouldn't be able to handle arguments and normal male frustration and anger, and now she had not only handled all three, she'd held her own. In fact, the fight had ended too soon, as far as she was concerned. A good fight was just what she needed to relieve some of the tension she felt right now.

He had even put his hands on her, and she hadn't flinched or cringed or even thought about being afraid, because she trusted him absolutely never to use his strength and size against her. Because he was Cleese, she thought, tempering her giddy self-congratulations with a little dose of reality.

She wasn't showing any sign of fear; if anything, she looked almost . . . cheerful. "You've gone to the police?"

She gave him a mild look. "Yes, I've gone to the police. After the second time, the phone company put one of those caller IDs on my phone." Raking a hand through her hair, she took a turn around the kitchen. "They said it's usually someone you know, and if he's confronted, he'll stop."

She didn't look cheerful now; she looked ill at the thought that it might be someone she knew, someone she liked. "Were you going to confront him?" His blood ran cold at the thought that she might have tried to deal with the bastard herself.

She shook her head with a humorless laugh. "No, I'm not that stupid. The phone company would have handled it, but the caller ID couldn't identify him. He's either got a device to block it on his phone, he's calling long-distance, or he's got a cellular phone. That's when I called the police. They put a tracer on my phone Monday." She glanced toward the refrigerator. "I better call and see what I'm supposed to do now."

Cleese saw the business card anchored under a magnet on the refrigerator door, and, because he was closer, he got to it first. Reading the name on the card, he nodded to himself in satisfaction. "I'll call while you put the rest of the groceries away."

Laurel didn't answer for a moment. She should call—it was her problem—but the knowledge that he was willing to share it, the relief that she wasn't facing this unknown enemy alone any longer, had silly tears stinging at the backs of her eyes, and the urge to let him handle it, just for a few minutes, was overwhelming. "All right." She achieved a fleeting smile. "Thank you, Cleese."

Listening to him on the phone a few minutes later brought another smile, one that came a little easier this time. A cynic might have said the cooperation he was getting was graphic proof that money talks, but it wasn't money talking, it was friendship. It took less than a minute of his side of the conversation for her to understand that he and the police lieutenant who'd given her his card were old friends, just as he was friends with "Duane," the man he called next to send someone right away to look at her car. Cleese Starrett was someone who kept his friendships, valued them, as, Laurel thought wryly, he'd demonstrated rather forcefully a few minutes ago.

The mechanic arrived first, and, from the sign on the side of the truck, Laurel realized that "Duane" owned the dealership where she had bought her four-wheel drive. She looked at the two men, one in a five-hundred-dollar suit, the other in greasy coveralls, talking easily as equals. It wasn't condescension on Cleese's part; the suit was a function of his job, just as the mechanic's coveralls were of his, and she suspected that, given a choice, Cleese would prefer Levi's. She smiled to herself. She knew she did.

As the service truck was pulling away, an unmarked police car took its place. Ty Burnett was only slightly smaller and slightly less good-looking than Cleese, and having both of them in the same room was almost more than a mere mortal woman could handle, she thought with a silent rueful laugh. Maybe thinking about Levi's and men who were too handsome for a woman's good was crazy at a time like this, but it was keeping the fear and the anger at bay.

Beyond a handshake, neither man wasted time on courtesies. "Did you have any luck tracing the call?" Cleese asked as he sat next to her on her living room sofa. She could feel the heat radiating from his body, smell his faint soap-and-spice scent, and was grateful for his warm solidity beside her.

The lieutenant sighed heavily. "Good and bad. He's local, but he's using a cellular phone. We can trace it to the closest transmission cell, but beyond that..." His grimace of frustration finished the sentence. "Once we have a suspect, we can check the record of his calls and get definite proof, but we have to have a name first."

"You don't have any names at all?" Cleese asked sharply.

Instead of answering, Ty Burnett looked at her. "Laurel, who did you give your number to this last time?"

"Only seven people," she answered immediately. "M. J. Tinnin, the secretary at Maxwell's, my brothers, my agent in New York, the vet, and Cleese. I wrote to my brothers. They probably won't have gotten the letters yet."

"You didn't give the number to anyone at the pharmacy?"

"Not this time. The vet called the prescription in, but I probably wouldn't have given it to them anyway." Cleese got up and left the room without explanation. Her curious eyes following him, she added, "Although I'm certain it isn't anyone connected with the pharmacy. Except for the delivery boys, everyone who works there is a woman, and it's been that way since I started going there five years ago. The owner's husband worked there occasionally, but, since they divorced last year, I haven't seen him. They owned two pharmacies. She kept the one I go to, and he took the other."

Cleese came back and silently showed the prescription bottle she had just picked up to Ty Burnett. "What?" Laurel asked.

"The pharmacy had your current phone number." Cleese let her see the label on the bottle, then handed it to the other man.

Puzzled, she looked from one man to the other. "How did they get it?"

"Let's find out." Ty pulled a mobile phone out of the holster on his hip. He wore his gun, Laurel had noted, under his arm. Cleese came back to the sofa, and they waited in silence while Ty had a brief conversation with the head pharmacist. "They got it from the vet," he said as soon as he hung up. "They ask routinely, just to make sure they have a current number, the same way they ask customers."

Cleese gave him a hooded look. "Have you checked out the vet and his staff?" His eyes, Laurel noticed absently, hadn't yet regained their usual lazy-big-cat look.

"The vet checks out fine—he doesn't even have a cellular phone, and the staff is all women."

"What about husbands and boyfriends?"

Ty gave him an assessing look. "You noticed that, too, did you?

Laurel looked at both men. "Noticed what?"

The two men exchanged a look, and Cleese gave the explanation. "The calls started at the same time as the PSAs you made began running on TV, and the caller accused you of meddling." He watched her face turn paler as she inevitably remembered the filth he had euphemistically called "meddling." "He's probably someone whose wife or girlfriend has left him, maybe brought charges against him after seeking help at Maxwell's or one of the other centers or shelters. He saw you on TV, already knew your name and probably had your phone number from some business dealing or other, and suddenly he had a target on whom to focus all the rage and frustration he's feeling because his woman had the sense to leave him. In his twisted mind, you're responsible."

Her face turned whiter, but her voice was strong. "How do we catch him?"

Ty looked briefly at Cleese before he spoke. "It isn't going to be easy. One way might be for you to try to set up a meeting with him the next time he calls."

Cleese's eyebrows instantly snapped into a solid dark V. "I don't like that idea at all."

"I didn't think you would," Laurel heard Ty murmur.

"I'm not too crazy about it myself," she told the man beside her wryly, "but if it will bring him out so the police can catch him, I'll do it. It's probably as you said, someone I really don't even know." The hideous irony that she had successfully dealt with one abuser only to be assaulted again by one she couldn't even confront or seemingly escape, no matter what she did, wasn't lost on her. She saw Cleese's mouth starting to open in immediate argument and overrode whatever he was going to say. "I'm frightened," she admitted frankly, "but even more, I'm mad. I hate being afraid to answer my own phone. I hate the ugly, obscene words, and I especially hate thinking it might be someone I know doing this. I want him stopped, Cleese, right now."

The desperation he heard under the anger tore at his gut. "I do, too, Laurel, but—" He broke off to glare at the front door and whoever was ringing the doorbell. Laurel got up immediately, but he still beat her to the door.

The mechanic stood on the other side. After declining her offer to come in, he looked at the man beside her. "You were right. There was something in the gas. Sugar, from the taste of it. The engine's a mess, but we'll be able to clean it out. It'll be fine, but it's going to take about a week," he warned.

Feeling suddenly chilled, Laurel looked past the mechanic to see her car hanging from the hook on the back of his tow truck, then back to him. "Thank you, and thanks for coming out." She found a smile for him. "I really appreciate it."

"It was nothing, ma'am." He handed her a copy of the work order. "Give us a call Monday. By then we'll have a better idea of when we'll have it ready for you." He looked from her to Cleese, who was still standing beside her, clearly not certain who he should be talking to. "I can arrange for a loaner."

"Thanks, I'll take care of it," Laurel told him. Cleese also thanked the man for making the trip out before shutting the door.

"You heard?" he asked Ty Burnett, who was standing at the edge of the entry behind them.

"I heard. This guy just got a lot scarier. Did you happen to get a name, Laurel, or remember the make of car, or notice anything else that might help identify the two guys who pushed your four-by-four out of the way?"

She shook her head impatiently. "They weren't the ones who sabotaged my car. They were just two young men driving by who stopped to help."

"Did they offer you a ride?" Cleese asked her.

"Yes," she said slowly, then added quickly as his expression turned harder and a little dangerous, "but they didn't seem disappointed that I said no, especially when they found out I was going in the opposite direction."

She might believe they hadn't been disappointed, Cleese thought, but he didn't. "Tell Ty what you remember about them, anyway."

Giving both of them a look that clearly said she was humoring them, she described the two men and their vehicle, then returned to the topic she wanted to discuss. "I want to keep this number and see if, when he calls again, I can talk him into meeting me."

Ty threw up a hand quickly in a manner reminiscent of his days as a traffic cop to halt the flow of angry protest he saw heading his way. "Twenty-four hours, and you *promise* me, Laurel, that you will call me immediately if he agrees. You are to do nothing on your own, even if he says he'll meet you in five minutes or not at all." She nodded. "Promise?"

"I promise," Laurel said, feeling as if she were five years old again.

The phone rang, and all three of them went still, Ty Burnett breathing a small, guilty sigh of relief at the reprieve from the six-foot-four steamroller that had been about to run him down.

Laurel made a move toward the kitchen, stopping short at the firm grip on her arm.

"I'll get it." Not waiting for her agreement, Cleese went to the back of the house.

He was back in less than a minute. "It's Edie from Maxwell's."

Cleese waited until he heard the murmur of her voice from the kitchen. "What's this twenty-four-hours crap, Ty? You know damned good and well this son of a bitch is dangerous. There's no way in hell she should get within ten miles of him, much less *meet* him."

"Frankly, I doubt he'll agree to a meeting, Cleese. His kind hasn't got the guts for that. But if, by some slim chance, he has, her phone will be monitored constantly. Even if she doesn't keep her promise, we'll be there." He rubbed his neck tiredly. "But I have to tell you, Cleese, I'm hoping he does agree. He's going to be damned hard to find otherwise, when all we know is he's got a cellular phone. I did run a computer check to see if anyone who works for the phone company has a record of domestic violence or making this kind of call and came up empty. It could be some guy, though, who has a way of accessing their system to find out her number."

Cleese grunted his frustration. He wanted to demand that Ty haul in every bastard in town who had ever mistreated a woman, but chances were the man wasn't even in their records. "Can you do anything?"

"I'll send a man to take prints off the gas cap of her car, but even if he gets a clear print, it'll probably be the mechanic's. I'll order extra patrols by her house—" his mouth twisted "—in between the various and sundry homicides, assaults, robberies and miscellaneous felonies, but..." He gestured his angry impotence.

Cleese clapped him on the shoulder as he opened the front door. "I know you'll do what you can, Ty." And I'll do what *I* can, he added silently.

Ty pulled the door shut behind them as they stepped out onto the porch. Both men stood facing the street, looking over the well-cared-for houses and lawns. "Nice neighborhood," he commented, and heard a grunt of agreement. "You two are pretty tight? I'd be bird-dogging?"

"You'd be bird-dogging," came the flat answer.

Watching a cat about to commit first-degree assault and battery on a robin across the street, Ty nodded. "She's a keeper, but if you should decide to throw her back..." He trailed off with a hint of a question.

"I won't be throwing her back." This answer was even flatter.

The lady of the house, a bird lover, judging by the evidence, was committing a little assault and battery of her own with a broom. Ty sighed deeply. "You know, you don't meet a lot of nice women in this job," he observed.

"Then change jobs." The advice was punctuated with a heartless-sounding laugh.

Ty sighed again. "I've been thinking about it." He turned abruptly to leave. "Keep a good eye on her, Cleese."

"I intend to," Cleese said softly.

When he let himself back into her house, she was standing in the middle of the living room. She had a fragile look about her that had him cursing under his breath. She'd gotten rid of one abusive piece of slime, rebuilt her life, and now another one was making her life miserable again. And, in a way, it was even worse this time, because, without knowing who he was, she couldn't get away from him. He'd never had a chance at Falco, but he would, Cleese promised himself, have a chance at this one. He made a show of looking at his watch. "How about going out for some dinner?"

She shook her head with a grimace. "Thanks, but I don't really feel like going out again."

"I can bring something back, and we can eat here."

"Why don't I just fix something?" He saw a shadow of a smile. "Out of two sacks of groceries, I ought to be able to throw something together—if you don't mind potluck?"

He wouldn't mind one of Frank's bones. "Whatever you want to fix is fine. I'll help."

With help like his, Laurel decided twenty minutes later, they would be lucky if they ate by midnight. He might be a genius in the boardroom, a champion roper and rider and just about the best bass fisherman she'd ever seen, but he was totally hopeless in the kitchen. "Why don't I just finish this up," she said, easing away the mangled loaf of French bread that he'd been supposed to be slicing and buttering before it became nothing but crumbs, "while you do the lettuce for the salad?" Resolutely she ignored the bizarrely sized green chunks soon flying into the salad bowl.

With leftover chicken wings for the appetizer, stewed tomatoes straight from the can doctored into spaghetti sauce, the Mutt and Jeff salad, and ice cream that was more cream than ice, the meal really lived down to its billing, but he didn't seem to care. With him around, leftovers would never be a problem again. Her hand paused over the dishwasher rack, her fingers frozen around the glass she had been about to set in it. Again? She placed the glass firmly in the rack. Once was not "again."

The phone rang as Cleese was finishing wiping down the counters. When she had stared at it through three rings, making no move to answer it, he asked quietly, "Would you like me to answer it?"

At the sound of his voice, she seemed to pull herself together. "No, I'll answer it."

He couldn't tell anything by her expression as she said hello, then listened to whatever the person on the other end was saying. Finally she spoke, her voice steady and composed. "Why don't we meet somewhere so we can talk in person?"

She listened for a second or so longer, then lowered the phone and looked at him with a small, wry laugh. "He hung up on me this time."

Cleese took the phone out of her hand and switched off the ringer before setting it back on the table. "The answering machine can get it the rest of the evening."

He said it as if he expected an argument, but he wasn't going to get one from her, Laurel thought with a silent, humorless laugh.

"What do you want to do now?"

"I have some work I really should catch up on," she said with an apologetic grimace that she had meant to be a smile.

She had handled the obscenely abusive caller with a coolness that amazed him, but the fragile look, which had faded during dinner, was back. "So do I. Will it disturb you if I work in your studio, or should I stay in the kitchen?"

"Cleese, you—" *Don't have to stay,* she was going to say, but the words wouldn't seem to come out. A faint shadow of beard darkened his jaw, and he'd taken his suit coat off to help with dinner and rolled the sleeves of his white dress shirt back over his powerful, hair-dusted forearms, all of which made him look even bigger and stronger and a lot rougher. She could understand now how so many refined Eastern schoolmarms had succumbed to uncivilized Texas cowboys. "You can work in the studio. It won't disturb me."

Chapter 7

It *had* disturbed her, and it was still disturbing her the following morning. He had brought in a briefcase, then proceeded to work in near-absolute silence on the papers he spread over the section of worktable she had cleared for him. She had never noticed before how the window-walls of her studio became near-perfect mirrors at night. While he had been busy reading, scribbling notes in margins, studying charts and what looked like topographical maps, making more notes and punching numbers into some kind of pocket computer, she had been busy, too—watching him read, scribble notes, study charts, et cetera.

After several hours and the four yawns she had smothered in as many minutes, he had abruptly gathered up his papers and announced that it was late and he should be going, making her wonder if perhaps he hadn't discovered the window's dual personality, too. He'd gone around the house making sure all the doors and windows were secure, thanked her politely for dinner at the front door, and then he had kissed her, long, lingeringly and with dizzying gentleness—

until he'd closed his hand around her throat, his thumb tilting her head so that her mouth met his even more perfectly. His mouth had then turned fierce and demanding, yet, oddly, still gentle. She remembered a low, animallike growl and had the suspicion it had come from her, not him. And that was what disturbed her most.

She heard the faint click of the answering machine as it answered her silent phone. It had taken her a long time to regain complete control of her life and herself, and now she was afraid she was losing control of both, Laurel thought as she put down the charcoal pencil she hadn't used in twenty minutes and went to answer the unsilent doorbell. Losing it to a faceless man—and to one whose face she knew better than her own.

"M.J.!" Laurel couldn't keep the surprise out of her voice, either at seeing M.J. when she would normally be in her office with a patient or at seeing the woman who wore tailored pajamas in grubbies even she wouldn't have worn. "This is a nice surprise. Come in." She said a silent thanks that Frank was already out in the garage. M.J. had a morbid fear of big dogs, and Frank, with the perversity of animals when they sensed that a human didn't care for them, always treated her like his long-lost love.

When Laurel paused in the living room, M.J. continued on to the kitchen, setting the box she had balanced on her hip on the table. "I brought some more stuff for the robot. This is the last of it, I'm afraid."

Taking an old chrome flashlight with a cracked lens out of the box, Laurel pressed the switch out of habit and was surprised to see that it still worked. "Did Jack finally clean out the garage?" she asked with a laugh.

M.J. pulled out a chair and sat down at the kitchen table. "No, I just won't be in the garage anymore." She took a deep breath. "Jack and I are getting a divorce."

The flashlight crash-landed atop the other junk in the box as Laurel dropped heavily into the chair opposite M.J. "Oh, M.J., no . . ." Blinking the instant tears out of her eyes, she reached for the other woman's hands across the table. "Does he have someone else?" she asked with a fierce frown.

M.J. shook her head. "No."

Laurel's frown eased. "Do you?" she asked hesitantly.

M.J. shook her head again, this time with a tiny laugh. "No. It's nothing like that. We just finally admitted that we shouldn't be married anymore."

Laurel squeezed the hands in hers. "What about a separation first? You don't want to rush into anything."

"We've been separated the past three months. I stayed at the house while Jack got an apartment, but I don't want it, and since I'll be moving anyway, I might as well move now." Seeing the hurt coming into the stricken look on Laurel's face, she added, "We didn't tell anyone, because if we managed to work things out, it didn't matter, and if we didn't..." Her shoulders rose and fell back into a slump. "If we didn't, everybody would know soon enough."

"What made you and Jack decide you shouldn't be married anymore?" Laurel looked at her helplessly. "You seemed so well suited."

Gently disengaging her hands, M.J. pushed her chair away from the table, stood up and began wandering around the kitchen. "At first I guess we were, but this isn't like the old days, when if you married a farmer, you knew he would always be a farmer and you would always be a farmer's wife and never have the opportunity or need to be anything else." She stopped to pull a dead leaf off the wandering Jew hanging over the sink. "Neither of us now is what the other signed on for ten years ago. Jack is going to run for state senator. He'll win and be very good. He wants to go farther, and he should." She stopped again, in front of the coffeemaker. "Do you want some coffee?"

Laurel started to shake her head no, then indicated yes when she realized M.J. needed something to do with her hands. Her own were knotted in her lap.

M.J. filled the carafe and poured the water into the coffeemaker, then added a filter and ground coffee to the brew basket. "He needs a wife who enjoys sitting on campaign platforms and smiling, who likes crowds and creamed chicken and keeps her opinions to herself. He doesn't need one who hates even the idea of political speeches and moving to Austin. And he especially doesn't need one who makes headlines of her own, testifying in one ugly, nasty abuse case after another." She was quiet while the coffee finished brewing, then poured two cups and brought them to the table. "So we're getting a divorce."

Taking a sip of her coffee, Laurel managed to choke it down, despite its triple strength. M.J., who usually just waved a coffee bean over her cup, didn't appear to notice; her cup was already almost empty. Despite her matter-of-fact tone, there was a shell-shocked look in M.J.'s eyes and a lost air about her. There was a great deal she was leaving out, but one of the requirements of friendship was knowing when not to ask. "Do you have a place to stay? You know you can stay here as long as you want."

M.J. looked at her over the rim of her cup. "I wouldn't want to be in the way."

It was a good thirty seconds before Laurel understood. "The only one sleeping here is me, M.J." she said evenly.

"Sleeping isn't what I was thinking about," M.J. muttered, draining her mug, then setting it down. "Thanks, but I've rented a place downtown, between my office and Maxwell's."

"If finances are a little tight," Laurel began delicately, "I'd be more than hap—"

M.J. waved away the offer. "Money's no problem, but thanks anyway." She was silent for a moment. "You know, the worst part has been dividing everything up, even friends. We finally decided that we'd each keep the ones we had before we got married. Up until a few weeks ago, that would have meant I got you and Jack got Cleese." Laurel saw a small but real grin. "Now I guess we'll have to have joint custody of the two of you."

Before Laurel could think of a good comeback, the sudden screech of an electric saw made both of them jump.

"Good Lord!" M.J.'s hand went to her heart. "What is that?"

"Oh, that's the carpenter Cleese sent over this morning. He put in new deadbolts and window locks, and now he's making a dog door for Frank." Laurel gestured behind her. "He's working in the backyard."

Propping her elbow on the table, M.J. dropped her head into her hand. "Oh, God, Laurel, I'm sorry," she said, shaking her head. "I didn't even think to ask you." She raised her head, a worried frown on her face. "Have the police caught that creep yet?"

"He called yesterday afternoon, but he's using a cellular phone, so they can't trace the call."

"Then it's good you finally told Cleese," M.J. told her, giving her a stern look.

Laurel made a wry face. "I didn't. He answered the phone yesterday."

"Men are very possessive," M.J. said, seemingly apropos of nothing. "They like the sense that something belongs to them, and when they think something is theirs, they take care of it. Good men, anyway."

Laurel wasn't sure if M.J. was trying to reassure her—or warn her.

When she saw M.J. again that afternoon in the hallway at Maxwell's, the other woman was back in one of her tailored suits, her earlier grubbiness a seeming illusion, except for the strain around her eyes and mouth.

"How did it go with Lina today?"

Laurel sighed in exasperation. "I don't think we're making much progress. About all we seem to have done so far is convince her that marriage is no longer a reliable way to make a living." She looked past the other woman to the little girl sitting alone on the bench down the hall. She was carefully, even lovingly, dressed in denim shorts, a pink and white striped top, sparkling white sneakers and white anklets with pink lace trim. The cheerful pink ribbons in her blond hair were at odds with the sad, almost hopeless expression on her thin face. "How are you doing with Amy?"

M.J.'s hand waggled a few times. "I sure hope we can convince Lina to let Amy and Randy testify, for their sakes, as well as hers. She still adamantly refuses, and without them as witnesses to their father's abusive behavior, the results of my evaluations could be attributed to having a 'crazy mother,' which backs up Renko's claim."

"And he would end up with custody," Laurel finished. The two of them frowned at each other in frustration.

He couldn't remember ever seeing any mention of men having biological clocks, Cleese thought, watching Laurel sit down beside the sad-looking little girl who had been sitting alone on a bench in the hall. She put her arm around the little girl and, after a couple of minutes, coaxed a smile and even a laugh out of her. The media seemed to focus only on women's clocks, which was why he was startled to suddenly hear his own ticking loud and clear.

He got to his feet as she said goodbye to the little girl and continued down the hall toward the lobby and him. Her smile was an equal mix of pleasure and surprise when she caught sight of him.

Maybe she should think seriously about doing that poster, Laurel laughed to herself. The women in the lobby—and there seemed to be quite a few more of them than usual—were giving him looks, covert and otherwise, that said they didn't see him as the enemy at all. He came to meet her, and they stepped out of the way at a wide spot in the hall.

"I came by so we could go to dinner," he said without preamble.

Once, in passing, she had mentioned her schedule at Maxwell's; she was amazed that he had remembered. "Oh, referendum—this will be only if and when the Government will have something to put before the people. There is no point in holding elections over an idea. The time for that is when the Government will have succeeded in reaching a negotiated agreement with Jordan on an arrangement acceptable to the Government. Only, prior to the final signature, the people must be consulted.

Question: There is some concern that the public may one day be facing accomplished facts in the Jordanian-Palestinian question.

Mr. Rabin: I can see no possible reason for such concern. I should be happy if we achieved peace with Jordan. I do not believe that there are members of the Government who are not guided by concern for our security. Fundamentally, the Government is bound to explore and decide on ways that may lead to peace pacts. As for Judaea and Samaria—there exists a definite undertaking on the part of the Government not to conclude any agreement without first holding elections. It follows that there are no grounds for concern over the possibility of accomplished facts. At present, my main concern is that, in case Jordan should consider Israel's position toward her too extreme, this might push Jordan toward Syria. To my mind, this concern is far more serious than the 'concern' over possible peace with Jordan.

Question: Minister Bar-Lev stated . . . that Israel was prepared to return most of the West Bank to Jordan. Is this also your position?

Mr. Rabin: I don't believe that now, before negotiations have started, is the time for drawing geographical lines. As far as any political subject is concerned, every Minister represents a political party. The Alignment has a platform on which it went to the electorate. This platform states clearly that Israel is prepared for territorial concessions against a true peace. I personally cannot see any point in defining now the extent of these concessions, their geographical and other details.

Question: Have you lately noted a certain erosion in the American stance on the Palestinian question?

Mr. Rabin: This is the situation on the main confrontation fronts in the Israel-Arab conflict: the main sectors of confrontation—Egypt, Syria and Jordan—are quiet. Such acts of hostility as are committed against Israel at present are carried out by the terrorist organizations. The result is the optical illusion of terrorist activity as the central problem. I have no evidence of an erosion in the American stance on the Jordanian-Palestinian question. I also believe that the U.S. feels concern about Jordan because of the affinity that exists between both nations, and I am certain that the U.S. does not wish to undermine the foundations of one of the friendly regimes in the Middle East.

Question: Mr. Prime Minister, without committing yourself—would you say there are fair prospects for reaching any kind of agreement with Jordan?

Mr. Rabin: My experience in the army and the Foreign Service, as well as my brief experience in my present office have driven me to the conclusion that one should not engage in prophecies. I prefer to seek ways to progress in directions I consider worthwhile.

Question: Do you believe that Egypt genuinely and sincerely wants some sort of settlement with Israel?

Mr. Rabin: As far as I know Egypt is willing to ⟨ on the basis of a complete Israeli withdrawal to t creation of a Palestinian State in Judaea, Samaria ⟨ ask me—won't such an arrangement bring survival?—My answer is clearly no. If you ask me arrive at a settlement with Israel, one which will g answer is again no. Therefore the course which we extent to which there is a prospect of bringing abo position, in their attitude to an overall settlement possible to advance toward an overall settlement w

Excerpt
Genera

Mr. Pr
Isra
holds
dispu
the gr
of the
citize
histor
Pales
equal
does
consi

ag

o
P
n
i
a

However, the Palestine community in general must in no way be equated with the terrorist organizations. From my own personal acquaintance with this community I refuse to identify it, or at least its great majority, with the terrorist grouping known as the PLO, which is not a national liberation movement but the roof organization of disunited and splintered terrorist groups whose pretensions and support do not spring from the broad masses of the Palestinian population. It is a fact that more Arabs than Israelis have been killed by these organizations. It is also a fact that more terrorists have been killed in the armed clashes between regular Arab forces and the terror gangs, and between the rival terror gangs themselves, than by the Israeli security forces.

These facts are obvious to anybody who cares to examine them. We refuse to recognize the PLO and we will not recognize it, because of its doctrines and of its deeds alike. The Palestine Charter which embodies the political ideology of the PLO stands in direct contradiction to the Charter of the United Nations. It denies absolutely the right of Israel to exist and postulates its destruction as a principal objective.

This ideology is accompanied by the criminal methods of warfare used by the organizations which make up the PLO, such as indiscriminate terror and deliberate murder of women and children, pupils and teachers, athletes at the Olympic Games, passengers on a Swiss airliner, chance visitors and Jewish and Christian pilgrims at airports, Arab women workers in Galilee. In reality the situation here is not that of a subject people trying to liberate itself with its own underground forces, but of gangs of desperadoes imposing themselves on a people and attempting to form and dominate it by means of the destruction of another people: this at a time when there is ample room for two states, Jewish and Arab, to co-exist in peace in the historic Land of Israel or Palestine on both sides of the Jordan, their common border being determined by negotiations.
Mr. President,

It is of course no secret that with the parliamentary situation existing in this General Assembly, the preconceived ideas held by a great number of those taking part here, and the irrelevant considerations which guide many delegations, a majority might concede the PLO demands. A resolution that would concede such demands will be regarded by Israel as an arbitrary resolution impinging on its fundamental rights, as illegal and not binding in any way. Every delegate here would reject a negative resolution which strikes at the foundation of his country's being. One cannot ask of any nation to agree to its own elimination or to commit suicide.

Understanding for the needs of the Palestinians—certainly; satisfaction of the demands of arch-murderers who appoint themselves as saviors—decidedly not!

I regret that many members of the United Nations do not delve into this problem thoroughly, with the consequence that, either deliberately or through misunderstanding, they reward these murderers and in so doing stoke the fires in the Middle East. Israel will not submit to violence and terror. Terrorism is an infectious disease which knows no national frontiers. Many states have already paid the price of submission to terrorism and I am afraid that the last word has not been said on the subject. Following the latest terrorist attacks in Paris and at the Hague, President Valery Giscard D'Estaing said: "Violence, which is sometimes presented and justified as an avant garde act is nothing but the rise to the surface of those depths of barbarism and primitive cruelty of which humanity has devoted all its efforts to rid itself." These are trenchant words, but there is need for action and for courageous co-operation in order to put an end to manifestations of terror before further disasters occur. The essence of the PLO is terror. It is no coincidence that whenever a concrete proposal for a political solution is put forward, the PLO leadership rises up against any such peace initiative. Their insistence on inscribing the question of Palestine on the agenda of this General Assembly is designed above all to destroy the prospects of the political efforts at the very beginning. A debate on this matter cannot fail to poison the international atmosphere. Acceptance of PLO demands may well condemn the prospects of the negotiating process to failure—just when the first ray of light has been glimpsed on the horizon.

Palestinians who wish to give constructive expression to their independent identity can be helped to do so in the context of the negotiations with Jordan. Moreover, I would not agree to a general settlement without including in it satisfaction of the needs of the Palestinians. It is after all not Israel which has prevented the crystallization of what is known as "Palestinian identity." To the extent that such a desire existed among the Palestinians it is the Arab states that have frustrated it during all these years. If not, how can one explain the fact the during 19 years of Arab rule in the Gaza Strip and on the West Bank, this identity never achieved any definite form or full expression?

The joint communique by Egypt, Syria and the PLO in Cairo on September 21, 1974, also deals a blow to the prospects of a constructive solution to the issue of Palestine identity. In the same way that the PLO bends all its efforts to prevent political progress in the area, certain Arab states are whittling down the hopes for a solution of the Palestinian question by granting the terrorist organizations the monopoly of representation of the Palestinians, when they know perfectly well that these organizations are not able to be a party to negotiations because of what they are.

Mr. President,

There is no sadder example of the heartless attitude of the Arab governments than the freeze which they have imposed on the status of the 1948 refugees. It is true that many of them have been absorbed in the economies of the Arab states in which they now live, but there has been a deliberate policy to prevent a constructive solution to this sore problem in order to exploit human suffering for political and propaganda ends. If the problem in itself were not so sad I would say that there is nothing more ludicrous than the annual fund raising efforts of UNRWA to make up the deficit in its budget—at a time when the Arab oil states command the biggest monetary reserves in the world.

Israel did not adopt this course: not toward the 600,000 Jewish refugees who fled the Arab states stripped of all their possessions, and not toward the survivors of the millions of Jews destroyed by the Nazis, with the blessing of the Mufti Hajj Amin el Hussaini who found refuge among his own kind in Nazi Berlin and fascist Rome. All of these were fully absorbed in Israel economically, socially and culturally.

In the light of the vast economic opportunities which now exist in the Middle East, the refugee problem must, and can, be solved. Far more difficult refugee situations in other parts of the world have been solved long ago. Given good will, without which no problem can be resolved, the question of compensation for both Arab and Jewish refugees can be settled. Israel is contributing, and will continue to contribute, its share in the solution of this painful human problem.

Palestinian Nationalism: An Established Fact

By Amnon Rubinstein

Sometimes there is a relation between a name and a fate: Had King Abdullah chosen the name of Palestinian Kingdom instead of the Hashemite Kingdom of Jordan, the Palestinian issue would not have had such powerful international resonance. If Israel shared its border with the Palestinian Kingdom, in which the majority of the population were Palestinian Arabs, the nature of the issue would be clearer to side spectators. The question would, in this case, have had the proper clarification: In the Arab Palestinian country, east of Israel, there are differences of opinion regarding the regime, and an internal struggle for the right of representation of the population's majority.

But King Abdullah did not name his kingdom Palestine and this marginal fact, together with other decisive political facts, gave rise to what is now known the world over as "the Palestinian problem."

The decisive political facts are: a constant conflict between sectors of the Palestinian population and the regime that is sustained by the Bedouin loyalty; a radicalization of Palestinian factors, with regard to Israel or to the Hashemite's pro-West policy; and Israel's continuing domination of the populated Palestinian territories. To this it should be added, of course, the extremist influence of the terrorist organizations which, as it were, brought the Palestinian message to the world's consciousness through abominable murders; these acts gave rise, along with the revulsion and the shock, to an adjustment to the horror and an understanding of what brought it about.

Of course, it is possible to rightly and most convincingly argue against overstating the Palestinian case: after all, even if there is Palestinian discontent, it cannot be compared to the suffering that is the lot of other peoples in our times. The

Palestinians are among their brethren, whose riches grow astronomically. They are not doomed to destruction by man or heaven. Their refugees, who were kept in their camps by the Arab countries, are afforded impressive and continued aid by the international community, the same that disregards famine and death in Africa and southeast Asia. When we compare the Palestinian suffering to that of others—and this while overlooking what the Jewish people have been through —one can sadly ponder upon the international hysteria over the Palestinian tragedy.

We know that when the terrorist organizations speak of this tragedy, they do not have in mind the human suffering of their brethren, but Israel's very existence here. The legitimate rights of the Palestinians, according to their formula, means the destruction of Israel.

But even if we argue, time and again, against the exaggeration of the question, even if we write self-convincing articles in our newspapers—the favorite sport of rightists—there still are facts we cannot eliminate. The first fact is the existence of Arab power. The Palestinian problem is now on the agenda of the international community first and foremost due to the Arab countries' enormous political and economic bargaining power. The Bangladesh refugees and the famished in Biafra, the Asians in East Africa and the Latvians in the Soviet empire have stronger arguments, both from the moral and the juridical point of view. But contrary to the Palestinians, they have no political support. For this reason, too, of the world's refugees, only the Arabs attained an extraordinary position, the refugees' descendants being given continuing aid to the end of time, regardless of their economic situation. It is possible and necessary to argue against this unfair order of priorities—and the writer of these lines has more than once done so in the foreign press—but the Arab power is a fact of life and no moralization in an Israel newspaper will ever reduce it.

Another fact is the strong Palestinian nationalistic feelings. Were it not for Arab power, this nationalism would never have become as strong as it has, but no power would have been able to create this nationalism if it did not exist. In fact, every observer knows that the Palestinian nationalism is a fact and finds its expression in a hundred and one ways: in writing and speech, in actions and wishes, in overt expression and disguised feelings. Again, it is not important how this national feeling arises and whether it has an "historic justification"; it is not important if the rights of this new nationalism are equal to those of Israel's; and none of this has bearing on whether it deserves the world's attention. The determining fact is that this nationalism is now a reality—and the fact that it thrives mainly on our very existence and on its opposition to Zionism, does not in the least detract from its own existence. So, in the background of Palestinian nationalism and Arab power, the Palestinian problem arose and made itself felt everywhere. Everywhere—except for Israel. Here, in the atmosphere of imaginary-power intoxication that existed before Yom Kippur, the political administration decided to disregard it altogether. In a proud world—again, unjustly, but no matter—the Palestinian wave and the consciousness of the new nationalism slowly penetrated until it reached formal declarations by countries friendly to us. More than one hundred—yes, this is no printing error—recognized the Palestinian Liberation Organization and in other countries its offices are opened as a matter of routine. From many aspects this murderous terrorist organization is given the same position the Jewish Agency held before the establishment of the State of Israel.

The recognition of the Palestinian problem spread beyond the New Left and liberal circles and even penetrated Jewish circles in the Diaspora. Even before President Nixon—who yesterday was the hero of the Israel right wing—spoke about the Palestinians' interests, it was clear that the day was not far when no politician in the world would disregard this combination of power, nationalism, and propaganda. Except for the Israel politician.

In fact, when the Palestinian wave swelled the world over, Israel's captains decided to determine—once and for all—that the problem itself does not exist, that there is no Palestinian nationalism, there is absolutely nothing.

Today this sounds strange and it's hard to remember that Prime Minister Golda Meir rejected the very concept of "Palestinian" and the use of this word was almost taboo at government meetings. Moshe Dayan went even further, and, in a series of appearances and speeches in June 1973, determined that there is no entity called "Palestinian." In his speech to Technion graduates, the then Minister of Defense declared that "politically, Palestine is finished." In those far off days — i.e., in 1973 — Mr. Dayan would repeatedly explain to his admiring followers the principles of his wonderful doctrine: there is no danger of war, there is no danger of invasion, there are no Palestinians, there is absolutely nothing.

It would be possible, somehow, to understand the governmental policy if the disregard of the Palestinian nationalism led to an agreement with the King of Jordan—i.e., to the known Hashemite solution." It would be possible to understand the disregard of the Arab power factor through the attempt to solve it by means of another power factor. But Mr. Dayan—who in fact shaped the policy of Meir's government—did not want this solution either. When he rejected the Palestinians' national existence, he advised King Hussein not to accept Israel's offer. He admitted that a "Hashemite solution" was possible, and even a peace agreement with Hussein was possible. But he strongly opposed any solution of this sort that was suggested. After rejecting the Palestinians and the possibility of an agreement with Jordan, he proposed his well known solution, by which Israel would have sovereignty over Judaea and Samaria whereas "sovereignty" over the population would be held by Jordan. This vision of an eternal Israel military rule over more than a million Arabs stemmed from Mr. Dayan's intoxication with his successes in the administration of the occupied territories. For lack of historic feeling and political understanding, the former Minister of Defense thought that it would be possible to change long-ranged political problems into an enlightened policy of conquest.

Today, so it seems, there is no room for a policy of absolutely nothing, which avoids both Israel's eastern border problems and the nature of the understanding that must be reached with Jordan and the Arab people on both sides of the river. Rabin's government is willing, contrary to its predecessor, to mention the forbidden name "Palestinian" and at least to discuss the subject. This means that there is an initial readiness to confront the question. This confrontation does not imply, to my mind, acceptance of the creation of a Palestinian entity or a separate Palestinian country in Judaea and Samaria, or negotiations with the organizations of terror and murder. What is implied is that Israel must consider the overall problems the Palestinian challenge faces Israelis with. There is no need for Israel to be—overtly or as a rule—the defenders of a certain regime. There is no need to become involved in the consolidation of political conceptions regarding Judaea and Samaria by forbidding political activity, as long as it does not deal with terror and sabotage; Israel must declare and inform the whole world that the Arab people on both sides of the Jordan has the right to define the nature of its regime and rule, as long as these do not go counter to Israel's security and peace. This is an apparently internal question of a neighboring country but for long-range political interests and for the immediate benefit of Israel's public image, she must recognize this right of the world living east of Israel.

Israelis must not be the only ones to deny the interest of the legitimate rights of the Palestinians, when the whole world recognizes them. On the contrary, we must join those who acknowledge these interests and define them in such a way that it may serve Israel's interest for security and peace. It should not apppear as if we are trying to prevent political organization in the occupied territories by means of administrative authorities. On the contrary, we must advise the territories' population to choose their representation as a part of the political power tactics inside Jordan. We must not determine beforehand who represents whom but on the contrary, we must put the cart before the horse and demand that the people on both sides of the river themselves determine the link between east and west Jordan. Of course, there is no assurance that this policy will bear good results. It may also be argued that Israel missed the precious opportunities that were lost during the period of imaginary power intoxication. But it is difficult to see how a realistic policy, which recognizes the Palestinian nationalism and considers it part of a Palestinian Jordanian country, could damage Israel more than a policy of blindness and sleight of hand.

I don't think so tonight." It was too soon after last night and its "disturbances."

Cleese considered the wisdom of pushing too hard and ignored it. "Have dinner with me."

"I really can't. I—have a lot of work to catch up on." She'd used that excuse last night, she remembered now, and it hadn't worked. Several women passed by, forcing them to move closer together.

"Have dinner with me."

Laurel looked down at her spotless linen dress. "I'd have to go home, get cleaned up, change clothes. You'd have to wait too long."

"Have dinner with me."

She looked at him, then away, while she chewed her bottom lip for inspiration, just as Lina Renko passed with Amy.

"Have dinner with him."

Laurel stared after Lina, hardly believing she had heard the other woman correctly, then looked up into laughing topaz eyes.

She had dinner with him.

It had been more than twenty years since he had considered holding hands at a movie a hot date, Cleese thought sardonically as he unlocked the door and opened it. "I see Frank figured out the dog door."

"It took him about thirty seconds."

With a little fancy footwork, he had expanded dinner into a movie afterward—a real date. "It looks like the carpenter did a good job," he said when they reached the kitchen. "How long did it take him?"

"Not very long, really. He was finished before lunch."

"He put locks on every window?" Leaning against the counter, he watched Frank take his hay fever pill, then demonstrate the dog door. He had deliberately cultivated an easygoing friendship with her, just like the ones he had with his male "fishing buddies," based on mutual interests and respect and a genuine liking. He had some friendships like that with women, too, with sex playing no part, but that wasn't what he wanted with Laurel, which no doubt explained why he had never been so sexually frustrated in his life. Sex—long, often, and a damned sight hotter than hand-holding—was most definitely going to play a part.

"He got all of them." She pulled back one of the kitchen curtains to show him the deadbolt-type lock on the window.

While she mixed up Frank's dinner, he spot-checked some of the windows. He was living with a perpetual ache, yet it was a peculiarly satisfying ache. Because there was no sexual bond between them—yet—the bond of friendship had had a chance to develop. She actually *had* become a fishing buddy, although, he conceded with a silent laugh, she would probably never have a man's ability to hold a conversation just by sharing bait. He sobered abruptly. Something else had happened, too. Last night she had asked him why he wanted to know when she was worried or upset or scared, and he had almost given her the real reason, a reason that had been a surprise to him and sure as hell would have surprised her. While he had been busy admitting himself to her life, he had been committing her to his heart. He had fallen in love with her—somewhere, he suspected, between the realization that his poacher was a woman and when she'd taken off her hat.

"Thanks again for sending the carpenter over," she said when he came back into the kitchen. "I wouldn't really have known who to call."

She wouldn't have called anybody. "It wasn't any trouble. Did he stay close to his estimate?" Again it had galled him that she, not he, paid. It wasn't the money—he knew she could afford it—it was that he felt it was his right to pay, just as he felt it was his right to protect her, when in reality he had no rights at all. It was now that he had to play her most carefully: she was hooked, but the hook wasn't set. If he kept the line too tight—let her know too soon just how much he wanted her—she would break the line and run.

"He charged me the estimate exactly."

He saw by her slightly puzzled look that his tone had been harsher than he'd realized and consciously softened it. "Good." After a last glance around, just to be absolutely sure the doors and windows were secure, he started for the front door. She had offered him coffee, but the faint shadows of fatigue under her eyes said she needed to get to bed. He thought of the narrow bed, with its pristine white coverlet, that he'd just seen in her bedroom. Alone—for now.

As they passed the hallway leading to the bedrooms, he saw her glance toward the alcove where she had her answering machine. The red message light was blinking. "Why don't you check it while I'm here?" He would have checked it himself, but that was another one of those rights he didn't have.

Her shoulders seemed to sag for a moment; then they straightened, and she moved to the machine and pushed the replay button.

There was only one message, from someone at the phone company with her new telephone number. Using a sheet from the pad by the answering machine, he scribbled it down and tucked the number in his pocket. "Who are you going to give it to?"

She looked up after writing the number down herself. "You, M.J., the secretary at Maxwell's, my agent, Lieutenant Burnett—if he doesn't already have it—and my brothers."

"Who've got to be wondering by now just what the hell is going on."

"If they've noticed." There was no rancor in her voice, just an easy acceptance of her brothers' indifference.

"You're not going to be giving it out at the vet's or the pharmacy, right?" Despite Ty's assurance that everyone connected with the veterinary clinic and the pharmacy checked out, the feeling persisted that the man they were looking for had a tie to one or the other.

"Or anywhere else," she said dryly.

He paused at the front door. "Okay, now, you have the number where you can reach me in Mexico City, and I'll call you every night. And be sure you keep the doors locked."

Laurel nodded dutifully. "I will, but don't worry. I have Frank, remember."

He hadn't forgotten Frank. Cleese looked down at the neon-yellow eyes staring back at him impassively. Frank could be a problem the next few minutes.

The dog tensed as Cleese took a half step toward her, bringing his hands slowly up to her shoulders. To his and the dog's satisfaction, she more than met him halfway.

Her response built rapidly, her hands weaving into his hair to hold his head still for her eager mouth's explorations. She nibbled at the corners of his lips, tracing just inside with a taunting tongue, giving him a taste of the passion waiting, impatiently, for release, and came too close to releasing his. Clamping one hand to the back of her skull, he took control of the kiss, holding her mouth to his with his probing tongue. She murmured low in her throat as her arms dropped to his shoulders, then twined around his neck, and he drew back a little to nip gently up the line of her jaw, feeling the small shivers that worked through her.

Locking one arm across her back, he eased his larger body over her much slighter one, rocking his hips, and a drawn-out, low moan of pleasure escaped Laurel as she arched her body against his, seeking to match rhythms. His big hand slid down, spread over her bottom and flexed, and for a moment the rhythm was perfect. Then, too soon—much too soon—his hand slid back up, his body went still, and her delighted sigh caught in her throat and became something that sounded like—but never could have been—a sob. For several long seconds he held her tight against him, and she stood motionless so that her body could absorb the hard steel feel of his, like a starving woman who, denied the feast, greedily grabbed up what scraps she could. Then, long before she'd had enough, he set her away from him with a brief, rough kiss.

"I'll see you Saturday," he murmured, and then he was gone.

Cleese turned the key and put the car in gear. He had left her hungry, and himself even hungrier. As he passed the plain sedan parked near the corner, the kind favored by Fort Worth's best private security firm, he slowed, acknowledging the nodded salute of the man sitting inside.

Rights be damned.

Chapter 8

Only in Texas would people dress up in tuxedos and ball gowns to eat barbecue. Laurel grinned as the Armani across the buffet table from her was saved by the timely napkin of her husband. The woman just laughed and added another rib to her plate.

Starrett, Inc. held a party for its stockholders every year, although "party" was a pale description. "Gala" or "bash" would be more accurate, or maybe "wingding"—as one double-barrel-chested, bowlegged older gentleman who would have looked exactly right climbing down off the seat of a chuck wagon a hundred years ago had called it. This year the party was being held in the huge ballroom of Fort Worth's finest hotel. Lead-crystal chandeliers glittered over a gold-seamed black marble floor and ivory-silk-hung walls that could have graced the castle in any fairy tale.

As the dance band began tuning up, she found a tiny table set back out of the mainstream where she could sit back and just watch for a few minutes. Laurel laughed softly as she looked over the crowd. Maybe wingding *was* the best word. All shareholders, whether they owned one share of stock or a thousand, had received invitations, and she would have bet nearly every one of them was here tonight. They'd gotten themselves all duded up—another contribution from the wingding man, whose wife had told her that his great-grandfather actually had driven a chuck wagon and had had the foresight, or plain dumb luck, to step down the final time onto one of the richest oil fields in central Texas. Rhinestones glittered beside diamonds, while designer rubbed elbows with department store, which was also typically Texas, although in this instance the host had more than a little to do with that democratic aspect.

Watching him over the rim of her champagne glass, she saw him introduce two couples whose incomes probably differed by several zeros. There were several men in the room taller than he was, and a few with broader shoulders, but there was none to equal him. He was wearing a Western-cut black tuxedo with a black satin string tie and a stark white shirt, and he was, quite simply, the most masculine, attractive man she had ever seen. She drained her glass and set it on the glass tabletop. And tonight she was joltingly, recklessly aware of it.

Almost as if he sensed that she was watching him, he turned his head suddenly and looked right at her, and unconsciously Laurel rose to her feet. Even from halfway across the ballroom, she saw the change in his eyes. The big cat was wide awake, hungry and on the prowl.

Without releasing his visual hold on her, Cleese dropped a departing comment to the group in general and started toward her. He'd kept her with him at first, worried that she would be overwhelmed by so many strangers, but he'd soon realized that she met and charmed strangers as easily as she charmed bass onto her line, and he'd let her go off on her own. He would have preferred that she stay beside him, but separating did serve the practical expedient of letting him get his hosting duties out of the way as fast as possible so that they could have the rest of the evening to themselves.

A passing waiter offered a tray of glasses, and he took one, emptying the glass absently to wet his dry mouth, not noticing or caring whether it was champagne or river water. Tonight she was the woman he'd seen in the newspaper clippings. An hour ago he had been wondering why the man he was speaking to abruptly broke off in midsentence to stare over his shoulder. Curious to see what had captured the man's attention, he'd turned, then understood. He would have had the same reaction if he hadn't had more time to get used to her. She looked like a woman who'd never even heard of hip boots, much less worn them. Her hair was half up and half down in an artful arrangement that looked artless, and her dress had the same deceptively sophisticated simplicity. It was a soft silk that clung lovingly to the curves of her breasts and waist and hips, then swirled around her long legs. Technically, he supposed, it was white, but the color was deceptive, too. It shimmered, splintering one moment into a thousand tiny prisms, then turning back to pure snow white the next. He didn't remember the dress from any of the clippings, and it didn't look as if it had been hanging in a closet for six years, which, trivial as it was, pleased him.

Gliding his hand down her neck and across her bare shoulder, he felt her slow shiver and saw growing sexual awareness turn her witch's eyes smoky. "Did I tell you how beautiful you look?" he murmured.

Laurel laughed up at him. "Yes, you did, but you can tell me again." She hadn't worn a dress like this since the night she had walked out of the house in Houston, leaving a closetful of them behind. Tonight, when she had looked in the mirror, it hadn't brought back any dark memories; instead, the reflection staring back at her had filled her with a strange lightness, as if she had been transformed for the night, freed of her usual self-constraints.

He tightened his hand on her shoulder, spreading heat under her bare skin, and turned her toward the middle of the ballroom, which was already filling with couples drawn by the vibrant rhythms of the band. "Come on." She heard a deeper rasp in his voice. "I've been waiting to dance with you all evening."

The band had mellowed, turning to slow ballads. Cleese crossed his arms behind her, one hand at the small of her back, inviting her into him. She accepted the invitation, shifting closer, so that their bodies created a slow, subtly arousing friction. A few men had tried to claim her for a dance at first, but his possessive hand—curved around her waist, a hip, her throat—had soon gotten the message across: She was his.

Laurel breathed in the familiar soap and spice and the sweetness of the jasmine scenting the soft warm night. The French doors in the ballroom had been opened to the walled patio outside, and someone had turned out the harsh white floodlights, leaving only moonshine, which gave the white angel wings of jasmine and the huge, creamy magnolia blossoms overhead a soft, unearthly incandescence. It was as if the flowers, the patio, her dress, the romantic music drifting out from the ballroom, had been sprinkled with fairy dust, she thought whimsically. "All night," she murmured, concentrating not on what she was saying, but on the warm pleasure trickling through her, "I've felt like Cinderella at the prince's ball."

Her high-heeled sandals had been kicked under a table half an hour ago. Rubbing his cheek against her silky hair, Cleese laughed softly. "Well, Cinderella, you've already lost both your slippers, so it shouldn't be hard for me to find you tomorrow." Hard. He laughed again, silently. Her left arm curled tighter around his neck, while her right sneaked under his open jacket to encircle his waist, and he molded her closer as he spun them in a slow turn.

His low laugh sent shivers shimmying down her spine to linger under his slowly circling hand. "Are we still dancing?" she asked in a softer murmur, eyes still closed.

"Mm-hmm..." Slowly he nuzzled down her neck as they swayed in place, their bodies rubbing lazily, rubbing in heat, rubbing in sweet aches. He nudged her head up with his chin, and her mouth met his as surely as if they'd done this a thousand times before. After a long, leisurely kiss, her body warm and pulsatingly alive against his, her lips drew away a fraction, and her eyes opened to his on a slow-breaking smile. "Are we still dancing?"

"No." His whisper was harsh. "We're leaving."

The door of the hotel suite locked behind them. Before the official party, the company officials had met here for a drink, and Laurel had forgotten her shawl. "I think I left it in the other room," she said.

"I'll get it."

While he went into the adjoining room, Laurel wandered to the tall window. Her sandals dangling from one hand, she gazed down on the city below. She heard him come back into the room, gauging his silent progress toward her over the thick carpet by the subtly increasing tension in her body. He stopped behind her, and she controlled a small shudder as his big hands, his palms rough and hot, cupped her bare shoulders. Her sandals fell unnoticed to the carpet. Raising her eyes from the lights below to their reflection in the darkened glass, she saw his expression, unsmiling, with a touch of ruthlessness around his hard-set mouth, and she didn't control the shudder so well this time. Her body began to resonate with the steady pulse of desire as her eyes met his in the dark mirror.

Cleese felt her heartbeat accelerate in the pulse thudding under his palms. Almost clinically, he appraised the darkening of her eyes and the speed of the breath hurrying over her parted lips. Deliberately he ran his hands down her bare arms, and she inhaled sharply; then, abruptly, she twisted around, her hands flattening on his skull to angle his mouth to hers.

She kissed with an erotic innocence that told him she might have been married, but she had never been aroused. He knew it was indefensibly chauvinistic to think that sexual fulfillment was all it took to mature a woman, but he was too human not to appreciate the opportunity he was being given, and far too human not to take advantage of it. No other man had ever given her this much; he was the first, and, with the right kind of ruthless determination, he would be the last. Pausing a moment to pray that he wasn't making an irremedial mistake, he abandoned the slow, careful planning of weeks and gave himself up to the risky luxury of surrendering to his own hungers and prodded her to satisfy hers. One hand dropped to her hips, urging—commanding—her into his body, while he treated himself to an endlessly gratifying taste of her dark, sweet mouth.

His mouth, no longer frustratingly passive, took hers, and, with a near sob of gratitude, Laurel traded taste for taste, stroke for lingering, deep stroke. His arms around her shifted, and she felt the powerful muscles of his body bunch as, maintaining the seal of their mouths, he lifted her.

Seconds later he set her down beside the bed in the other room. Soft light from the bedside lamp suffused the room, but she was only dimly aware of it as her hands impatiently pushed his jacket off his shoulders; then her fingers undid the silk tie around his neck before moving down to release the studs in his shirt one by one. Spreading the edges of the white linen, she whimpered slightly as her palms molded themselves in a mat of dark, surprisingly soft hair.

Cleese swept one hand up over the silk-covered swell of her hip and stopped, just under her breast. He heard her breath catch, and her hands clenched on his chest as she waited, but he paused for a few seconds longer, letting them both savor the anticipation. Finally he spread his hand and let it close over the warm, firm weight. Her eyes glazed and closed as she breathed out raggedly. Her mouth against his went slack as she arched, pressing into his hand. He watched his thumb against the white fabric, dark, rubbing, feeling soft flesh tauten, seeing a small swelling rise hard and greedy under the smooth silk. With his free hand, he brushed the nothing straps off her shoulders, then found the hidden zipper under her left arm.

There was a sudden whisper of cool air over her back and chest, and vaguely Laurel was aware that he'd dragged her dress down, exposing her breasts, but she didn't want to think; she just wanted to feel the incredible pleasure that intensified with every stroke of his rough, callused thumb, to cede control of her body to him so that she could float forever in this delicious limbo. His arm tightened across her bare back, dragging her other nipple through the mat of hair on his chest, which didn't feel quite so soft now to her ultrasensitized skin, but a little abrasive instead and fantastically arousing.

Her open, hungry mouth devoured his, and he felt her knee sliding up the inside of his thigh. It nudged higher, and he couldn't help groaning harshly. He heard her questioning murmur and answered by dragging her hand down his body. He felt her go rigid and began to pull her frozen hand away, cursing himself in lurid silence, when her fingers suddenly flexed, and he felt his zipper sliding down. It was his turn to go rigid as his breath hissed out, and he was suspended in agonized anticipation while her fingers slipped inside and closed over him, soft and so cool. She hadn't freed the button, so his trousers were still tight around his waist, the open fly like a secret, her hand inside surreptitious and stealthy. The almost furtive aspect of it gave the act a forbidden quality that only incited his arousal. Her cool palm slid down, cupped him, then started a slow, hard slide back up, and he swallowed his moan, his teeth grinding with the effort to keep control.

He shoved her dress down out of the way, then skimmed his hand up the inside of her thigh. She wasn't wearing panty hose or a garter belt; she had on thigh-high stockings that left his way free and clear, but he was too intent on his goal to appreciate that, or the silk-soft skin under his palm.

He ground his knuckles gently against the satin-covered heat between her thighs, and her hand convulsed on him, nearly driving him over the edge, before her arm fell limply to her side.

An electric shock arced through her, scorching her belly and thighs and melting her knees, leaving her limp body supported only by his arm across her back and his hand between her legs. There was a brief resentment that he'd stopped her from satisfying her curiosity—he had been so hot, so strong, so *alive* in her hand—but another jolt, sharper than the last, obliterated it. His hand was inside her panties, and if she had thought his callused thumb had felt deliciously rough on her sensitive nipple, it was nothing compared to the unbearably exquisitive sensation she felt now as it found another, tinier, harder nub. She clutched at him wildly as a roaring sound filled her ears. Barely coherent, she understood that she was hearing her own blood pounding the craving of her body for his through every capillary, every cell. His other hand glided around to her breast, the searing heat dissolving into icy-hot shivers under her skin. He took the nipple into his mouth, and she lost another remnant of her rapidly disintegrating sanity to his rasping tongue and hungry suction. His wickedly talented mouth and hands seemed to have found every erogenous nerve, sending shock waves of sizzling heat through her, and she lost the last shred of conscious, rational thought.

He probed, and dampness, hot and slick, glazed his finger, snapping all but the last thread of his control. Yet for a moment he just looked down at the woman whose body pulsed under his hands. Her cheeks and beautiful breasts were flushed, her nipples were wet and rosy, and her closed, dark lashes fluttered in time with the breath jerking over her moist, slightly swollen lips, giving him a sense of power he'd never had before with a woman. Then her witch's eyes opened, and the last thread snapped.

Tumbling her down to the bed, he dropped down over her. Laurel was so lost in a passionate fog that only the sensation of falling and the presence of a large, male body penetrated. With conscious thought shut down, her subconscious interpreted what was happening, relying on an old memory of being thrown onto a bed, and another big, overpowering man. The palace clock tolled midnight, and Cinderella's enchanted evening came to an end.

"No! No, don't! Please don't!"

Lost in his own haze of desire, Cleese didn't hear the words at first, only the voice, and it didn't get through any faster that the woman in his arms was scratching and clawing not to get closer, but to get away. When at last it did, he reared back off the bed. "Laurel! What the hell—?"

The red mist of lust finally cleared, and what he saw almost made him sick to his stomach. The small, frightened animal he'd glimpsed the day she'd flinched was now panicked beyond all rational thought, the fear he had dreaded seeing once before filling and widening her eyes as she crouched at bay in the middle of the bed, one arm raised to ward him off. "Laurel. Laurel, it's all right. Everything's okay, honey." Speaking quietly, he raised his hands slowly and took one careful step toward her.

"No! Leave me alone!" The pins had come out of her hair, and it was a wild tangle around her head as she cowered back against the headboard, her terror-stricken eyes sweeping the room frantically for an escape. Trapped as she was in some kind of waking nightmare, quiet and careful wasn't going to get through to her, he understood grimly. "Laurel. Laurel, wake up," he said strongly. She still stared at him, not seeing him, seeing only the monster from her two-year nightmare. He moved toward her without warning, raising his hands only at the last second. "Laurel, it's all right. It's me, Cleese," he said as he caught her.

"No!" Her voice rose to a near scream on the word as she tried frantically to scramble away from him. "Don't! Please don't hurt me!"

She fought him, struggling so furiously to get away that there was a real danger she was going to hurt herself. He controlled her by the simple expedient of wrapping himself around her, trapping her arms between their bodies and her thrashing legs between his. Moving one hand, he risked enough pressure to bend her stiff neck so that he could cradle her head against his heaving chest. "Shh, sweetheart. It's Cleese, darlin'," he murmured soothingly. "Stop fighting me. Everything is okay. Just be still for a minute." He rubbed her back slowly, smoothing his hand up over her tangled hair, then down again, repeating the gentling motions over and over. Drawing a deep, ragged breath, he bent his head back and tried to swallow the bitter bile in his throat while he blinked away the moisture in his eyes that her last desperate plea had brought. All that he had imagined wasn't one tenth—one thousandth—as bad as that one *Please don't hurt me.* Laying his cheek on her hair, he closed his eyes wearily. The words would echo in his soul until the day he died.

Gradually the awful shuddering of her body stilled, and their rasping breathing grew easier. "You can let me go now," she said, her voice dead. "I won't fight you."

He eased his tight hold fractionally. "Who am I, Laurel?" he asked quietly.

"I know who you are, Cleese," she answered, in the same flat tone.

He released her, then bent to pick up her dress and held it out to her. His body, to his disgust, had not forgotten that she was virtually naked, especially when her bare breasts had been flattened against his chest. Trying to shield herself with one arm, she took the dress, her eyes meeting his for a scant split second before she turned her back, but it was long enough to see the horrified shock in them. He hadn't lost her, he promised himself grimly. She hadn't broken the line or thrown the hook; she'd just taken it and run with it. He would bring her back.

Feeling excruciatingly awkward, Laurel stepped into her dress and yanked it up over her hips and breasts. Her eyes flickered to the large mirror over the low dresser as she jerked the straps over her shoulders. He wasn't showing any sign of awkwardness or embarrassment at all. He was matter-of-factly doing up the studs in his shirt. His slacks were open and barely hanging on his lean hips. He must have just been ready to shove them down when— She felt the panic rising again and couldn't let the thought continue. His eyes never leaving her, he tucked his shirt down inside his open pants, then briskly zipped and buttoned them. After fastening her zipper, she took a deep breath that didn't make it past the middle of her chest and turned around to face him. She'd just undone the work of six long, hard years in the space of a heartbeat, leaving her humiliated and, worse—so much worse—terrified by her failure. "This was a mistake."

His topaz eyes were hooded. "It was a mistake tonight."

"It was a mistake any night. I don't want—" her hand jerked toward the bed "—this. It can't happen again."

Her gesture was too broad, on the verge of being out of control, but his own control wasn't what it should be, either. "I'm going to make sure it does."

She looked at him, her eyes wide with appalled dismay. "What are you saying? We're friends! We're going to forget this ever happened." She shook her head angrily, like a petulant child. She was being a child, she knew, but knowing it didn't help.

"Friends?" He snorted derisively. "'Fishing buddies,' maybe? Is that what you think we are, Laurel?"

She gave him a furious glare. "It's so comforting to know that the fishing trips were just a sleazy try to get me into bed."

He felt himself flush, with shame or anger, he wasn't sure—probably both. He *had* been trying to get her into bed, true, but his motive was hardly sleazy. "We're not going to forget about this, Laurel," he said, more calmly. More than the shimmer of tears in her eyes, the childish thinness of her voice and the pleading desperation that he'd prayed never to hear again helped him regain control. He held up an implacable hand to silence her denial before she could get out the first bitter word. "It's late, and neither one of us is in any shape to discuss anything right now. I'm taking you home. We'll talk about it tomorrow."

Laurel ripped her stare away from his broad shoulder, appalled and disgusted with herself for even thinking of how comfortable it would be there, his strong arms tight around— She fled the bedroom and began looking around for her purse. "I'll take a cab."

"I'm taking you home." He'd followed her, of course.

She risked meeting his eyes. "I'd prefer not to have to see you for a while."

His shrug as he pocketed her small evening bag told her that her preferences were of no importance at the moment.

Late the next morning, he walked into her kitchen. If looks could kill, he would have died the second he set foot in the room.

"You don't knock anymore?"

Black machine grease was smeared across her right temple and cheek, matching the smudge on her right hand and contrasting with the purplish shadows under her eyes. She hadn't slept any more than he had. "Your front door was unlocked."

"A mistake you can be sure I won't make again."

"Good." The barb was aimed at him, of course, but the flicker of alarm in her eyes assured him that she wouldn't be so careless again. Frank, who had met him at the front door, brushed by his leg. He glanced down automatically and, although he'd rarely felt less like laughing, almost did. He could have sworn the dog gave him a sympathetic look as he went by.

"I thought I wasn't going to see you for a while." She couldn't help contrasting his Levi's and boots this morning with the elegant tuxedo of last night. Last night... Picking up an orange gasket, Laurel examined it minutely for invisible flaws. The last person—after herself—that she wanted to see this morning was him.

Deciding an answer to her implied complaint was redundant, since she *was* seeing him, he ignored it. Crossing his arms over his chest, he leaned one shoulder against the wall. "Do you always take out your hostility on the household appliances?" he asked interestedly. Wearing faded blue shorts and an equally ancient T-shirt advertising a salmon-fishing derby in Nanaimo, British Columbia, her hair in a haphazard ponytail, she was sitting crossed-legged on the kitchen floor, beside her disemboweled dishwasher. On a once-clean sheet in front of her were the greasy insides, meticulously laid out to match the diagram propped up against the base of a cabinet.

"I am *fixing* it." Leaning into the empty carcass, she carefully placed the gasket, then pulled back out to consult the diagram before selecting what looked like the pump housing from the autopsied guts spread out on the sheet.

Shoving himself away from the wall, he dropped to a squat a foot or so away from her. Idly he picked up a sliver of bone lying beside a screwdriver. "This is what was caught in it?"

She glanced at him only long enough to see what he was holding up. "Yes."

Picking up a pair of channel-lock pliers, she began to tighten the bolts that attached the pump housing to the body of the machine to form a watertight seal. He saw her knuckles turn white on the grips as she strained to get the bolts as tight as possible. "Don't you have any socket wrenches?"

"Not a metric set."

Her voice was breathless, and a little huskier than usual. Backing out of the dishwasher, she set down the channel-locks, flexing her hand as if to relieve a cramp, then swiped it across her forehead to brush a wisp of hair out of her eyes, smearing the grease a little more. That was when he saw the salt dried at the corner of her eye. "How many times have you put it back together?"

She picked the pliers up again. "Four."

"And it leaked every time?"

He saw her shoulders slump just for a second before she started back into the machine. "Yes."

As she was reaching for the next bolt, big hands closed on her hips and, gently but inexorably, she was pulled back. The hands were removed as she sat back on her heels.

His mouth was tight as his eyes scanned her face. "Have you had anything to eat today?"

"No."

Nodding, his mouth tighter, he reached into his back pocket and pulled out his wallet. "I noticed a Chinese place a few blocks over. Why don't you go get us something to eat while I take a shot at the dishwasher?"

It was phrased as a question, but he wasn't asking. Laurel stared down at the twenty-dollar bill he was holding out. Having already proved she could be a fool with the best of them, there really wasn't any need for further evidence. "What do you want?" she asked, taking the bill as she stood up.

Releasing a silent breath, he stood up, too. "Anything but soup. It always tastes like cardboard." He put his hand into his front pocket and pulled out his car keys. "Here, you'll need these. I've got you blocked in."

Cleese punched the replay button on the answering machine. The phone had rung while he was putting the tools away, and by the time he'd tracked it down, the machine had picked up the call. There had been no more abusive calls, Ty had turned up nothing, and the security firm hadn't reported anything out of the ordinary, but the faint warning prickle along his backbone hadn't eased. If anything, it had grown stronger during the last week. The caller wasn't finished with her.

She needed, he thought absently as M. J. Tinnin asked Laurel to call her, a couple of phones that stayed in one damn place. That was going to be one of the first things he— He wasn't planning past lunch, Cleese reminded himself caustically.

As always, he was drawn to her studio, partly because of the revelations it made about the woman who worked there and partly because he was so fascinated by her work that he was always curious to see what she was doing. With a smile, he counted four pair of shoes scattered under and around the worktable. The huaraches seemed to be a permanent fixture, although they were never in the same place twice, indicating that she must wear them at least long enough to kick them off again.

He went through the stack of blank drawing sheets on the worktable, hoping for, but not really surprised when he didn't find, any L. J. Matlocks. The book had been gone from the bookcase the next time he'd come over, too. He'd been waiting to present his copy for L.J.'s personal autograph, but the right moment hadn't presented itself yet. She was so careful about L.J.'s identity that he was certain the magazine editors and probably even the book publisher didn't know who L. J. Matlock was. He laughed softly as he straightened the stack of paper. What would the editors say if they found out that ol' L.J. was really a redhead named Laurel Jane who would knock their collective fishing hats off?

The robot was gone, likely down in the playroom at Maxwell's, but the illustrations were still spread out on the worktable, finished now. As he'd thought she would, she had the girls and boys working together by the end. The robot had gained a few more parts, an old brass colander for a helmet and what looked like the head of a toy microphone—a kids' version of a karaoke machine—as a mouth. She'd decided to use the broken fishing rod as an antenna, sticking it in one of the colander's holes. The last addition was a flashlight, which made its first appearance on the preceding page when a ray of sunlight reflecting off the cracked lens shone like a spotlight on the ceiling, drawing the kids' attention to its hiding place under an old dresser. The kids wired the flashlight onto the helmet like a headlight, switched it on, and magically switched on the robot, too. The book ended there, and Cleese laughed again when he realized he was wishing she would do a sequel so that he could see what the kids would do with the robot next.

Frank stood up suddenly, his pointed ears alert, and a few seconds later Cleese heard his pickup pull into the driveway. "Come on, boy," he said. "She's home."

As she entered the kitchen, Laurel glanced at the dishwasher, now reassembled and chugging quietly—without leaks. The dial showed it was in midcycle, meaning he must have had it fixed almost as soon as she walked out the door. "How did you get it to stop leaking?"

He looked up as he began taking white cartons out of the sacks he'd taken from her at the door, then opening them. "The bolts weren't quite tight enough. It just needed a little more hand strength."

Laurel nodded in depressed confirmation. Taking out plates and a bowl, she noticed the miniature white cotton balls on the plant growing down the side of the cabinet. Somehow it didn't surprise her that today was the day she noticed the Swedish ivy had mealybugs again.

When they began to eat, she saw his look as she dipped a spoon into her soup bowl. "I happen to like the taste of cardboard," she informed him, getting a brief, dry grin in response. There was an edge to him today. Mentally Laurel shook her head at herself. When had she begun lying to herself—and believing it? There had always been an edge to him, hard, tough, more than a little dangerous. She'd seen it the second she met him that morning on the riverbank, but she'd pretended that she hadn't, just as she'd pretended that his only interest in her was as a fishing partner.

Not that many minutes later, there was a neat stack of empty cartons in the middle of the table. No leftovers again, she thought distractedly. Glancing across the table, she saw his mouth harden, and she knew he was about to broach the subject that had been carefully avoided ever since he'd walked into the kitchen. He had her blocked in in more ways than one. She'd sensed that he was keeping his impatience in check in order to let her gain some strength from the simple act of putting food into her empty stomach, and she appreciated that. A cowardly part of her would also appreciate putting off the next few minutes forever, but she was responsible for last night's fiasco. There had been no slow, endless lead-in, no sweet, coaxing words; he'd treated her like an adult woman, and she'd reacted like a raw teenager. The least she could do was be an adult now.

"I'm sorry about last night," she began, forcing herself to meet his eyes.

"Aside from the last ten minutes, I'm not." His dark amber eyes were at full power—as they would be from now on, she was certain. He wasn't hiding his true self or his intentions any longer.

To her astonishment, she felt her mouth curve in a real smile. "Me either."

The tiny smile vanished as fast as it had come, and the sober, almost bleak expression returned, but it *had* been a smile, Cleese assured himself.

"I imagine you've made some guesses about my marriage—from that cringe and the fact that, if you asked Jack Tinnin, about all he could tell you was the name of the man I married." His nod didn't surprise her. "I met Paul Falco a month after I lost my dad, and I still wasn't thinking straight enough to see past handsome and charming. The charm began wearing thin the night of our wedding." Her mouth twisted in nothing that resembled a smile. "I was one of those rather rare phenomena on my wedding night—a virgin. I thought things would get better as I got more experience. They didn't."

He was listening in silence, and she could tell nothing of what he was thinking from his expression. Incongruous as it seemed, especially after last night, it would be easier to talk if she could have some small physical reassurance, just a touch, Laurel thought. As if by some magical telepathy, he suddenly reached across the tabletop, and tears burned at the back of her throat as his big, strong, rough hand closed around hers. "The verbal abuse started almost immediately. Like so many women, I kept telling myself that I just needed to figure out what I was doing wrong, and he would stop. And," she added softly, "I was afraid of being alone, too." She paused for a moment, then continued, her voice stronger. "He didn't stop, of course. He got worse. He began drinking more and more, and I blamed his behavior on that, but alcohol is never the cause, it's just an excuse. Two days before our second wedding anniversary, I finally faced reality. He wasn't going to stop."

Her fingers gripped his harder, and Cleese braced himself for what was coming.

"He was out, as he was most nights by then, and I forgot to lock my door." Hearing the last six words, Cleese's blood ran cold; what was coming was going to be even worse than he had thought. "I woke up when I felt his hands. Suddenly I couldn't bear him touching me even one more time. I managed to get off the bed, but I got tangled up in the bedspread, and he threw me back down on the bed. He'd used force before, but he'd never hit me until then." His eyes went automatically to the scar at the corner of her mouth, but she didn't notice. She was staring past him, seeing a bedroom, not her cheerful, comfortable kitchen, but the bedroom whose door she had kept locked. Her voice was flat, almost a monotone, and he wanted to tell her to stop, that he didn't need to listen to any more—he wasn't sure he *could* listen to any more—but if she didn't finish, whatever chance they had had ended last night.

"When he left, I got up and got dressed. There was a hospital not too far from the house, and I went to the emergency room." Her free hand came up and touched the scar at the corner of her mouth. Before it could drop back into her lap, he caught it, wrapping both his hands around hers in the middle of the table. "I checked into a motel afterward, and in the morning I looked through the listings in the phone book for a lawyer who specialized in divorce. By that afternoon, I was filling out the preliminary paperwork."

"You didn't go to the emergency room just for the cut on your face, did you?" Cleese hardly recognized the harsh rasp as his own voice. She shook her head, and he swallowed hard. As bad as his imaginings had been, rape hadn't been part of them.

Her voice regained animation as she looked at him again. "He died in a single-car accident two days later, which the newspapers kindly attributed to poor weather conditions. The charges I'd filed against him hadn't gotten out to the papers yet, and, with his death, they would have been old news, anyway. His mother begged me to go to the funeral, to keep up the public front I had maintained for the past two years." Her faint smile twisted off center. "And I did, but not for his family. For myself. It was easier than answering a lot of questions."

"You'd gone to his family for help?" He asked the question even though he was already certain of the answer.

"His mother. That's when I found out abusive husbands were a Falco family tradition. She told me I'd get used to it." Cleese indulged in a childishly satisfying fantasy of revenge while she shook her head and gave a small, humorless laugh. "You know, people think abuse is limited to the so-called lower classes, but that's not true. And the ironic thing is, the more well-to-do, the better educated, a woman is, the less likely she is to seek help, because she thinks she has more to lose financially and can't face the social humiliation."

She tugged on her hands, and he let one go, reluctantly. She might have needed the contact more at first, but now, he suspected, he was the one who needed it. "After the funeral, I came straight back to Fort Worth, bought a house, restarted my life and, after a few months, realized I wasn't doing as well as I thought I was. I needed to talk to someone, but—" she grimaced ruefully "—I didn't want to just pick another name out of the phone book. Finally I thought of the hospice counselor who had helped my father and me so much those last few months." Her fleeting smile was soft. "It was early afternoon when I went over to his house, and pitch-dark when I left. Somewhere during all that time I mentioned that I was going to donate the money from Paul's estate to a women's shelter, and he got me to promise to actually go and look the place over and not just make an anonymous donation, like I'd been planning." She smiled again as she met his steady gaze. "He was counting on what he hoped would happen actually occurring, I think, and it did."

"You decided to give more than a check."

Her smile was wry this time, like her short laugh. "Yes, and not for such altruistic reasons, either. I had been feeling pretty sorry for myself, thinking I must have had the worst marriage in the world. I couldn't understand, either, how I could have been so stupid as to stay in it as long as I did. The clients at the shelter ended up helping me at least as much as I did them. I found out there were much worse marriages than mine, hideously obscene ones, and that none of us stayed in them because we were stupid or because there was something so wrong with us that we couldn't do or didn't deserve any better. It didn't take me long to realize that I had been much luckier than the women I met. I was financially secure, I had made the decision to leave the marriage on my own, and I had my life back together."

Even hearing from her own lips what had happened—and she'd left a hell of a lot out, he knew—he had a hard time reconciling that the woman of sunshine and laughter he knew had spent years in darkness and fear. Objectively, he agreed with her—she'd had little reason to feel sorry for herself, compared to other women whose marriages had been much worse. But, subjectively, he couldn't help but feel sorry for her. He didn't know those other women, didn't love them. The concept was still new enough that it had the power to shock him. Maybe he could get used to the idea faster, he thought sardonically, if he could say the words out loud.

He looked at her across the table. She didn't want or need his sympathy, though. She had done an admirable job of self-recovery—in all areas but one. Which they were about to tackle now, he saw as she withdrew her hand from his and folded it carefully with the other on the table in front of her. It was the first sign of nervousness he'd seen from her today, and, perversely, it made him happy as hell, because it meant that what happened in the next few minutes was as important to her as it was to him. She didn't talk about her years with Falco to anyone—strangers or old friends—not because she was embarrassed or ashamed, but because she was an intensely private person. He appreciated the gift of trust she had just given him, and he appreciated even more that the reason why she'd made it, whether she was ready to admit it or not, was that *he* was important to her.

"I don't talk about my marriage very often." Her small, crooked smile mocked the understatement. "But I wanted you to understand that what happened last night wasn't your fault. I reacted instinctively when—when we fell on the bed." She gestured in frustration. God, she hated feeling like a gauche thirteen-year-old. "I guess I haven't made as much progress as I thought in that area."

"Sex."

She nodded abruptly.

"Then I guess we'll have to see you make some progress real quick." Her response was a startled blink. "Oh, hell, Laurel—" he raked an impatient hand through his hair "—if I'd had a little more finesse last night, we wouldn't even be having this conversation right now. We wouldn't even be out of bed yet, and you'd have made all the 'progress' you could want."

One eyebrow lifted. "Boy, you must really be good."

One corner of his mouth quirked upward. "I'm not asking you to take it on faith."

Coloring a little, she snorted in disgust and looked away. When she looked back at him, the bleakness was back in her eyes. "I'm almost thirty-three years old, Cleese, and I've never had a normal relationship. I don't even know if I have anything to give one." Shoving back her chair, she stood up. He remained seated and quiet as she paced a few aimless steps away, then back again. Gripping the back of her chair, she faced him. "I know that sex is supposed to be fun, pleasurable, but that hasn't been my experience. I'm not sure it ever will be, and I'm not sure I even want to try." She glared at him with a mix of defiance, despair and desire.

Slowly Cleese pushed back his chair and stood up. He couldn't ignore her very real fears, and he couldn't discount her monstrous experience with Falco. In fact, it amazed him that she was willing to trust a man again, but she did trust at least one—him—and he was going to take advantage of that trust for both of them. He was convinced that the way to deal with last night was the same theory as getting right back on a horse after you fell off. On the other hand, you didn't put an inexperienced rider back up on an unbroken stallion, either. You chose an easy, slow old plug instead. He winced mentally at the description, since it was going to have to apply to him for a while. And she was worse than an inexperienced rider, he reminded himself, because what experience she did have was all bad.

He came around the table and stopped a few feet away from her, the chair between them. "I'm sure enough for both of us, Laurel." Reaching out, he drew her away from the chair, letting his hands rest lightly on her shoulders. "And I don't have any doubts that you can give a relationship all a man could ask for and more."

She looked up at him, her expression open and unguarded. "What we have now means... a great deal to me, Cleese. I don't want to lose that." Her expression and voice took on a childlike wistfulness. "Can't we just go on being fishing buddies?"

His hands slipped up to frame her face, his thumbs caressing the shadows under her eyes as he smiled down at her. "We'll still be fishing buddies, but neither one of us can be satisfied with only that much. I've wanted you since the morning I caught you stealing my fish." He saw her small, reluctant grin. "And you want me, too. I can see it in your eyes." He brushed a fingertip over one delicate eyebrow. "And feel it in your arms." His hands smoothed down her bare arms, his fingers locking through hers. "And taste it in your mouth." He dropped a soft kiss on her mouth. Her lips parted under his, and he drew her arms around his waist, then closed his around her, bringing their bodies together until they were tight against each other from breast to thigh. Bending his head, he took what he'd been needing for hours.

She tensed at the first slow penetration of his tongue, but her small moan, as much as her near-instant response, told him she had been hungry and needing, too. Yet he felt her wariness in the tense line of her body and saw it in her eyes when he finally pulled back. Tucking her head against his shoulder, he rubbed his cheek over her soft hair, closing his eyes as he inhaled her subtle sweetness. "We'll take it slow, Laurel," he murmured. "We'll take it slow."

Chapter 9

Cleese scanned the passengers exiting the jetway. When he'd said they would take it slow, he hadn't realized just how slow "slow" was going to be. Bright and early the next morning, she had called to say she was going to New York. A publisher wanted her to do the illustrations in a ten-book series, and, after trying to make sense of the details over the phone with her agent, she had decided the only thing to do was go and see if they made any more sense in person. The yearly booksellers' convention was about to happen, too, and her attendance at that was necessary, as well. She'd been gone two weeks—the longest year, he thought with dry self-derision, of his life.

Finally she came through the door, walking with a leaden shamble, her face white except for garish clown spots of color on her cheeks and winestain shadows under her eyes. Roughly he shouldered his way against the tide of arriving passengers and their relatives, reaching her just in time to slide his arm around her waist as she stumbled over a loose bit of carpet. Wordlessly he guided her into the nearest chair, then squatted down in front of her. "Laurel, what's wrong with you? You look like hell."

"What a charming greeting! And here I was expecting something conventional, like, 'Hi, Laurel, I missed you,' or 'Gee, I'm glad you're home.'"

Her voice was so hoarse and thin, he hardly recognized it. He'd talked to her last night and thought she sounded a little odd then, but he'd put it down to a bad connection. He started to say something, but suddenly she was seized by a coughing fit that left her so limp he had to grab her arms to keep her in the chair so that she didn't slide right out. Even through the jacket of her suit and the blouse she wore underneath, he could feel the unnatural heat of her body. Propping her up with one hand, he pressed the back of the other against her forehead. Her skin felt parched and much too hot. "Damn it, Laurel! What—"

"I'm just tired, Cleese." The smile she tried came off looking more like a skeleton's rictus. "The convention was exhausting, and then I forgot to put on an airsick patch last night, so I had to stay awake on the plane to concentrate on not throwing up." She had to pause to take a breath. "I think I have a touch of the flu, too."

"More than a touch, I'd say. Do you think you can make it down to pick up your luggage, or do you want me just to take you out to the car and have it delivered?"

With an effort, Laurel focused on his worried eyes and grim mouth. She would have liked nothing better than to just collapse right where she was, consigning her luggage to the hell he'd said she looked like, but she would be home in an hour. Hold on that long and you can have the luxury of collapsing in your own bed, she made a deal with herself. "Sure," she said with what she thought was adequate brightness, but from the grimmer look on his face, she knew she didn't quite pull it off.

Cleese hailed a passing passenger shuttle and knew she was even sicker than he'd thought when she gave him a grateful look instead of an argument. He left her on a bench near the baggage carousel, and even over the noise of the conveyer and the chatter around him, he heard her cough. She stood up as he came back with her suitcases. Her eyes suddenly seemed to lose focus at the same time he heard her raw croak.

"Cleese . . . I think I'm going to faint."

A shivering spasm jerked her awake. She was lying across Cleese's lap, his left arm cradling her away from the door. He had the window rolled down, and the cool air washing over her felt wonderful. "How can you drive like this?" she asked, struggling to sit up. His arm tightened, and she stayed where she was.

"Plenty of practice when I was in high school. It's very handy at stoplights." Braking for a red light, he demonstrated, dropping a quick kiss on her forehead. "How are you doing?" he asked softly.

She grimaced. "My head hurts. Did I hit the bench?"

"Missed it by almost an inch." The light changed, and he accelerated. "Laurel—" he glanced down at her "—this doesn't seem like exhaustion or the flu."

"I went to my agent's doctor a few days ago. He says there's a lot of whatever this is going around. I took a couple of aspirin and some of the cough syrup he prescribed just before we landed." She paused for a cough that wracked her whole body. "It doesn't work too well."

He gave her another glance, which she didn't see, since her eyes were closed. "I noticed. How about you go to the doctor again, first thing in the morning?"

He got a sleepy-sounding murmur of agreement and didn't say any more. It was better that she napped instead of talked, for several reasons, he thought, cutting the lights before he pulled into her driveway, in case she woke up. She wasn't in any shape tonight to deal with why her garage door had a new coat of paint.

Frank was waiting at the front door, and Cleese paused to see if he was going to have a problem with the dog because a man had a hold on his mistress. Frank whined softly, his bushy eyebrows drawing into a worried frown, but he made no move to attack. Cleese had been looking after the dog after he found out that Laurel had planned to leave him at home in the care of a neighbor who was too terrified of him to do more than throw food over the fence occasionally. Kennels, she'd said, took one look at him and showed them the door.

She didn't wake up, so he carried her into her bedroom and left her under Frank's watchful eye while he went back for her luggage. When he returned, she hadn't moved, and she didn't even twitch when he spoke to her. Bending down, he eased an arm under her and raised her hot, limp body enough to pull the spread and top sheet out from under her. She needed to get some clothes off, not just for comfort, but also because she needed to cool off. The aspirin she'd said she'd taken hadn't kicked in yet, apparently. After pulling off her shoes, he let them drop on the floor, then worked off the jacket of her suit. He dealt with her blouse and shirt with the same impersonal briskness; it wasn't until he reached up under her slip, which looked as if it were made of silk and cobwebs, to pull down her panty hose that "brisk and impersonal" quit working. She wasn't wearing panty hose, but the same garterless thigh-high stockings she'd worn the night of the stockholders' party. They were, for reasons he wouldn't think about right now, incredibly sexy. He was half disgusted with himself for even noticing, and for noticing the pink silk and lace a little higher up, and even more disgusted that he had to force his hands to peel the stockings down her legs quickly when they wanted to take their time with the job. Just as quickly, he pulled the top sheet up over her, then sat on the bed beside her. Carefully he straightened her tangled hair and spread it over the pillow, then slicked the damp tendrils clinging to her cheeks and forehead back. A smile curved her mouth as she turned toward him in her sleep. Leaning down, he pressed a soft kiss on her hot cheek. "Sleep tight, love."

* * *

At 3:36—according to the green numbers that seemed to be floating a few inches above the bedside table—Laurel jolted awake again. She'd lost count of how many times it had been. She was going to have to stay up for a while this time, but she didn't want to lie in that bed. It was either a charcoal grill or a frozen-food locker, depending on whether it was reflecting back her fever or her chills. Right now it was saturated with ice-cold perspiration, as well, and she didn't have any more clean sheets.

She stumbled into the bathroom and swallowed three more aspirin, gagging a little on the sour taste as one caught at the back of her raw throat. She'd lost count of how many times she'd done this, too; she would probably OD on the things before she found out what was really wrong with her.

Her last nightgown joined the rest in the bathtub, along with the sheets. Naked, shivering and weaving slightly, she stood in front of the linen closet and peered at the shelves until one multicolored mass finally resolved itself into the old log-cabin quilt that had covered her bed as a child. Wrapping the quilt around herself, she went into the living room. Ignoring the lights, she switched on the TV and curled up between the plump arms of an overstuffed chair, drawing the soft, comforting cotton tighter around herself.

As one of the living near-dead herself, she watched in morbid sympathy as *The Brides of Dracula* trailed from coffin to coffin across the screen. Frank watched briefly, but, there not being even a werewolf in the movie, he went to sleep on the floor beside her chair. During a lull in the spooky music while the count stalked his next victim, she heard what sounded like a metallic scrabbling at her front door and glanced in that direction. There was only the bluish, flickering light from the television, but it was enough for her to see that the doorknob was turning. In terrified fascination, she watched as the knob revolved slowly to the open position.

The eerie music rose to a crescendo as the door swung open and a man in black stepped into the spectral gloom. The victim's death scream resounded through the living room, echoed by Laurel's hoarse shriek, a loud, startled yelp from the rudely awakened Frank, and an equally loud and startled roar from the man.

Cleese recovered first. Striding across the living room, he snapped the lights on and the television off. "For God's sake, Laurel," he raggedly demanded of the two huge eyes staring at him out of an old patchwork quilt, "why the hell aren't you in bed?"

Laurel struggled with the quilt, finally managing to sit up. He wasn't really wearing black; his Levi's and dark T-shirt had just looked black in the bad light. "How'd you get in?" Her voice came out in a squeak.

He glanced impatiently at his hand before stuffing it in his pocket. "I've got the key you gave me for Frank, remember?" He glanced in the dog's direction. Frank's fur was still in the process of lying back down. "Why aren't you in bed?" he repeated, crouching down in front of her chair. He laid his palm on her forehead. "Good God, you're burning up!"

That news was so old it didn't rate a comment. "What are you doing here?" Now her voice sounded more like a squawk, Laurel observed clinically.

"I was worried about you," he said shortly as he began gathering her in his arms. He stood up easily and started for her bedroom. "And you still haven't told me why you aren't in bed."

Laurel gave him a hazy smile as she looked up. He was good-looking even when he was scowling. "I was getting delirious, so I had to get up for a while," she said with complete reasonableness.

Cleese froze at the door to her bedroom. "What do you mean, you were getting delirious?" he asked her carefully.

"I get delirious when I get much of a fever," she said, unconcerned. "I always know when it's starting. First there are little rocks on my bed, then they grow into huge boulders, and finally I'm being crushed by earthmovers, cement trucks." Her hand untangled from the quilt to flop weakly. "You know, big machines. Then the room starts spinning." Her hand patted back a yawn. "But that didn't happen this time. I got up when the rocks started growing."

Cleese stared down at her. Her explanation was probably hilarious, but he was too worried to appreciate it fully. "So you probably shouldn't go back to bed now?" The heat from her feverish body was radiating through the quilt as if it were tissue paper.

She shook her head apologetically, as if she were afraid she was disappointing him badly. "I'm afraid not."

He returned her to the chair. "Where do you keep your thermometer?"

"I dropped it a couple of hours ago in the bathroom sink. It broke," she added unnecessarily.

He glanced around the room, then back to her. "Do you have any idea where your phone is, Laurel?" he asked with careful patience.

She peered up at him owlishly, as if she were trying to focus on him, or maybe on the question. Probably both, he thought grimly. "No," she said finally.

Laurel watched him disappear in the direction of her studio, muttering under his breath. Wondering belatedly why he wanted to wake someone up in the middle of the night, she tried to eavesdrop when he began talking—in the kitchen, she thought—but a sudden coughing fit drowned out his half of the conversation. After a minute or so she collapsed back in the chair, trying to catch her breath and ignore the pain wracking her rib cage every time she inhaled. He hung up and came back through the living room without saying anything, disappearing again, down the hall this time, before she had a chance to ask him who he'd called.

He was back in a few minutes, or maybe it was an hour—her sense of time seemed to be a little vague, suddenly—with a towel, a wet washcloth and what looked like the bottle of rubbing alcohol from her medicine cabinet. He detoured to flip on the porch light before squatting down in front of her.

"Who did you call?"

He opened the bottle, pouring some of the contents into the washcloth, and she smelled an unmistakable odor that confirmed her guess and pleased her ridiculously.

"Wick McCloud, a friend of mine. He's a doctor. He'll be here in about twenty minutes."

Wick McCloud, Ty Burnett, Cleese Starrett—they all sounded like characters from Louis L'Amour novels. She started to giggle, then she remembered the rest of what he'd said. "A doctor's coming? Now? No—" Her protest died in another coughing fit. He held her until it eased, then laid her back in the chair.

"Keep still, Laurel."

There was a pleading note mixed in with the exasperation. Exhausted as she was by the coughing, it was a minute before she realized what his hands were doing. "Cleese! I don't have anything on underneath." She was back to squeaking, Laurel realized distractedly as she tried to bat his hands away.

Meeting her fever-bright eyes, Cleese deliberately opened the quilt to her waist. "It's hardly new territory, Laurel," he reminded her, "and Wick says we've got to start getting your fever down right away." It wasn't new territory, he reminded himself again as he began sweeping the alcohol-soaked cloth across her bare shoulders and down her arms. He poured a little more alcohol on the cloth, then wiped it down her throat and chest. Her nipples drew up tight like small berries from the cooling evaporation of the alcohol. They were the same beautiful deep pink of the shell she'd found that day on the beach. He pulled her forward onto his chest, swiping the cloth up her straight, narrow back. Her nipples pushed through his T-shirt into his chest, hard and warm. He laughed in silent self-disgust—he needed a distraction, a different one.

"Laurel, honey, why is your bathtub full of sheets and nighties?"

He was talking to her again in that overly patient tone people used with a five-year-old, but she didn't care as long as he kept up the wonderfully cooling rhythm of his hand. "I was sweating so much, my nightgown and the sheets kept getting wet, and that gave me chills," she murmured, eyes closed. "I changed them until I ran out."

Wick McCloud didn't look like a doctor any more than his name sounded like one's, but he kept his stethoscope in the refrigerator just like a real doctor, Laurel thought, suppressing a shudder as the frigid metal disk made contact with her hot chest. Tall and rangy, wearing cowboy boots and Levi's, he bore enough of a resemblance to Cleese and Ty Burnett that she had to wonder if he wasn't another cousin. His examination was professional and thorough, though, and Cleese sat on the arm of her chair through it all.

"Who's your regular doctor, Laurel?" Wick asked when the exam was finished and he was sitting on her couch, writing on a prescription pad.

She told him, and he wrote that down, too. "I'll give her a call in the morning," he muttered, then looked up as he capped his pen and stuck it back in his black bag. Laurel waited, Cleese's big hand around hers, for his diagnosis and his version of "Take two aspirin and call me in the morning." Neither was what she was expecting.

"I'm not surprised you're delirious. Your fever is a hundred and three, even after the alcohol bath. You've got double pneumonia, Laurel, and I suspect it's not the usual garden variety. You're going to the hospital, honey."

"I don't need—" This protest was cut short, too, by another attack of coughing, the worst one yet. As she lay against Cleese's shoulder, wondering if breathing was possible yet, she saw the two men exchange a look of perverse satisfaction.

"I'll call the hospital so they're expecting her. Where's the phone?" the doctor asked Cleese.

"In the kitchen." Cleese saw Wick's wary look at Frank, who had made sure Wick knew he had teeth. "I'll show you." Leaning down, he tucked the quilt tighter around her. "I'll be right back, sweetheart, and then you can tell me what I'll need to get together for you to take to the hospital." She wasn't too sick to glare at him, he noticed.

He accompanied Wick to the kitchen, then stood by to make sure Frank, who'd followed them, behaved.

Waiting for his call to be transferred, Wick murmured, "She's a knockout, Cleese."

"I thought you doctors didn't notice things like that," Cleese growled.

Giving him a disbelieving look, Wick laughed hard. "Only the dead ones."

L.J. was going to suffer an accident while fishing sometime in the next couple of issues, Laurel decided, and spend a little time imprisoned in a scanty hospital gown with full back view under the tender care of a clone of Big Nurse, from *One Flew Over the Cuckoo's Nest*. She lay on her back and counted to see if there were still sixty-three holes in the ceiling tile directly over her head. Yep, still sixty-three, same as yesterday and the day before that. She rolled her head on the concrete pillow and looked across the narrow room. A cellmate would have been nice, but Cleese had insisted on a private room, and anyway, the poor woman would have had to be stone-deaf, because of her cough. She looked out the nice big window with the view of nice dirty brick, then up at the television. It was true that television series never died; they lived on—and on and on—in reruns, often on two or three different channels at once.

She entertained herself for a few minutes by trying to draw air into her congested lungs while performing her

retching cough. Afterward, she reminisced about some of
the more fun experiences she was having: not being able to
wash her hair, the IV puncture in her hand that itched like
a dozen mosquito bites, the graduate of the Marquis de Sade
School of Inhalation Therapy, who stuffed her sinuses three
times a day, and, of course, the highlight, half-hourly trips
to the bathroom—one of which was due now.

Between the endless IV bottles and the ice water the nurses
cheerfully forced on her to combat dehydration from the
pneumonia's persistent fever, she knew every crack in the
bathroom wall by heart. Unplugging the intravenous stand,
she began to trundle it toward the bath as fast as the defec-
tive grocery-cart wheels would go. The alarm on the regu-
lator squealed on her, alerting the guards that the
troublesome prisoner in cell 417 had broken out again.
Muttering a graphic description of the machine's ancestry,
she managed to shut the bathroom door just before Big
Nurse II could remind her about bedpans.

When she came out of the bathroom, M.J. was sitting on
the bed. "M.J.," she said happily. She plugged in the IV
stand again and jabbed the alarm-reset button before
climbing back into bed. "Did you just come from Maxwell's?" she asked as she pushed the button to elevate the
head of her bed.

M.J. shook her head. "I was in court all morning. How
are you doing today?"

"I'm still here," she said disgustedly.

"Did I ever tell you about my cousin Janine?"

Used to M.J.'s habit of seeming non sequiturs that turned
out to have a point after all, Laurel just shook her head.
"I've met all your cousins at one time or another. You don't
have one named Janine."

"Not anymore," M.J. agreed. "Not since she got pneumonia when she was nineteen."

Laurel favored her with an irked look. "You must be such
a comfort to your patients, M.J." The other woman

laughed, then Laurel asked a question of her own. "How are *you* doing?"

M.J. considered for a moment. "Okay. Not great, but okay." Getting up from the bed, she lifted the cover on the lunch tray that had been delivered while Laurel was in the bathroom. "Mmm... Lunch looks good."

Laurel made a face at the tray. "If you like boiled cardboard and watery tempera paint."

Laughing again, M.J. bent to sniff one of the roses in the big mixed bouquet on the bedside table. "Has Cleese been by today?"

"He came in early this morning—mainly, I think, to catch the doctor when he made his rounds." Although she had made a visit, her doctor had deferred to Wick McCloud, since, it turned out, his specialty was infectious diseases. "Cleese doesn't believe *me* when I tell him I'm doing better," she said in an aggrieved tone.

M.J. sat down in the room's only chair. "I've noticed women don't accept nurturing very well, because they aren't comfortable as the nurturee. Their expected role is as the nurturer, while men accept nurturing much better than they give it because that's their expected role." She smoothed the skirt of her linen suit, and Laurel knew the point was coming. "It's very rare, and lucky, to find a nurturing man."

Laurel smiled at the man who had just walked into her hospital room and made it suddenly feel even smaller. What with the man who was already there, it was tiny. "Cleese," she said to the newcomer, "this is my brother, Robb. I believe—" her smile remained, although her voice took on a slight edge "—you've already met on the phone."

She waited while the two men shook hands. There was no particular physical similarity between them, unless it was height; Robb was probably only an inch or two shorter, although it was hard to tell in his navy flight suit and boots. After dropping an easy kiss on her cheek, Cleese sat down on the bed, and she drew her knees up to make more room. "How did you know where to call?" she asked him.

He heard the annoyance under the smile. "I found the numbers in your address book on your desk. I knew you'd get around to letting your brothers know eventually, but I figured they'd like to know right away that their sister was in the hospital."

Cleese's voice took on a subtle but unmistakable edge, too, as he directed his last comment toward the man sitting in the chair. She saw Robb's gray eyes narrow slightly, not so much at what Cleese had said, she suspected, as at the sight of his casually possessive hand on her knee. There was another similarity between them, she thought, although she'd never noticed it about Robb before; they both had the same toughness about them.

Robb returned his look. "We'd always want to know something like that right away."

Laurel's look moved between the two men; clearly they were saying more to each other than what she was hearing. "It's wonderful to see you, Robb, but you didn't need to come all this way. I'm really not that sick. Whatever—" she shot the man sitting on the bed a look "—Cleese told you."

"Either Jim or I would have been here in the next few days, anyway, to find out why we were getting postcards every week with a new phone number for you. Jim's still out on that oil rig, and I needed to get in some flying time, so we decided I'd come."

Cleese's hand tightened on her knee. "You haven't told your brothers why you needed new phone numbers?"

"I did," she hedged. "A few minutes ago. There wasn't much they could do about it long-distance."

"We still should have known, Laurel."

There was a third similarity between them; both of their mouths could take on that same tight, hard look.

"Laurel told you about her car, as well as the calls?"

Her brother nodded. "There hasn't been anything else?"

"No."

From the subtle, indefinable change in Robb's expression, Laurel sensed that there had been some silent addition to Cleese's brief response, but when she glanced up at him, she couldn't tell what.

The inhalation therapist chose that moment to arrive for another torture session, and the two men stepped out into the hall, leaving her to his untender mercies.

"What else happened?" Robb Drew asked as soon as Cleese pulled the door shut behind them.

"While she was in New York, he painted some of the garbage he's been giving her over the phone on her garage door. It was dark when she came home, and she was too sick to notice that the door had been repainted." His voice went flat. "The man who was supposed to be watching her place knew she was gone and decided it wouldn't hurt if he knocked off a few hours early. The new one won't."

"She still has that killer dog, doesn't she? Frank?"

"She does, but he's not at her house right now. I've taken him out to my ranch for the time being." He paused. "I'll be taking her, too, as soon as she's out of the hospital."

Robb Drew gave him a long look. "Did you know Falco, her husband?"

He shook his head once. "No."

"My brother and I didn't know him as well as we should have."

"No, you didn't," he agreed.

"We won't make that mistake again."

Cleese returned the other man's hard stare. "Good."

Absorbed in her pencil, moving rapidly over a sheet of drawing paper, she wasn't aware of him at all as he stood just inside the door, Cleese knew. She paused for a few seconds, her lips pursed slightly as she studied what she'd drawn. What would it be like to be the object of that kind of total concentration? Would she make love with the same absorption? The pencil began moving again. Would she lose herself as completely in him?

As he stepped farther into the hospital room, she looked up, smiling as soon as she saw who it was. "Hi."

He reassured himself of her recovery with a long, gentle kiss, taking her sweetness to neutralize the bitter worry of the past week. She leaned into him, drawing him down on the bed, and the kiss became longer and not quite so gentle.

"What were you working on?" he asked when she sat back. The instant she'd seen him, the drawing had disappeared into the stack of paper he'd brought her.

She dismissed the drawing with a wave of her hand and a guileless smile. "I was just doodling."

"Um-hmm... What else did you do today besides doodle?" He'd caught just a glimpse of the "doodle": L.J. in a skimpy hospital gown.

She wrinkled her nose. "Mostly slept and watched TV. The highlight of my day was learning how to do pintucking on 'Sewing with Nancy.'" She shook her head gravely. "It was pretty much downhill after that. Radar went home on one channel; Henry Blake got shot down on another, and Miss Kitty left Dodge."

"I see." He tried to match her gravity, but he couldn't, and she grinned at him as he laughed.

"How's Frank adjusting?" she asked after a minute.

"He settled right in." His hand, rubbing her shoulder, found the too-sharp bones, a result of the weight she'd lost the past week. She'd probably lost a good ten pounds, and her color still wasn't good, but at least what little she had wasn't coming from the fever any longer. "He's trying to start something with the foreman's sheepdog, but she's playing hard to get."

It was her turn to laugh as a knock on the half-closed door announced Wick McCloud, followed a few seconds later by a lanky, gray-haired woman whom Laurel introduced as Hattie Sparks. He had been frankly amazed by the virtual parade of women he'd met over the past week, some from Maxwell's, all of them friends. She seemed surprised by their concern, something that hadn't surprised him at all.

The three of them made small talk while Wick went over her chart. She had been agitating to get out of the hospital for the past two days, and he suspected Wick was about to grant her wish. He just wondered how she was going to react to the next phase of her recuperation.

Wick scribbled something on the chart, then slid it back into the holder on the door. "Well, Laurel, how would you like to blow this Popsicle stand?"

"Now?"

"Now."

Laurel wasted no time in starting off the bed to get dressed before he could change his mind, but his next words brought her up short.

"There's just one problem. You live alone, and you need somebody around for the next week or two, to make sure you don't try to do too much and put yourself right back in here."

"She's coming home with me, to the ranch."

Laurel snapped her head back to the big dark man on the bed. He stared back impassively.

Wick McCloud nodded his satisfaction. "Good. I'll give the release order, and somebody'll be up with the paperwork in just a few minutes."

She didn't even spare him a glance. "No. I'll have M.J. stay with me." Laurel didn't like the bitchy tone in her voice, but she also didn't like the sense that she was losing even more control of her life. And beyond that, she didn't like the fact that she liked the idea of going "home" with him too much.

Hattie spoke up. "M.J. can't, Laurel. She just found out that she has to go to San Antonio. She's been recalled to give more testimony in a trial up there."

The dark amber burned hotter as his eyes held hers. Both of them were ignoring their audience. "You're coming home with me, Laurel. I want you, and I'm not too particular at the moment how I get you."

Chapter 10

Laurel walked across the dusty yard toward the corrals. It was amazing how familiar everything seemed after only two weeks; it was as if his ranch really were home. A very temporary one, she amended, refusing to pursue the thought in the most obvious direction. She hadn't seen her house in almost a month, and she did miss it, but not enough to insist that Cleese take her when he'd gone to pick up some materials from her studio or when he went periodically to check on things. It was he who had thought of the sheets and nightgowns she'd left in the bathtub long before she finally remembered them, which was long after they would have become a mildewed mess. She smiled unconsciously. She just wished he had thought to pack a few of those nightgowns with the rest of the clothes he'd brought her.

After worrying about losing control of her life, she was oddly content just to stay there, at first spending an embarrassing amount of time sleeping, then being accepted with surprising swiftness into the ranch community. Passing the swimming pool, she returned the waves of the several small children and one watchful mother enjoying the water. The ranch, she had discovered, was really more like a village, with about a dozen families living in the houses scattered over it. Most of them were clustered behind the main house, added gradually as the bachelors in the bunkhouse had been replaced by men with families. The men all worked on the ranch, as did two of the wives. Some of them worked in nearby Weatherford and Mineral Wells, while others worked at home, just like anywhere else. What was unusual was the congeniality and loyalty of the ranch population. Several of the families living there now were second- and third-generation, and Laurel hadn't been surprised to learn that aunts, uncles, sisters, brothers, cousins and children worked in other Starrett holdings. There was strong allegiance to the Starrett name.

And to the current holder of the name, Laurel knew, as she caught sight of him by the second corral. A large complex of barns and corrals sat behind the housing area, and she paused in the shade of the first barn. She wasn't spying on him; it was just so seldom that she got the chance to simply look at him as much as she wanted without him being aware of it. Even after the past two weeks, it still was astonishing how easily he made the transition from tycoon to working cowboy. She'd known that he worked one or two days a week on the ranch, but she'd thought he just oversaw what everyone else did. She had been surprised to see the boss work as hard and long and get just as dirty as everyone else. She laughed softly. Then again, maybe the two roles weren't so different after all, just the clothes. Both involved a lot of rounding-up, a good bit of poking, prodding and cajolery, dealing with bullheadedness and manure—more in boardrooms, she suspected—and plain hard work.

Shifting against the corral rails, he turned a little more toward her. He and the foreman, Lonnie Cottrell—another Louis L'Amour name, she thought with a smile—were leaning against the corral discussing something. He was dressed in the usual old Levi's and boots, a wide leather belt, a sweat-streaked plaid cowboy shirt with the sleeves rolled up over his forearms and half the pearl snaps undone down his chest, short leather gloves and a beat-up straw Stetson pushed back on his dark head. She had thought about drawing him like that, but she didn't have the talent to begin to do him justice. With an unconscious sigh, she stepped out of the shade. She hadn't looked enough to be satisfied, but somebody was bound to notice sooner or later if she stood in the same place for hours.

She returned Lonnie's silent nod as she reached the two men. After a quick but thorough look, Cleese wrapped an arm around her shoulders while he continued talking, and she suppressed a wince at the needle of pain threading along a rib. She'd felt it every time she tried to take a deep breath or moved the wrong way for almost three weeks. The conversation wrapped up a minute later, and Lonnie tipped his hat to her and took himself off.

Cleese turned to her immediately. "Your ribs are still hurting, aren't they?"

So much for trying to hide it. "Yeah," she said ruefully.

"Come on." Taking her by the hand, he opened the outside door to the tack room in the horse barn, then locked it behind them, and she gave him a puzzled look.

"I think you've got a dislocated rib from all that damned coughing." He pulled a stool out from under the workbench. "Hop up."

She didn't hop, but she got on the stool. "Wick says it's a pulled muscle," she told him over her shoulder as he took up a position behind her, pulling off his gloves.

"Yeah, well, Wick never did any steer wrestling," he muttered. "Look straight ahead."

She felt him pull her T-shirt loose from her shorts, then his fingers were under her shirt, warm and rough, working along her spine. They paused for a second, then traced one right rib from her backbone to almost under her breast. His fingertips were raspy on her bare, ticklish skin, but she felt no inclination to laugh. They backtracked an inch or so with the lightest of touches, then pressed hard. "Here?"

"There!" she gasped.

"Your rib's dislocated, just like I thought. I'm going to punch you right here—" his fist nudged just to the right of her spine "—and it will stop hurting by this time tomorrow."

She gave him a sardonic look over her shoulder. "Punching me will make it stop hurting?

He grinned at her. "Trust me, it works."

"Okay, but if it doesn't, I get to punch you—this time tomorrow."

He laughed. "Fair enough." Cleese braced her with his other hand and pulled back his fist for a short jab, then paused. Trust me, he'd said, and she did. He was going to hit her—and she was going to let him. They'd come a long way, and they had only a little farther to go.

"Ow!"

When she frowned blackly at him over her shoulder, he kissed her until her perturbed mouth softened. The rest of her body swiveled slowly on the stool toward his. He let his arms rest easily around her waist, and hers came up to link loosely around his neck. "Did the lab call?" he murmured against her lips. Nudging her knees apart, he stepped between them.

"Mm-hmm... The X ray was clear. I'm officially cured," she murmured back. As she shifted forward on the stool, her knees tightened around his thighs, snugging their lower bodies closer, soft warmth seeking hard, and finding it as they shared tastes for a long, leisurely moment. His mouth left hers, and while his tongue traced the delicate bones at the base of her throat, his right hand drifted up and cradled her breast, the softness not quite filling his hand as it had before. He felt her long sigh as much as heard it as her fingers sifted through his hair, and he heard the faint scrape of his hat hitting the floor. His thumb rasped lazily, and she nudged his head back up with her chin, joining their mouths again. Her legs shifted tighter around his, drawing their hips into a slow bump and grind. Her tongue searched deep, and he tightened his arm around her—and felt her slight flinch when he inadvertently squeezed her sore rib.

She made a sound of denial when he loosened his hold. "Shhh... It's okay." Easing his mouth and body away, he held her to him gently and closed his eyes. It felt so good to just hold her that it was enough—for now. "Shhh..." he whispered again. "Tomorrow."

It was tomorrow. Laurel pushed off with the toe of her sneaker to set the front porch swing in motion, breathing in the watermelon smell of freshly mown grass lingering in the still air. They'd cleaned up the kitchen together after dinner—the past few days she'd taken over the cooking from Lonnie's wife, Merle, who acted as Cleese's housekeeper, though not without some "discussion"—then he had gone off to catch up on faxes. With only occasional trips into Fort Worth, he'd spent the past two weeks here with her, a fax, the phone and a computer making it possible for him to keep in touch with his office. It couldn't be easy or convenient, but he'd given no indication that he would rather be anywhere else. Neither would she.

It was tomorrow. The soft purple light of early evening filtered through the branches of the ancient live oak overseeing the front yard, and a cricket began fiddling its two-note repertoire. Behind her the house began settling in for the night with discreet creaks and groans, like an elderly woman settling into bed. Weathered red brick with dark-green-and-white gingerbread, the house was a huge Victorian from the last century, surviving quite nicely, thank you, in this one. She had fallen in love with its rambling elegance the moment she'd seen it.

Frank climbed up onto the porch, laying his head in her lap, and she petted him. Like all wonderful old houses, there were wonderful stories that went with this one, and Cleese had shared them with her, just as he shared his house with her. The first Starrett family home had been a log cabin, built by his great-great-grandfather, John. When John had decided to go hunting for a wife in St. Louis, he'd covered the logs with white clapboard and the river-rock chimney with red brick, and put glass in the windows and rugs on the new oak floors, but one of the original features he hadn't been able to camouflage. Agatha Starrett, the new bride, had spent her first night in her new home wide-awake, with a bottle of kerosene handy for the bedbugs. No matter what new remodeling and eradication efforts had been undertaken, the bedbugs had survived, and when the house burned to the ground twenty years later, Agatha had been the chief suspect, although she had denied it, of course. Whatever had happened, Agatha had gotten a new, bedbugless house out of it—this one.

Frank went off to a corner of the porch to lie down, and she gave the swing another push, glancing down at the white marble steps leading up to the porch. They had survived the fire along with a few things that Agatha had rescued—a priceless photo album, a silver candelabra, an ormolu clock, a gold-trimmed handpainted china gravy boat and an antler-and-brass chandelier. Privately, she doubted that Agatha had risked her life for the latter. Cleese had shared these family treasures with her, too, making her feel that, somehow, they were also hers. With the friendly ranch community, the grand old house, the stories and the treasures, she felt so comfortable here, felt such a sense of belonging, although it was really the man, she knew. Perhaps that was why, yesterday, when Merle had asked him if he'd renewed the lease on his town house yet and he'd said he was still thinking about it, the offer to share her house had been on the tip of her tongue before she had even thought about it. Then she *had* thought about it, about the details like utility bills, housework, groceries, who got the bathroom first every morning, who slept on which side of the bed... It was that last that had kept her mouth shut. She felt the same bubble of hysterical laughter trying to escape once again.

Weren't you supposed to sleep together at least once before you lived together?

It was tomorrow. "Tomorrow," he'd said yesterday, and she'd known what he meant. He was going to make good on the threat—the promise—he'd made over a month ago. And about time, too. If she hadn't gotten sick, she would already know who slept on which side of the bed. Instead, the sexual tension had built up inside her to the point that she was ready to scream with frustration. And whimper with fear. All the worries and dreads had had a chance to build up, too. Over the past six years, she had successfully restored her self-confidence in all areas but one. Sexually, she didn't have a drop. His wife had refused to live on the ranch, and he had never brought another woman here, Merle had told her with a casualness that wasn't casual at all. The other woman had meant to reassure her, Laurel knew, and she had—and also terrified her, because she realized how important she must be to him, and she was so afraid she was going to disappoint both of them. She wished now that she'd indulged in some good old meaningless sex the past few years so that she would have more experience—which only went to show, she thought with a laugh of silent disgust, what a mixed-up mess she was.

An approaching thunderstorm electrified the horizon, while a handful of lightning bugs put on their own pyrotechnic display over the lawn. She heard the screen door screak behind her, then the creak of the porch floor, before a large body settled on the swing beside her. Cleese took over the locomotion of the swing. His arm eased around her right side, and she laid her head on his shoulder.

"The pain's still gone?"

"For good. I guess I don't get to punch you after all," she murmured.

She heard his quiet chuckle, then they drifted to and fro in easy silence, his hand idly playing with her hair. The evening had darkened to deep indigo, bringing the moon garden planted at the corner of the porch to life. All the flowers

in the night garden were pale gold or white, the white ones
so white, like the moon, that they were ethereal, seemingly
unreal—miniature angels' trumpets mingling with the big
bass trumpets of jimson, golden-spurred columbine, evening primroses, cleome puffs and spicy stock. Hawkmoths
fluttered over them on their soft, soundless wings, gray
shadows sipping the sweet nectar.

With the light ebbing, colors ebbed, too, making a world
of dark and scent, touch and feel. The storm gusted the first
downdrafts of cool air across the porch, bringing the smell
of rain to mingle with the sweet primrose and spicy stock.
Goose bumps shivered over her bare arms and legs, and he
shifted her to his lap, his arms wrapping around her to share
the heat of his big, hard body, and new scents were added,
soap and the tang she recognized as uniquely his. She felt his
head lower, and his lips touched her cheek, a moth-wing
kiss, soft, silent. She turned her head, and their mouths
fused. Their tongues touched and flicked in play before they
became serious, exploring, withdrawing, in the same easy
rhythm as the swing. Her hand curled loosely against his
chest, then opened, her fingertip brushing a hard little nub
under the soft cotton of his shirt. Delighting in the tiny
shock tingling her fingertip, she scraped lightly, the nub becoming smaller and harder, and felt a corresponding hardness under her hip. His hand rubbed up her bare thigh and
across her stomach pausing just under her breast, but instead of continuing upward, it slipped back to her waist.
Abruptly, his mouth left hers, and he held her to his suddenly tensed body for several long seconds before he spoke
quietly over her head. "I'm going upstairs, Laurel. Don't
stay out here much longer. It's too cold." His mouth came
back to hers in a kiss that was as hard and hungry as it was
short; then he set her on her feet and turned to go inside. A
lightning flash illuminated the dark porch as he opened the
door, and she caught a glimpse of his expression, sober, set
and, oddly, a little vulnerable.

The inky dampness swirled around her as the storm settled over the house. Laurel leaned over the porch railing, the first erratic raindrops matching her heartbeat. It would be so much easier if he had simply carried her off to bed, but the lead in their long mating dance had been his. Now he was letting her take it for the last step, because he needed to know that she made her choice freely, because she truly wanted him.

She washed up by rote, then pulled on fresh panties and the T-shirt he had given her to sleep in, wishing he had packed just one of her pretty nightgowns. She switched off the light in the bathroom; then, taking a deep breath that was only a little ragged, she crossed the hall.

Pausing just inside the door to his bedroom, she reached to switch off the small, dim lamp on his dresser, then pulled her hand back. It would be easier in the dark, but if she was going to do this, she was going to do it right.

Propped up against the pillows, Cleese watched her cross his room. She had surprised him when she didn't turn out the light. She stopped a foot or so from the edge of his bed and shivered as if she were cold, but the shiver wasn't due to a chill, he knew.

He came up on his knees in the middle of the bed and silently held out his hand. Her eyes darted down his body, almost as if she couldn't help it, and he almost smiled at the flicker of relief when she saw that he was wearing briefs. She put her ice-cold hand in his, and he tugged her gently forward.

Her knees bumped the edge of the bed, and she stopped again. Laurel watched his hands come up to the hem of the T-shirt and begin to draw it up her body, the backs of his fingers brushing up her ribs and the sides of her breasts with torturous delay.

He hadn't noticed the flies, the heat, the sweat, the smell, all day, too lost in imagining the night. Cleese pulled the shirt over her head, letting it fall to the floor, then closed his hands gently over her bare shoulders to bring her mouth to his. He waited until her arms came around him, then glided one hand down to the edge of her panties, pressing her into his hips. He rocked their bodies slowly, while his open mouth trailed moistly up her throat until her neck suddenly went lax and her head tilted, giving him better access. He ran the tip of his tongue around the delicate edge of her ear, his teeth nipping softly at the lobe, then back down to the pounding pulse at the base of her throat.

Laurel heard herself moan quietly. Her hands caressed tentatively around his waist, then clutched at his hips as his tongue tracked wetly down and around one breast. It circled maddeningly, drawing the circle tighter and tighter, slowing even more to lap and suckle the swollen tip to an exquisite aching. His mouth sauntered across to the other nipple to tease and tug and madden again, while his hands slipped under the elastic of her panties, his hard palms heating the curves they cupped, his long, blunt fingers kneading, urging her closer, until scalding hardness surged against cushioned satin.

She moaned again, deep in her throat, as her bones melted, her body flowing over his. His mouth back on hers, his tongue thrust and retreated, inviting hers to play the imitative game. When it did, he slid her panties down over slim hips as satiny as their covering. They skimmed down her long legs to puddle at her feet.

Hazily Laurel watched his dark head rise. His topaz eyes burned leisurely over her naked body, and she felt the heat spread under her skin. "You're so lovely, Laurel." His voice was almost a growl. "And I've waited so long to have you like this." His mouth returned to hers in another thirsting kiss. The rough hair on his thighs brushed against the smoothness of hers as one big, warm, rough hand began to slide down over her belly, seeking her heat, and she flinched.

"Damn!" Embarrassed, furious with herself and frustrated almost beyond bearing, Laurel spun away from the bed. She'd hardly made half a turn when his hands caught her by the shoulders.

"Easy, Laurel." His raspy voice calmed her. "Easy, now." Her resistance eased, and he turned her to face him.

She shut her eyes on a convulsive swallow. "Damn," she said again. "I'm sorry." Hot tears clogged her throat and dampened her lashes. "I promised myself I would be sophisticated and cool. I'm not succeeding very well, am I?"

Her shaky laugh broke, almost breaking his heart along with it. Carefully he eased her against him, and her eyelashes, like wet butterfly wings, fluttered against his shoulder. "Shh..." He stroked her hair away from her damp face. "It's okay, sweetheart." It wasn't okay. He could feel the random, jerky twitching of her body still, as if her nerves were growing out of her skin and being rubbed raw. If she were a virgin, they would have only her fearful imaginings of what might be to deal with. But she had real memories of what had been. No matter how slowly he went, how much care he took with her, the specter of another man, another night, might always stand between them.

He held her until she relaxed, then let her go and lay back on the bed. She looked down at him, clearly puzzled by his action, and he laughed to himself grimly. Better puzzled than terrified. "Touch me, Laurel." Her hands came up after a long minute to hover over him nervously as she raised uncertain eyes to his. If she but knew it, he thought with another silent laugh, this was new territory for him, as well. He had never let a woman initiate their sexual relationship before. He considered telling her that, but decided it would only make her more nervous.

"Touch me," he repeated, need roughening his voice even more. One hand finally touched his chest, but then seemed to freeze. Laying his hand over hers, he guided her cool palm and quivering fingers down his body, traveling slowly across his chest, over his belly, stopping at the waistband of his briefs. His hand fell away, as, her wide eyes locked on his, her hand returned to its starting point.

Her gaze dropped to her fingers as they followed the silky ribbon of dark hair that bisected his rock-hard, flat stomach as far as they dared to go. Her hand came back up again, and she unconsciously eased onto the bed beside him while her other hand came up to join its better-traveled twin. Together they explored the mat of hair on his chest, finding tiny tight nipples, then skimmed down the surprisingly soft skin over his ribs. His breathing changed, slowing and deepening as a faint flush spread under his bronze skin. She twisted a nipple gently, and his powerful body shuddered. Fascinated by his reactions, she knelt over him, her hair whispering across his belly. Her hands moved lower, one pausing to investigate his navel, while the other continued on, not stopping at the band of his briefs this time. Watching his face, she knew they both felt the same galvanic jolt when her hand touched the pulsing warmth under the white cotton. His eyes glazed and closed as his breath seemed to rush out of his body.

Hooking her fingers in the waistband of his briefs, she eased them over his arousal, then dragged them down his strong thighs and calves and finally over his long, surprisingly narrow feet. Running a hand back up the inside of his thigh, she cupped him and heard his strangled intake of air as his fingers spread convulsively on the sheet. Her hand slid higher, closing around hot, smooth, steel hardness, and she measured him, slowly. Leaning down, she touched her tongue to his nipple, then moved her mouth down his chest, journeying languorously, detouring to learn and savor with lips and tongue and teeth while her hand deliberately intensified his need—and her own—even more.

Suddenly, ferocious hands hauled her upward, stretching her body along his. "God, woman, you're driving me insane."

He rolled her under him, his mouth taking hers, igniting a fuse that burned through her veins, incinerating all worries, all fears. Her fingers tangled in his hair to hold his ruthless mouth in place. Dimly she felt his hand graze the inside of her thigh, and suddenly her whole body was throbbing, bombarded by sensation that was almost more than she could survive. One long finger deepened and accelerated the rhythm, and her hands dropped to clutch desperately at his heavy shoulders. "No!" Just for an instant, fear returned, the fear of being completely out of control. "No, I can't...."

"Yes, you can."

"No..." She rolled her head frantically on the pillow as she felt herself slipping away. "I've never..."

"I know."

His name was a long scream as she lost herself in a climax so absolute, so all-consuming, that for long minutes she wasn't sure she had survived. Finally she opened her eyes to see him still above her, a faint smile on his face. Wordlessly he slid his hands under her hips, and just that, the feel of his callused, hot hands, brought an instant response she wouldn't have thought her body capable of for hours, days even.

She arched beneath him, taking him as completely as he took her. He was huge inside her, and for a moment she felt an almost unendurable, stretching fullness; then her body seemed to adjust, and he started to move, stronger, deeper, with each stroke, as his hoarse whisper encouraged and praised. Her gaze followed his to the joining of their bodies, his dark and quintessentially the aggressive male, hers light, the receptive female. It was the most erotic sight she had ever seen.

He raised his eyes, holding her gaze as he thrust again, gauging every nuance of the expressions crossing her face— joy, agonized pleasure, shocked delight, but no fear. Her hands drew him closer, her ankles locking over his calves, and he felt her begin to tighten around him. His own control at the outer limit, he urged her on with hard, quick strokes. She cried out, her body convulsing around his, and without warning an incandescent, gushing release flooded through him, washing him beyond pleasure, to a place he'd never visited before—pure sensation, pure freedom, pure love.

Chapter 11

Laurel lay totally limp, every bone, every muscle, in her body vaporized. She could never describe in words what had just happened to her, and, if she tried to draw it, all the paper would have on it would be a giant mushroom cloud. Random spasms still jerked through her, into the large male body that was mashing hers so splendidly. The body began to shift away from hers, despite her best—and pitifully weak—efforts to keep it, and she realized there was a small aspect of it that she could describe, after all. It had been an exorcism.

Cleese looked down into eyes that were still unnaturally dark, still had tears seeping at the corners, still looked too shocked to fully comprehend what had just happened to her. Unfortunately, he did.

"Laurel, I'm sorry."

He was *sorry?* Laurel stared up at him, now sitting away from her, no longer touching her in any way. How could their perceptions be so completely opposite? But, no matter how, they obviously were. His mouth had that harsh, tight line she knew too well to mistake. First she had lost his wonderful body; now she was losing the ecstatic happiness that had been hers far too briefly. In a desperate bid to save it, she blurted out the perfect response, which was not the one she would have made if she'd taken time to think about it.

"Why?"

For a moment she didn't think he was going to answer her. "I wanted you to have the control, Laurel, to be gentle and careful. Instead, I was no better than—"

His voice was raw as his mouth thinned even more in self-disgust. He had been haunted by the same ghost, Laurel understood in a sudden flash of insight. As quickly, she found the energy to sit up in an adrenaline surge of very real fear. "No, Cleese!" Her hand on his mouth silenced the awful—and wholly mistaken—self-accusation he was about to make. "It couldn't be gentle and careful for us the first time. We'd had to wait too long. It had to be wild and a little rough. And, as for control—" she smiled a little "—just as a matter of practicality, you had to take it. You were the one who was sure of what to do next."

Kissing her fingertips, Cleese took her hand gently from his mouth. Immediately, her hand turned, and her fingers curled fiercely around his as his eyes searched her face. "Are you sure, Laurel?"

Her smile almost blinded him. "It was the most incredible experience of my life."

A tightness squeezed his chest and throat. "Mine, too," he said in a harsh whisper. Why didn't he just come right out and tell her? Because, he thought caustically, every instinct told him that any mention of the word "love" and she would run, breaking the fragile line connecting them. He needed—*they* needed—more time to strengthen it. His thumb brushed the two iridescent tears from the corners of her cloudy eyes, then paused for a second on the scar at the corner of her mouth. "And the best part is, it will only get better," he promised her softly.

For a second her smile became even more radiant, if that was possible, and then it turned crooked as her eyes no longer quite met his. "I read once," she mentioned, "that a man has a hundred or so minutes of, ah—potential a night."

Choking back a startled laugh of delight, he considered the information thoughtfully. "I don't believe I've ever heard that particular theory, but it shouldn't be too difficult to prove."

Her eyes came back to his, and he saw a wicked glint. "Or disprove."

"Which salad dressing do you want?" They'd proved the theory.

"Honey mustard." How many nights constituted proof? Was three enough? And did day count as night if you didn't pause in between? He'd proved something else, too—unbelievably, it did get better.

Cleese set the honey mustard and Thousand Island dressings on the maple trestle table, along with the butter, sour cream and strawberry jam he'd taken from the refrigerator. "I'll get the potatoes and biscuits out of the oven." It would take time before she made love without a few reservations, a little embarrassment, but each time she was a little more eager, a little less self-conscious. She was learning the intricacies of rhythm, response—his and hers—learning what she liked and how to ask for it. What she lacked in experience she more than made up for in instinct and imagination, and, as he'd already known, she had a very creative imagination.

Laurel transferred green beans to a serving bowl. "Can you get the fish, too? I stuck the platter in there to keep them warm." The past week she had drowned in sensuality. Whether it was instinctive or calculated on his part, she didn't know or care. All that mattered was that he'd known just what she needed: a total voluptuous, erotic immersion in him. Whatever residual fears and hang-ups she had were being cured as she learned what she should already have known about herself and filled in the gaps in her sexual experience. Making love wasn't like it was in the movies—two perfectly choreographed pretty bodies falling gracefully into a beautifully made bed. It was sloppy, chaotic, instinctual; it was messy and animalistic; it wrecked the bed—when they used a bed—and she loved it. Making love with Cleese Starrett was beyond wonderful, light-years beyond.

He added the contents of the oven to the table. "What else do we need?" She was teaching him a few things, too. Besides finding out that her eyes were darker when she woke up in the morning and that she preferred showers, he'd learned that he'd never made love before. He'd had sex, making sure that his partner was satisfied, but no more. Or, more often than he liked to admit, he'd indulged in the commonly, and rightly, named obscenity—selfish, physical exercise where anyone would do, the woman little more than a faceless object, as he was to her. With Laurel, he had discovered the opposite of the obscenity: making love. It was the ultimate in generosity and sharing—pleasure, tenderness and caring—and no woman would do but Laurel. She touched him as if he were gold, a precious gem, and he'd never felt so desired, so wanted, so chosen, before. Not knowing he could feel that way, he'd never missed it. Now that he did know, he craved her touch as a miser craved more wealth to add to his hoard. And, like the miser, he wondered if he would ever have enough.

She looked over the table before smiling up at him. "I think we have everything we need." As a lover, he was himself: physical, arrogant and aggressive. He was also tender, gentle and more careful of her than she was of herself. He was the one who worried that she wasn't getting enough sleep, that her unaccustomed body needed more time to recover from one bout of lovemaking before initiating another.

Returning her smile, he pulled out her chair. "Good. Let's eat." They'd proved another theory, too—the better the friend, the better the sex. Yet physical possession was only a part of his craving. He grinned at the top of her head as she took her seat. A very important part, but not everything. He craved the nonsexual, too. Rarely did she pass up an opportunity to touch, to hold, to stroke, him—like now, when her hand grazed his as he held her chair. It wasn't sexual, although it was just as intimate. The intimacy was different and unique, warm and loving as opposed to hot and exciting, and it almost scared him how good those touches and strokes and hugs felt. No matter how gentle and careful, sex still involved power, and the simple facts of biology and anatomy gave it to the man. By their natures, men saw the world in terms of power, and if a man didn't have it in a particular situation or relationship, that must mean the other person did. Women saw the world more in terms of equality, because power didn't seem to matter so much to them, and she was teaching him that, a much more important lesson than any he was teaching her. Maybe that was why intimacy that didn't lead to sex almost frightened him, Cleese decided. It was going against all those ancient male instincts to always try to be the one in power. Intimacy without sex made the man and woman equal, and he had discovered he needed that kind of intimacy as much as he needed the sexual. He needed warmth and loving embraces—*her* warmth, *her* loving embraces. He would have cherished her for that alone, for loving him whether he held the power or not.

"Thanks," Laurel murmured as she sat down. As a lover, he was also carnal, sophisticated, uninhibited, as generous with his own body as he was demanding of hers, and she was gradually finding the nerve to make some demands of her own. She had come to understand that he would be tender but not controlled; he would give, but he would take, as well, sometimes with a stunning speed that left her feeling as if she'd been caught up in a tornado, helpless to do anything but go along for the wild, terrifyingly exciting ride. Sometimes the loving was hours long, slow and easy and seemingly endless; and sometimes it was as it had been just before dawn this morning, when he'd used every part of his body—hands, mouth, arms, legs, all of him—to arouse her almost beyond all bearing, dragging her after him down into a dark, mysterious world of pure physical sensation. She'd caught up and raced with him, in step every throbbing beat of the way. However it was, she loved the heat and weight of him, the hot, musky smell of him, the tangy taste of him, almost as much as she loved the man himself.

It was his turn to say thanks as she filled his glass with iced tea, while he took the chair across the narrow table from her. She did love him, whether she was ready to admit it or not. Love was in her every word, every touch, every look. He held out the sugar bowl. "Want some?" he dead-panned. She was one of those who liked a little tea or coffee with her sugar. She took the bowl with the same cheeky grin he'd seen that morning, when they'd gotten up. He'd tossed her the old green T-shirt he had pulled on after his shower the night before, and she'd held it between her thumb and forefinger, giving it a disdainful look, before suddenly grinning at him and plopping it over her head. The shirt had skimmed the middle of her sleek thighs, and he had marveled at how right she looked wearing his shirt...in his bedroom...in his house...his woman. He had caught her, netted her, held her at last in his hands. He hoped she realized there was no way in hell he was going to let her go.

Laurel dumped sugar in her glass and stirred. She did love him, even if she was far from ready to admit it to him. She'd only recently admitted it to herself, although the actual fall had taken place early on—probably somewhere around the time she'd first noticed what a good advertisement he was for Levi's, she thought wryly. She had been so concerned, so *overwhelmed*, with the physical aspects of their relationship that she had ignored the emotional. Or maybe that had been a deliberate diversionary tactic she had used to protect herself because the emotional aspects were even more disturbing than the physical.

"Did any of the kids go fishing with you?"

Laurel accepted the platter of cornmeal-fried panfish from him. "Janey did." Behind the barns and corrals was a good-size pond stocked with crappie, perch, sunfish, and a few lunker bass who kept the pond population under control by cannibalizing their small cousins and gave someone an occasional thrill by taking a jig. She slanted him a look as she slid a fish onto her plate. "She said you got skunked when she went with you."

He smiled sweetly. "It was her first time. I didn't want to show her up."

She let a delicate snort speak for her, mainly to make him grin, but the truth was, he probably had made sure he didn't catch anything to ensure that little Janey had a great time on her first fishing trip. She'd learned that he had taught all the ranch kids to fish. He obviously liked children, was very good with them, and the ranch kids adored him, of course. He really ought to have a few of his own, she thought, and an oddly sweet pain pierced her.

He eyed the second fish she put on her plate. "That one was a little small, wasn't it?" he said chattily.

Implying, of course, that he would never have kept such a minnow. "It was a hoo— It swallowed the hook," she said with great dignity.

"Hmm... A hook swallower." Cleese hid his grin behind his glass of iced tea. She had almost called the little fish the name from one of L. J. Matlock's funniest pieces, the one that had defined the terms to use to lie convincingly about a lousy catch. He had been waiting for the right moment.... Sobering his expression, he lowered his glass. "What did you catch them on?"

Her eyes narrowed on him for a second, then she shook her head slightly, as if dismissing the suspicion, and he had to take another drink of tea. "A suicide jig."

He nodded. "That one always works. You know," he went on in the same conversational tone, "you don't look old enough to have 'roamed the world the past forty years with a fishing rod in your hand.' "

Damn! She'd known that "hook swallower" crack had sounded too innocent, but she could bluff her way out of this, Laurel assured herself. He had no real proof, only that drawing, which had gone into the trash, and a book that now thousands—hopefully—had. "Cleese, what in the world are you talking about?"

Oh, she was good. Both her tone and the puzzled frown suggested that he'd gone quietly nuts in the past two minutes. He didn't bother to hide his grin this time. "I know who L.J. is, Laurel Jane."

As you were supposed to do with crazy people, she agreed with him. "So do I, Cleese. He's some old fisherman, seventy-five at least, if he's a day."

His deep laugh contained an extremely annoying degree of smugness. "I know," he repeated himself. Quite unnecessarily, she thought. "The only thing I don't know is where you got the 'Matlock' from."

She considered him for a long minute. "It was my mother's maiden name," she said finally, with a small, lopsided smile. "No one else knows, by the way, and I'd like to keep it that way. I'm not too sure L.J. could survive a sex change."

"I'm sure his editors couldn't," he agreed dryly. It was plain high school, but sharing a secret with her pleased the hell out of him. "I won't tell anyone—if you autograph my book for me. Since I'll have the only signed copy in existence, it ought to be worth something someday."

"Yeah," she told him wryly. "About two dollars at a used bookstore."

He laughed again, then his grin blurred to a soft smile. "I've enjoyed your stories more than I can ever tell you, Laurel. They bring back so many good memories of my dad."

In her answering smile, he saw complete, shared understanding. "I'm glad," she said simply.

* * *

"If we take him, we're going to have to buy him one, too. Frank has a thing for ice-cream cones."

Cleese slapped the dropped tailgate on his pickup. "The sheepdog dumped him for a German shepherd, and he needs cheering up. Don't you, boy?"

He addressed his last comment to her lovelorn dog, who needed no urging to hop up into the back of the truck. Laurel watched Cleese slam the tailgate closed and Frank butt his head against his hand for a pat. Cleese obliged, and Frank's eyes closed blissfully. Like mistress, like dog, she thought with a silent, half-despairing laugh.

The trip for ice cream was for "predessert," with the peach pie she'd made to be the real dessert later. The truly funny part was that he had made the pronouncement with a perfectly straight face. She still marveled at the amount of food he put away, but, having seen him work, she knew why he could eat like that and never gain an ounce. It was his intention that she gain many ounces, however, which was another reason for two desserts. She had heard the admonition to eat "a little more" so many times that finally she'd "Yes, Mothered" him. He'd laughed uproariously—then told her to take more potatoes.

Once they were on the road, he reached across the cab and matter-of-factly slid her across the bench seat to his side. She no longer tried to come up with silly reasons to explain away the electric thrill, just accepted it as normal now, the way she accepted as normal the sense of security and happiness that came with his strong arm around her shoulders . . . and ignored the tiny worm of doubt.

"What does Frank want? Vanilla?

Laurel looked down her nose at him. "Frank is a connoisseur," she informed him. She scanned the offerings in the freezer case. "Pink bubble gum, a small one."

It was his turn to give her a disparaging look for her parsimoniousness as he ordered a jumbo bubble gum cone. She considered warning him, but decided he wouldn't believe her; he would have to see for himself why small was better.

The expression on his face a few minutes later was priceless as he watched Frank, who didn't gulp down the giant cone as any normal dog could be expected to do, but took a delicate lick of the pink ice cream. He gave her an unbelieving look as Frank continued to lick daintily at the cone. After a dozen or so licks, he pulled back and regarded the man with a faintly reproachful air.

"What now?" Cleese's "air" was more exasperation.

"You're not turning it so he can lick all around and catch the drips," she explained solemnly.

With another disbelieving look, he turned the cone, and Frank went back to licking. Burying her giggles in her rocky road, she watched as Cleese ate his own butter pecan while, wearing an expression of long-suffering patience, he slowly rotated the pink bubble gum cone.

Frank was still happily slurping when a pickup load of Little Leaguers pulled up in the empty space on the other side of the truck. "Hi, Mr. Starrett," several of the kids called out as they piled out of the back of the truck. He returned their greetings, then introduced her as the kids came over and, in response to the elbow nudgings and smothered giggles, gravely introduced Frank. Frank ignored them in favor of his ice-cream cone.

The driver and the other man, the coaches, she assumed, followed. "Hey, Cleese," said the driver.

"Cleese," echoed the other man.

"Gaylan, Bobby." Again he introduced her and, with a grin acknowledging theirs at seeing the big tough guy holding an ice-cream cone—a *pink* one, for God's sake—for a dog, introduced Frank, identifying him as hers, which made their grins even broader. Most men would have handed the cone off to her when they saw anyone they knew coming, if they'd ever gotten into such a ridiculous position in the first place, but he clearly didn't feel any need to spare himself embarrassment. Because he didn't feel any. Cleese Starrett

was too confident and secure in himself to be concerned over
the absurd picture he and Frank made; instead, he was enjoying the laugh at himself more than anyone else.

The men had tipped their baseball caps to her, showing
the same old-fashioned courtesy that had him pulling out
her chair for her every time they sat down to eat. That and
the other little politenesses he showed her still came naturally to men here, and she appreciated them. Another part
of that courtesy was eschewing overt curiosity, but she had
seen the covert speculation in Gaylan's and Bobby's eyes
before Cleese had introduced her. When he had, he'd given
no explanation of their relationship, not that one was necessary in this situation, but he'd done the same on the ranch,
where everyone had good reason to wonder just who she was
to him. Yet, by not explaining, he had explained, by indicating that it should be so obvious that it needed no explanation. For a moment she thought of the baseball cap he'd
given her—and which she still wore. His "explanation"
would have bothered her, if she hadn't seen, following the
speculations, the understanding that he wore her brand, too.

Gaylan and Bobby left to rescue the besieged ice-cream
store clerk about the time Frank licked his pink bubble gum
down to the rim of the cone. Cleese's fingers shifted to the
bottom of the cone, as if he thought Frank was now going
to chomp the remainder, finally, in one bite. He didn't.
Prissily he began lapping ice cream out of the cone, and
Cleese began to laugh helplessly. Taking pity on him, Laurel climbed into the cab of the truck and opened the sliding
back window. "Here," she said, reaching for the cone. "I'll
take it."

A couple of minutes later, Cleese turned onto the narrow
blacktopped road that led back to the ranch, a chuckle es-
caping him every time he glanced sideways and saw Laurel
with her hand stuck through the back window, calmly
holding the ice cream cone for Frank. Finally the ice-cream
was gone, and the dog dispatched the empty cone in a single gulp. "Where did you get him, anyway?"

"He was hanging around Maxwell's a few years ago. He was just a puppy, but he was already so big and homely, I knew if we took him to the pound nobody would adopt him." She laughed sheepishly. "So I did."

He grinned as his arm reached out, and she leaned her head back against his shoulder to watch the oaks and large mesquites pass by, their green fading to a silvery gray in the twilight. The scents of the wild clover growing along the road and dust mingled with soap and man, and she drifted in simple contentment.

At the sudden slowing of the pickup and his muttered oath, she sat away from him and peered ahead. About a dozen "world-champion-bloodline Charolais"—as she'd been informed the first time she'd called them "cows"— blocked the road, all wearing an eartag she'd come to recognize. World champions were *not* branded, she'd also been informed. It was just dark enough for headlights, and the huge white cattle, caught in the bright lights, looked oddly ghostlike as they walked toward them out of the gloom. "How did they get out?" she asked, glancing at him.

"There's a gate with a tricky latch about a half mile down the road. It's been on the 'when somebody gets around to it' list to be replaced, but—" twisting around, he took the top half of his fly rod from the gun rack across the back window "—it just moved to the top of the 'do it yesterday' list." Letting the truck creep forward, he stuck the fly rod section out the window and began swatting broad backs and broader rumps while he whistled and yelled. Laurel grabbed the bottom half of the rod and began prodding and swatting on her side of the truck, adding her own whoops and hollers, while Frank contributed several choruses of deep, baying barks. The startled cows jumped around in confusion, then the largest started ambling back in the direction from which they'd come, and the rest slowly followed.

Full darkness had fallen by the time she pushed the gate shut behind the last cow. Cleese twisted the baling wire that he'd taken from the toolbox behind the truck seat through the gate and around the fencepost several times, then pushed hard on the gate. The wire held, and they started back toward the pickup. His arm settling around her waist, he pulled her easily to his side and lowered his head automatically for a quick kiss, halting abruptly when he saw the expression of profound sadness on her upturned face. "What's the matter, honey? Did you get stepped on? Damn it, I knew you should have stayed—"

"I didn't get stepped on, Cleese. It's just that you've shattered the last of my illusions," she told him somberly. "Roundup by pickup." She shook her head sadly. "I don't know what the West is coming to." Actually, she had seen him "rounding up" on horseback several times. If ever she was asked to illustrate a book of Greek myths, she knew exactly what the centaur would look like.

He grinned at the laughter in her enchantress eyes. "It's coming to air-conditioning and seats with lumbar supports." He fulfilled his intention, giving her a smacking kiss, then returning for another, softer, longer, hungrier one when her lips parted immediately beneath his. Raising his head, he looked down to see desire in her eyes and love in the smile that curved that lush, giving mouth. Friend plus mistress . . . equaled wife. The words were constantly on the tip of his tongue, like the body hunger that never seemed to be satisfied, no matter how many times he had her. But there was something else in her eyes, too, a faint, almost invisible shadow. Doubt? Fear? Something he couldn't put a name to. He loosened his arm slightly and started them walking again, silent. Until he could name it, he didn't know how to get rid of it, and until he did, the words would have to stay where they were.

Sliding behind the wheel, he asked casually, "Do you still want to go into town tomorrow?" She'd mentioned it at breakfast.

"Yes. Lina Renko's divorce trial starts in two days, and I'd like to sit in on the practice session." Counting the trips in to see Wick McCloud, she'd been to town only three times, and the first two times she'd only gone to the doctor's office. Cleese had been picking up her mail every few days when he checked on her house. "Frank needs a refill on his allergy prescription, too, and I really ought to make at least a token visit to my house."

He started the pickup and pulled back onto the road. "We can go in together, or you can take one of the pickups."

It was too dark to see his expression clearly, and there was nothing in his voice to tell her which idea he preferred. Either plan would result in her return to the ranch tomorrow evening, however. "I think I'll go in with you," she said slowly. "That way I can pick up my car."

"Good idea. If it sits much longer, the battery will probably need recharging." Actually, even though he knew it was irrational, he thought it was a lousy idea. But he told himself that just because she had her own car didn't mean she'd be running off to her own house for good. In fact, it probably *was* a good idea. If she had her own car, she wouldn't feel so dependent on him, and maybe she wouldn't be in any hurry to go "home."

There was something else she had almost forgotten, besides her house, Laurel thought dryly. She'd been calling her answering machine for messages, and there had been, blessedly, none from the abusive caller, allowing her—almost—to forget the whole nightmarish episode. "I think I may have heard the last from my unknown caller," she murmured, putting her thoughts into words.

"I'm not so sure." He'd been about to slide her across the seat, but delayed so that he could watch her reaction. "He left you a message on your garage door." A decision was being forced on him that he conceded he should have made sooner on his own. "While you were in New York."

Her expression suddenly stark, he saw her sorting through all the questions in her mind to decide which one to ask first. "What was the message?"

Her choice let him relax a little. "The same trash as the ones on the phone, in black spray paint. I painted it out the same day. You didn't notice the night you got back because you were too sick."

She nodded slowly. "Why didn't you tell me sooner?"

"I didn't want to upset you once I realized how sick you were, and afterward—" he shrugged slightly "—when nothing else happened, there didn't seem to be any hurry. I'd already taken care of it."

At that last statement, the tiny, insidious worm grew another segment. "Perhaps so, and I do thank you for taking care of it, Cleese, but you should have told me sooner. It is my house."

And that was something else he didn't like. He didn't like "my" and "your"—irrational as that, too, might be. He wanted "our." Her tone was mild enough, but there was a firm line to her unsmiling mouth and a sharp glitter in her eyes that he hadn't seen since the night she had insisted on leaving her phone number unchanged so that she might have a chance at catching the obscene caller. "You're right. I should have."

He admitted it readily; he did understand that she took care of her own life, Laurel assured herself. The worm raised its head, and ruthlessly she squashed it.

Blue and white soothed, Laurel thought, glancing around the room. The combination renewed and uplifted. She would never know Cleese's mother, yet, oddly, in this room she felt a friendship with the long-dead woman. It was on the second floor, a back corner room with a large window on each outside wall, so that sunshine poured in during the day, starshine at night. In the side window, a lovely etched rose bloomed surrounded by beveled, leaded panes, while the back window overlooked real roses, whose big, old-fashioned white and pink blossoms looked like the tissue roses she'd made in third grade and smelled like heaven. His mother had been a quilter, and this had been her work-room, Cleese had said when he suggested that she might want to use it for a studio after she asked him to bring her drawing materials and watercolors so that she didn't fall too far behind schedule.

None of his mother's personal possessions remained in the room, so she had no sense of intruding, or of lingering ghosts. Instead, she felt as if the room had been ... bequeathed to her by someone who knew her well, because it suited her so perfectly. The walls were painted a soft white that picked up warmth from the polished wood floor. A blue-and-white rag rug lay on the floor by the daybed, the blue in the rug matching the blue in the floral and geometric quilt covering it. White lace shades and darker blue curtains, billowing a little in the soft, rain-sweet breeze coming through the windows, added to the feminine sense of the room without making it aggressively cloying or cute.

Reaching up, she adjusted the shade on the brass swing arm lamp clamped to the old drawing table to throw more light on the paper. As her pencil started moving again, she heard a faint creak and smiled unconsciously. That was the fifth step on the staircase. Cleese said he'd spent his high school years avoiding it, sneaking in late at night. Her unconscious smile faded. They had parted just inside the front door, with him going to catch up on the faxes and phone messages that were waiting for him, reminding her again of the dual life he led. Once the financial gap between them had made her a little uncomfortable, but after seeing how hard he worked and how much responsibility he carried, the gap had become unimportant as she saw it was the man, not the money, that was exceptional. He would be the same man if he had one broken-down bull, three dry cows and a tar-paper shack—although he wouldn't have so little for long, she thought with a dry laugh.

Cleese looked at the huaraches lying half under the daybed with a grin. The only room she looked more right in was his bedroom. She turned to smile at him as he crossed the room toward her, and when he stopped beside her stool, his arm dropped easily across her shoulders. "Which month is that?"

After another second or two of simply enjoying looking at him, she turned to look at the drawing she had been working on. "September." She felt his hand drop down her back, then a slight tugging on her hair, and she realized he had removed the elastic band as his fingers began unraveling the braid at the nape of her neck.

"That's always been one of my favorites," he murmured. The advance orders on "L.J.'s" book had been so heavy that the publisher had decided to capitalize on its popularity by having Laurel do a calendar with each month illustrated by a particularly funny scene from one of her stories. September's page recounted the time Flea/Flee had decided to play matador with a huge bull he, L.J. and Doc had encountered unexpectedly. A couple of sentences from the story provided the setup of the dog ramming the bull and discovering that he'd run into a wall of solid, furious beef. Her illustration showed what had happened next, as the dog lived up to his second name and cowered behind the two men while the enraged bull pawed and snorted. She'd cleverly drawn the bull's one visible eye so that it looked directly at the viewer, the animal's sly expression conveying that he knew he was going to scare the holy crap out of the trespassers and enjoy every second of it.

"Mine, too," Laurel replied, just above a whisper. His fingers were combing through her loose hair now, freeing the tangles and sending slow tingles down her back.

"You finished the watercolor." With his free hand, he took the painting at the top of the drafting table carefully by an edge and drew it into the pool of brighter light. The painting was to be the cover of a mystery for older children. She had drawn a preteen boy and girl, the girl bending down to pick up a capped bottle that had washed up on the beach, with what looked like a piece of paper inside. He might have thought that she had only recreated the scene of them finding the bottle on Padre Island, just downsizing him and herself into the kids, except that she had reversed the hair color, making the boy a redhead with dark eyes and the girl dark-haired with pale blue eyes. He glanced down at the top of her head as she seemed to study the picture. Almost... almost as if she were drawing, not them, but their children? His hand clenched in her hair, and he had to force his fingers open to release the silky mass.

"Y—" she had to clear her throat. "Yes, I did it this morning." Finished with her hair, his fingers now were working down her spine, where it was exposed above the low back of the sundress she was wearing, finding each bone, loosening it, so that she was beginning to feel disconnected, limp, with no bones at all.

Her head turned slowly, as if she were drugged, and she looked up at him. The sun she'd gotten the past few weeks had turned her skin a light honey-gold, heightening the contrast with her eyes and intensifying their almost opalescent glow. Just as slowly, his head bent, savoring the anticipation of tasting her mouth and the satisfaction of knowing that he would have more than a taste of her mouth, of her.

He'd had a piece of the peach pie, Laurel thought vaguely as he explored her mouth leisurely, and she tasted the sweet fruit, a trace of cinnamon and the darker tang of him. The kiss was unhurried and thorough, and somewhere in the middle of it they traded places, so that he sat on the stool and she on his lap.

He spread his hand over her breast and felt the nipple peak against his palm. Bending her back over his arm, he took the tight nub between his teeth until she moaned softly, then licked it through the thin, dark cotton. Her fingers spread and clenched in his hair as he moved his mouth to the other nipple.

"Laurel." He stroked the dampened fabric, rubbing it over the peaks of her breasts while his mouth moved back to claim hers again.

He worked his palm down a stroke at a time, over her belly, lower, until the heel of his hand reached the spot that changed anticipation into ravenous hunger. He intensified it, his hot, hard palm kneading through her clothes, sure and deliberate, in counterpoint to his tongue, which stroked deep, with devastating dominance. His arms shifted, and hers locked around his wide shoulders as he stood up and began moving, their mouths never losing contact with each other.

He set her down beside his bed, pausing to pull down the covers and snap on the bedside lamp, then reaching again for her. Some dresses were made to put on, and some were made to take off. The one she was wearing now was made to take off. Long, with skinny straps, it was made like a slip, but buttoned all the way down the side from under the arm to just above the knee. It wasn't one she had requested, but it was one he had known he would bring the minute he saw it hanging in her closet. He reached down for the lowest button and freed it. He would watch her unbutton it some-time, preferably some hot afternoon, with the curtains drawn to make the room dim and cool, and when she could take a lifetime with the sixteen white buttons, but he didn't have the patience for a lifetime now, and unbuttoning the sixteen buttons himself was another fantasy that was every bit as good.

Freeing the next few, he slid his palm up the outside of her smooth, silky thigh. She was wearing only panties under the dress, he knew, but he forced himself to find enough pa-tience to wait to reach them until he'd undone a few more buttons. He slid his hand down slowly, drew it out from be-tween the open edges of her dress and released five more of the buttons. Easing his hand inside again, he ran it up to the cool silk covering her hip, then brushed the knuckles of his hand along the edge of the silk until it changed from cool to warm and damp. Her thighs shifted to give him access, but, teasing both of them, he pulled his hand out from under her dress again and unbuttoned it up to her waist. His finger explored under the lower edge of the silk this time, pausing a scant moment to rub and probe. Her arms fell limply to his shoulders, and her head dropped to the hollow of his shoulder, where her quick, ragged breath was cool on his neck. He ran his finger inside the waist of her panties and felt the warm, smooth skin quiver and jump in response.

He rubbed the backs of his fingers over the side of her breast through the cloth before undoing the next buttons, and Laurel felt a melting spill of pleasure. Only the strong arm across her back was keeping her on her feet, she knew; her knees had given out with the third button. His hand slipped inside her dress again, then inside the waistband of her panties, his roughened fingertips feathering down her stomach, and she widened her stance in invitation, then groaned in disappointment when he didn't accept it. Finally he undid the last three buttons, and the soft cotton rubbed with almost unbearable friction over her stiff, near-painful nipples when her dress fell open. Both hands came inside her dress, and her panties skimmed down her legs. She stepped free of them automatically as his big, callused hands smoothed over her hips and cupped her buttocks, pulling her up high and tight against him. She groaned again, rubbing against him, trying to relieve some of the aches. The furtive, hidden quality of making love beneath her clothes was so erotic and arousing that she didn't know how much longer she could stand it.

As if he sensed that she was near the end of her endurance, he whisked her dress up over her head abruptly, and less than a second later she felt the cool, crisp sheet underneath her. It seemed like only seconds afterward that she felt his big, warm, naked body join hers on the bed. His hands and mouth seemed to be determined to snap her sanity, and she tried to return the delicious torture, but when she reached for him, a heavy thigh stilled her restless legs and her wrists were seized in one large, inexorable fist. He stretched her arms up over her head, leaving her body completely exposed and vulnerable.

"No," he said quietly. "This time I'll do everything."

There was, Laurel realized dimly as his mouth strung openmouthed kisses down between her breasts, an element of bondage in submitting to pleasure, selfishly taking and giving nothing back but the sense of power, perhaps, or the selfless giving that humans needed to offer from time to time. What once would have panicked her only made her more greedy now.

"You taste like nothing else in the world, Laurel." Her breath shattered as his mouth moved lower. "I don't think I'll ever get enough."

Chapter 12

"You let this so-called abuse continue. You cooperated by staying with Charles. The marriage couldn't have been so bad or you would have asked for a divorce a long time ago. So why are you complaining now, Lina? What is the real reason why you're asking for a divorce? Is it because you've decided you want to marry your lover, so you've trumped up these accusations against your husband to try to get more money out of him when, in fact, you're the one who's guilty—of adultery?"

Laurel shifted, trying to find a more comfortable spot on the hard wooden bench. Sometimes she suspected Hattie had always secretly wanted to be an actress, the way she threw herself into these trial rehearsals with such enthusiasm.

"I have no lover, and I've never committed adultery, Mr. Mitchell." Lina's response from the witness stand was so soft that Laurel could barely hear her in the first row.

"Louder and stronger, Lina," Olivia called from the back row.

Lina repeated her answer, louder and stronger, then added, "The marriage has been awful for years, but I was too frightened, too browbeaten, to admit how badly my husband was treating me. Finally, one morning, after he had spent an hour screaming at me, telling me how stupid and worthless I was because he couldn't find his car keys when he'd locked them in the car himself the night before, I sat down after he left and counted the days that month that I'd been unhappy because he was angry with me. Then I counted how many days I had been happy, had felt loved and appreciated. There were none. I couldn't remember the last time there had been a day like that."

Laurel gave Lina a thumbs-up. For many of the women who came through Maxwell's, their divorce hearing or the assault trial of their abuser was the first time they had ever seen the inside of a courtroom. That initial experience could be unsettling even in the most innocuous circumstances; it could be terrifying when the woman had to face her attacker, as well. That was why two of the conference rooms had been combined and remodeled into a miniature courtroom, complete with judge's bench, witness stand, attorneys' tables and several rows of spectators' benches. With someone—frequently Hattie—from Maxwell's playing the abuser's attorney, the woman and her attorney could enact mock trial scenes to get the victim used to the physical setting of a courtroom while preparing her to testify and deal with the opposition's questions.

"Everybody's unhappy in their marriage sometimes, Lina," Hattie said in the tone of a kindly uncle dispensing advice. "Couldn't part of the problem be that you're just not . . ." Hattie paused as if she were trying to be delicate. "The intellectual equal of your husband?" Most of the divorce attorneys in Fort Worth knew each other, at least by reputation, if not personally, so the woman's lawyer usually had a good idea what tack the opposing attorney would take. Larry Mitchell, Charles Renko's attorney, took the lowest tack he could, apparently.

"You're right, Mr. Mitchell," Lina said, with a smile so faint Laurel wasn't sure it was a smile. "I'm not the intellectual equal of my husband. I graduated summa cum laude from college. Charles dropped out after his freshman year."

There was a titter of laughter, and even Hattie wasn't actress enough to hide a grin, but there was an unfunny truth illustrated by Lina's quip. Overachievers were often the easiest victims, because they conscientiously assumed responsibility for everything. A smart abuser played on that, blaming the victim for his own abusive behavior, knowing she would accept the blame and the responsibility, as Lina had.

"You're aware that your husband was badly mistreated as a child, that his father beat him, abused him for years," Hattie said, returning to the script. Lina's attorney apparently thought Mitchell would try the "abused abuser" tack, too. It was an old ploy, one all abusers practiced, whether they abused drugs, alcohol or people. They tried to snare everyone, even their victims, into excusing their addiction because of "inner demons they couldn't control," an excuse still accepted all too often. Making someone miserable was the verbal abuser's "fix," and, like all addicts, he never got enough.

"Yes." Lina's thin voice carried no expression.

"Don't you think that, given how he was treated, how he suffered as a child, his occasional outbursts at you are understandable?" Hattie softened her voice. "Even forgivable?" Hattie had seen Mitchell in action, too, which helped her performance enormously, to the point that Laurel heartily disliked her for a moment.

"N-no, it's not forgivable. I'm sorry Charles's father abused him, but th-that doesn't give him the right to abuse me. I'm not the one who mis-mistreated him." Most of Lina's hard-won composure and—worse—certainty seemed to have deserted her. If this were the real trial, Mitchell would only have to hammer one or two more strokes before

Lina crumbled, Laurel thought grimly. As she'd feared, Lina wasn't ready yet.

Wiley Otis, Lina's attorney, stood up, looking agitated, but Hattie shook her head at him before he had a chance to speak. "I think that's probably enough for today," she said briskly, Hattie once again. Instead of leaving the courtroom, though, she pulled out a chair at one of the attorneys' tables and sat down. Laurel, Olivia and M.J., who had come into the practice session just in time to see Lina's near disintegration, came through the swinging gate to drag chairs from the other table over to Hattie's and sit down, too.

There were still two empty chairs, and Wiley Otis was moving to take one when another headshake from Hattie warned him off again. He looked for a moment as if he were going to argue, but then he shrugged slightly and turned toward his client, who was stepping down from the witness stand. "Well, Lina," he said with a cheerfulness Laurel knew none of them felt, "I'll see you tomorrow morning, nine o'clock sharp."

Lina managed a wan smile, then, after he'd left, followed everyone else's unsubtle example and sat down at the table. She grimaced tiredly. "I blew it, didn't I?"

"You did fine. You were just a little shaky at the end," Hattie said, uncharacteristically glossing over the truth.

Lina's dry look told her that she knew it, too. "Why did I do that?" she asked the table in general, shaking her head in bewildered disbelief.

Olivia answered her. "Because a small part of you still wants to believe that he loves you, that he doesn't want to treat you badly but just can't help himself."

Lina was listening with her head down, but, seated next to her, Laurel saw her eyes slowly fill with tears. Love died hard, but she sensed—she hoped—that the tears were part of the grieving process for what her marriage should have been and not so much for the man himself.

"We women seem to suffer the delusion that all men are capable of giving the love we want, and that if we are only patient and giving enough, try hard enough, we'll get it. But the truth is, you can't get gold from lead, Lina," Laurel told her quietly.

Sweeping a hand across her eyes, Lina drew a deep breath before she looked up. "And, boy, was he lead," she said with a small shaky laugh.

Everyone around the table smiled in rueful agreement, but nobody said anything, because nobody, Laurel suspected, knew what to say. Lina was still so fragile that saying the wrong thing might shatter her resolve and courage. The silence grew as the four women exchanged a helpless look.

"You know," Lina said after a minute, "when I first met him, he was so charming. He called, sent me flowers, seemed to think about me twenty-four hours a day. It was very flattering." Her brief smile was wistfully hazy. "He was very good with the grand gestures, too. For my birthday, he had a violinist play 'Happy Birthday' at our table while the waiter brought out a cake with sparklers instead of candles. It was very romantic."

Laurel saw the alarmed look on Hattie's face and, sensing she was about to speak, made a small, sharp gesture with her hand.

"It was a long time before I realized what he was doing to me." Lina seemed to be talking to herself now, oblivious of the rest of them. "By then, I was so isolated, because he'd cut me off from all my friends and my family, that I didn't have anyone but him to turn to." Lina's sad brown eyes suddenly focused on her. "He never did love me, did he?"

"No, Lina, he never did," Laurel agreed gently. "What he did to you had nothing to do with love. It was about power and dominance." She glanced toward the big, dark man who was just taking a seat at the back of the courtroom and acknowledged his presence with an almost imperceptible nod. He'd come in quietly, and, as focused as everyone was on Lina, she knew she was the only one aware of him. Deaf and blind, she would still be aware of him.

Lina turned to Olivia. "You warned me, Olivia, that just because he didn't hit me, it didn't mean that he wouldn't start, but the other day I realized he had started, in his own way. There've been all these little 'accidental' bumps and knocks and falls. He told me it was because I was clumsy, but he was causing them."

Laurel knew that Lina's husband's "way" wasn't that uncommon. Olivia, clearly uncertain what to say, wisely said nothing, just nodded.

Her eyes drifting, Lina stared at nothing. "He knew I was afraid of gaining weight—the women in my family have a problem with that—so he was always needling me every time I ate a piece of candy or had a little bit of cake or a cookie. Finally I gave up eating anything that had many calories."

Which explained why Lina had been almost anorectically thin when she'd first come to Maxwell's. She'd gained weight since, but she was still too thin. It was natural when you loved someone to open yourself to that person, revealing your secret fears and worries. Lina had done that, and her husband had had yet another weapon to use against her. Charles Renko had missed few of the abuser's standard tricks, all of them designed to reduce the victim to a state of helplessness. The "tricks" often began when the abuser was a boy, doing something like standing under the stairs to look up girls' skirts or making sexual taunts about their developing bodies. That kind of behavior was still sometimes dismissed under the heading of "boys will be boys." Her glance cut across the courtroom. Cleese's sons would never be boys like that.

"It's funny, you know." Lina's harsh, humorless laugh belied her words. "If a stranger had said the things to me that Charles did, he would have been prosecuted, maybe even sent to prison, but a husband can say them to his wife and the worst that can happen is that he'll be divorced, lose his marriage, something he didn't care about anyway."

Lina was absolutely right. Abusive husbands cared nothing about their marriages; the only reason Charles Renko was contesting the divorce was that he didn't want to lose his victim. "Things have improved, even though it doesn't seem like it sometimes," Laurel said wryly. "Do you know how the saying 'rule of thumb' originated?" The other woman shook her head. "It used to be legal in the U.S. for a man to beat his wife as long as the stick he used was no thicker than his thumb."

There was a wisp of humor in Lina's laugh this time. Laurel glanced around the table. M.J. looked mystified by Lina's seeming ramblings, and Hattie worried, but Laurel knew what Lina was doing, and so, she expected, did Olivia. Lina was talking through her grief and, at the same time, reinforcing her conviction that she was doing the right thing in divorcing her husband. As she talked, she sat a little straighter, her voice grew a little stronger, her dull eyes a little brighter.

"Mary said one day her husband was stuck in the 'terrible twos,' throwing tantrums, always demanding attention," Lina said, taking off on another apparent ramble.

"The Mom-on-the-phone syndrome," Olivia interjected dryly.

"Yeah." Lina smiled fleetingly. "That's really what Charles is—still that little boy abused by his father. He's stuck there."

Laurel tensed and knew that Olivia, M.J. and Hattie had, too, as all of them realized what Lina had been working around to. She was right; Charles Renko, like all abusers, was emotionally stunted. He was a scared, insecure toddler trying to control the world that so frightened him, and, because his own self-concept was so poor, the only way he could feel secure and powerful was by controlling and demeaning someone else, the way he had been controlled and demeaned. They had discussed his arrested emotional development and its cause before, but, as she'd shown during the trial rehearsal a few minutes ago, Lina couldn't seem to resolve her conflicting feelings. Now she had, finally. The question was, had the toxic situation she'd been living in so poisoned her that her sympathy for the little boy would let her excuse the man?

"How do you feel about that, Lina?" Hattie asked quietly, proving she had more courage than the rest of them, Laurel thought.

Lina frowned at her, as if puzzled by the question. "I understand why he is the way he is, but I don't condone his behavior, and it isn't my responsibility to correct it." She smiled crookedly. "I'm going to do what Mary does with her 'terrible two.' Put him in time-out—permanently."

Their laughter came more from sheer relief than from Lina's wit. Despite its humorous connotation, time-out— isolation of the abuser—was the recommended response, just as it was for a tantrum-throwing child. Since the adult couldn't be sent to his room, the victim left—in most cases, for good.

Lina's laughter died abruptly. "What's the matter, Lina?" M.J. asked her softly.

"Oh, I just thought of a joke my sister made, about me marrying again." Lina shook her head with a rueful grimace. "I can't even imagine marrying again."

Laurel answered her unspoken question. "The same thing won't happen again, Lina, if you just remember to ask yourself a few questions. Does he make you happy? Does he have your welfare at heart? Is he your friend? Are you a better person for being with him?"

A corner of Hattie's mouth turned up wryly. "The answers are supposed to be yes, Lina. There are two kinds of power in a relationship, the kind that kills the spirit— Charles's kind—and the kind that nourishes it. You can't make a nourishing, nurturing relationship, you can only share one, because you both have to want it."

With the first question, Laurel had looked instinctively toward the back of the courtroom. Throughout her questions and Hattie's response, his amber eyes had burned bright and clear and strong on hers.

A few minutes later, Cleese watched her walk back through the mock courtroom toward him. Until today, he hadn't fully appreciated just what she did at Maxwell's. She had told him about the women in the group she worked with, and he knew she'd kept in touch with them by phone while she'd been recuperating, but not until the last half hour had he realized how hard it was, and how much stronger she was than he. For his own selfish reasons, he wished the Renkos had timed their divorce a little better and that Laurel, for now, anyway, wasn't associated in any way with Maxwell's. He wanted her thinking about marriage positively, not negatively. Listening to Lina Renko describe the obscenity that was her marriage had sickened him, and he'd found himself in complete agreement with her when she'd said she couldn't imagine marrying again. After what she'd been through, how could she? Yet Laurel, who had had her own obscenity, besides listening to dozens of others, didn't. He just wished he knew if she had recently asked herself the same questions she had posed to Lina. And, if he'd seen what he'd thought he'd seen in her eyes the last time she'd looked across the room at him, that the answers had been yes.

She stopped in front of him with, incredibly, a smile. "How about going fishing? There are still a few hours of daylight left," he said.

Taking his hand as automatically as she glanced out the window to check the weather, she gave the logical answer of a true fisherman—*woman.* "Where?"

"Well, we could go truck fishing."

"Truck fishing?" She frowned at him. "What is that? What do you use?"

"Mostly Fords and Chevies. You park in the river and throw a line out the window." He grinned at her pained look. "How about your favorite poaching spot, then?"

She considered him. "No rocks?"

"No rocks," he swore solemnly.

She'd needed this, Laurel thought, looking over the wild garden of bluebonnet and red Indian paintbrush, their blossoms that they were riding through, planted by the wind and watered by the rain. She'd needed sun and open space and natural beauty to help dispel the close atmosphere of the mock courtroom at Maxwell's and all the misery caught within its walls. She was even glad Cleese had suggested cutting cross-country on horseback rather than going the long way around in his pickup, even if, she thought with a silent laugh as she shifted once again in the saddle, she rode a pickup better than a horse.

They stopped at a small meadow that she remembered was about a half mile below the stump where the giant bass lived. The horses began contentedly cropping grass while he untied their fly rods from behind his saddle and they rigged their lines. Frank, courting a Saint Bernard now, had elected to stay back at the house.

Cleese watched her open an old leather fly wallet. "Are you going to use your Weedless Willard?"

She studied the river, which was running high and a little murky—perfect conditions for her mutant yellow fly. "Why, yes," she said with a sinless smile, "I am."

An hour later, Laurel thanked whatever gods of fishing were listening for giving her the idea of that yellow fly. Without it, she thought, watching Cleese cast with a metronomic precision that never faltered, she would have been thoroughly embarrassed by now. She had decided he was the best bass fisherman she'd ever seen; after the past hour's demonstration, she would have to take off the species qualifier. He was the best. He'd coaxed fish out of every spot he'd tried, but he hadn't, she thought smugly, coaxed out Ol' Stump, giving the big bass he'd been dueling with over the years her own private name.

As he approached, she got up from the spot on the bank where she'd been watching. "He's all yours," he said with more than a trace of disgust.

Laurel stood on the riverbank, trying to decide how to make the best presentation. He hadn't brought her waders along with her fly rod, but, to keep things even, he hadn't brought his along, either. It was too soon to be standing hours on end in cold water, but the lack of them did make catching the fish more difficult, as he'd just proved.

It took her all of two casts. Cleese watched with a mixture of disgusted disbelief and reluctant admiration as the bull bass tail-danced across the water, trying to shake the hook. Then he dived deep, heading back toward the stump and the chance to wrap the line around one of the submerged roots and break it. But he never made it. Playing the fish with that uncanny skill that almost made him think she was half fish herself, she anticipated every trick, every move, the wily fish had developed over the years. Finally, out of moves and tricks, the bass surrendered, and she reeled him in.

"What do you think?" she asked, holding the fish up. "Eleven pounds?"

"More like thirteen," honesty forced him to admit.

"He'd make a nice fish fry, wouldn't he?" Laurel enjoyed the aghast look on his face that reflected the horror all true-believer bass fishermen displayed whenever the ignorant committed the ultimate sin of suggesting actually *eating* one. "No? Well..." She knelt down and, placing the fish back in the water, gently unhooked him. "Then I guess I'll have to let him go." Realizing he was free, the huge bass wasted no time disappearing.

Sliding his hand into the back pocket of her jeans, he looked down at her as they ambled back toward the horses. "You only caught him because of that one-of-a-kind fly," he pointed out with a superior smirk.

She smiled seraphically. "I know. The one I have and you don't."

* * *

She had needed this, too, Laurel thought, waking up slowly. Back at the meadow, she had spread out the blanket Cleese had brought along and the sandwiches she'd made while he retrieved the bottles of beer he'd left cooling in the river. Afterward, too lazy to even think about riding back, they'd lain on the blanket, shoes and boots off, enjoying the late-afternoon sun, talking about nothing, until they'd drifted into a nap. Unconsciously she snuggled into the hard heat at her back, and his heavy arm tightened around her waist. Maybe sleeping together was the most intimate thing two people could do, she thought—no sex, just sleeping together. Because of the vulnerability and exposure when one was sleeping, doing it with someone else implied paramount trust . . . contentment . . . love.

The arm around her waist tightened a little more as his hand exerted a gentle pressure, and she rolled over to face him. While they had slept, twilight had come and gone, the dusk deepening into true darkness. Stars burned tiny holes through the black-velvet sky overhead, the full moon had risen, and a few fireflies had winked on. The river song played quietly, while a lonely bullfrog added his deep voice to the soprano chorus of crickets. A light breeze teased their hair, bringing the far-off scent of new-cut alfalfa. They lay on the blanket, looking at each other, silent, letting the anticipation build.

His hand came up and slowly flicked open the pearl snaps on his shirt. Her hand moved just as slowly, sifting through the dark cloud of hair on his chest. After a little more time, she felt his hands on the hem of her T-shirt, then it was gone, the soft hair on the backs of his fingers brushing the cleft between her breasts as he unclasped her bra. Smoothing aside the wisp of lace and silk, one hand captured a breast, while his other hand slid leisurely down. His palm rested, unmoving, on the triangle between her thighs, warmth penetrating through the denim, heating. Without haste, she eased off his shirt; then her hands drifted over his broad shoulders, down his ribs and circled back together at his waist. The soft popping of the buttons closing his fly was loud in the dark quiet.

His palm began to move, almost imperceptibly at first, radiating heat in ever-expanding circles, his fingers molding through the denim, caressing slow and deep.

She sat up, her eyes glowing with the luminescence of the moon. Hooking her fingers in his belt loops, she took her time pulling down his Levi's, and he shifted to help her. His shorts went with his jeans and socks, and he felt the soft breeze on his naked body. Her fingers skittered up his arch, around his ankle and up his calf like a moth, so light. They tickled behind his knee and up along the inside of his thigh. She was playing with him! Reaching up, he touched one moon-misted breast, just to reassure himself that she wasn't a perfect phantasm his deepest cravings had conjured up. He heard her small sigh, and saw the nipple tighten and rise. Then she bent, the ends of her sweet-scented hair sweeping his chest and belly as her tongue and teeth, rowdy and bold, like her hand between his thighs, played with his nipples, and he knew the pace wouldn't be slow and easy much longer.

At the quiet sound of the snap on her jeans opening, Laurel moved onto another plane of awareness. All of her senses—were there only five?—heightened, suffusing her body with more messages than she could possibly assimilate. She could only focus on isolated snatches, freeze-frames of brilliant sensation.

Touch—raspy denim sliding down; rough hair on long, muscled legs; powerful muscles and tendons that clenched and relaxed under damp, quivering skin; fingers finding warm, secret places, delving, measuring; a cool, arrogant mouth, nipping, tugging; a wet, velvet-slubbed tongue polishing, soothing, seeking.

Taste tangled with scent—musky, salty, tart-sweet, grass newly crushed, the scent of each on the other.

Sound—sighs, gasps, skin sliding over skin, sharp cries, soft moans, and words. So many words. Husky praise, hoarse pleas, sweet encouragement, growled prayers and curses, whispered promises.

And sight—long browned fingers on white skin, lean graceful, masculine symmetry, wide shoulders outlined in the moonlight, sharp planes and shadows of a beloved face.

The sensory overload became too much, and it exploded in a shimmering rush of ecstasy that seemed to go on and on, forever.

Cleese drifted in that netherworld between consciousness and oblivion, a timeless world with no clocks, no schedules, no commitments to keep, except to the woman lying in his arms, her body boneless and warm, filling them perfectly. His arms tightened their possessive cradle, and her right leg shifted across his hip and thigh, her narrow foot tucking under his left knee—her nakedness against his, in intimate trust. He lay for a while longer, then kissed the milky skin of her shoulder, moistening it with his tongue before buffing it dry with his lips. They rose and dressed, and he lifted her onto his horse in front of him. They rode home in silence under the moon's benevolent gaze.

Laurel snapped a fresh sheet over the bed—their bed. She could call it that now, she guessed, now that they were officially living together. Somehow she had thought the decision would generate a little more discussion, maybe even a little celebration, but she couldn't complain, since the idea had been hers. The real estate agent handling the nearly expired lease on his condo in town had called to leave the message that he really had to make a decision on renewing. When she had given him the message, she had also heard herself blurt out the suggestion that perhaps he might want to exchange his condo for her house. Since they spent so much time together anyway, and since she had the room, it didn't seem to make much sense for him to lease a place in town when hers was available. It would be a "practical" living arrangement, and he'd agreed. And so it was settled, just like that.

She tucked in the corners of the sheet. There had been no talk of marriage in all of this, of course. It was just "practical." She had nothing against the notion of living together. She just wasn't sure it was right for her; everything seemed too... practical . She hadn't expected a proposal of marriage, of course. Despite her past experience with it, she did still believe in marriage, but she could understand if he didn't. His last experience with it had virtually ruined him.

Pulling up the spread, she tucked it beneath the pillows. No, if she had doubts, she would keep them to herself. She couldn't say she didn't want to live with him, when she did, and he wanted it just as much. A week ago, when she had, as a matter of form, asked if he didn't think it was time she went back to her own house, he had said no, simply and flatly, and she hadn't pursued the topic, because she didn't want her to go back to her own house, either. Each trip he made to her house, he brought back a few more of her clothes, another fishing rod or reel, more art supplies, until she suspected more of her belongings were here than there. She knew what he was doing—moving her in, belonging by belonging, and she was going along with it because she *did* belong here. So, really, what could she say? *Cleese, I know living together was my idea, but now I'm having second thoughts because this is all just a little too casual?* He would say, *Well, what would you like? Something in writing? A pre-living together contract?*

And then she might blurt out what, despite the ugly little worm, she was beginning to think she did want, and that wouldn't be "practical" at all.

Glancing at the clock on the nightstand, she headed for the closet and a dress to change into. The judge in Lina's divorce trial was giving his decision at one o'clock today, and no one had a clue what it would be. Larry Mitchell, Charles Renko's attorney, had hammered Lina with every point they had been afraid he would, earning him M.J.'s nomination as poster boy for the National Shoot a Sleazy Lawyer Society. Lina had maintained her composure, though. Each side had produced their expert witnesses, with M.J. testifying for Lina concerning the effects of their mother's abuse on her children. Lina hadn't allowed her children to testify, and Mitchell had known better than to call them as witnesses for his side. What it had finally boiled down to was Lina's word against Charles's, and which one of them the judge believed.

She pulled a tailored navy linen shirtwaist over her head. Cleese had promised to be there, but she wasn't going to hold him to it. The phone had rung before first light, and he'd left not long after that. He'd murmured something, but she had been half-asleep and hadn't heard it. She expected it was a business emergency, probably something to do with the labor contracts he was negotiating for an oil-drilling project in Mexico. There had been continual snags. At first she'd thought he talked to her about business just to be polite, but she'd soon realized that he discussed problems with her because he valued and respected her opinion and wanted to hear it.

Stepping into her heels, she paused for a moment, staring at the bed. The reason he hadn't left right after the phone call was that he'd come back to bed. He had shown her that making love could be teasingly playful, raunchy, overpoweringly erotic or so tenderly beautiful that she wept. In the misty blue predawn light of this morning, she had learned that it could also be almost violent, single-minded physical possession. His urgent, skilled hands and mouth had rapidly created an insistent, voracious hunger in her to match his. He had taken her before she was fully awake, satisfying that hunger with an incendiary paroxysm, then let her slip back into sleep before she was sure she wasn't dreaming.

"All rise." Those seated in the courtroom obeyed the bailiff's command, then sat again, waiting while the judge

Join the celebration....

April

REGAN'S PRIDE
by Diana Palmer

MARRY ME AGAIN
by Suzanne Carey

May

THE BEST IS YET TO BE
by Tracy Sinclair

CAUTION: BABY AHEAD
by Marie Ferrarella

June

THE BACHELOR PRINCE
by Debbie Macomber

A ROGUE'S HEART
by Laurie Paige

July

IMPROMPTU BRIDE
by Annette Broadrick

THE FORGOTTEN HUSBAND
by Elizabeth August

It's our 1000th Silhouette Romance and we're celebrating!

Join us for a special collection of love stories by the authors you've loved for years, and new favorites you've just discovered.
Silhouette Romance....
Vibrant, fun and emotionally rich! Take another look at us!
With this special bookmark you'll be sure not to miss any of these wonderful titles...
only from
Silhouette Romance.

You'll fall in love all over again with

shuffled papers. Someone sat down on the bench beside her, and Laurel turned from a whispered conversation with M.J. to smile at Cleese as he took her hand.

It was odd, Cleese thought, that sitting in this courtroom, listening to testimony designed to break a marriage up, had strengthened his belief in marriage and made him realize what a treasure a good marriage was, a treasure that too many people undervalued. It was a precious cache of love and companionship, and it made an empty house a home of comfort, respite and deep fulfillment. It was something that he would teach his children to value so that they would understand why it was worth the effort and work to keep it. And it was something, he thought as he gently squeezed the small hand nestled in his, that he was more determined than ever that he would have.

The judge cleared his throat, and Cleese felt the hand in his tense.

Cleese put his arm around her as she came back to him from the small crowd around Lina Renko. "She won," he said, tightening his arm around her briefly. "You all did a good job."

With a small grimace, Laurel shook her head. "She survived. *Now* we have to make sure she wins."

They paused again outside, on the courthouse steps. "Where are you going now?" Cleese asked her. "Back to the ranch?" He would go with her, to make sure that she did, but his silent pager had just vibrated, giving him a message that he was needed back at his office immediately.

Laurel nodded. "I have to pick up Frank first, but then I'm going back." Frank had spent the night at the vet's, recuperating from the anesthesia necessary to put him out for his annual teeth cleaning. "Do you need me to pick up something for you?"

"No." I just need you to be waiting for me tonight, and every night, he thought. He gave her a swift kiss. "I'll see you about six-thirty."

Laurel watched him disappear rapidly around the corner, then turned in the opposite direction. Now that she thought about it, as long as she was going to be in the vicinity, picking up Frank, she probably ought to stop by her house, too. When she'd gone by yesterday to pick up her mail and her dress, she'd forgotten to measure the bedroom to make absolutely sure the king-size bed they had ordered to replace her single one would fit. Too, she ought to see how much room was left in the garage after M.J. had stored all of her craft and sewing paraphernalia in there, in case she needed to store a few things of her own to make room for his.

She wasn't sure why they needed a king-size bed, she thought with an unconscious smile as she turned down her street. She'd found out what side of the bed each of them slept on—the middle.

Her smile turned abruptly into a frown when she saw the crowd of pickups with toolboxes and ladders and what looked like Ty Burnett's unmarked police car parked at her house.

Cursing steadily, Cleese slammed the door of his car and sprinted up the sidewalk. She saw him the second he rounded the back corner of the house. Leaving the carpenter who had installed the window locks and dog door, she marched toward him.

"Why didn't you tell me what that phone call this morning was about, Cleese?"

Her voice, low-pitched instead of raised in a shout, told him just how angry she was. He'd always wondered if there was a temper under that red hair, but this was not the time or circumstances he would have chosen to find out. Not caring to have an audience, he took her arm to pull her into her studio. She shook off his hand but was right on his heels when he stepped through the empty window frame. A look from him sent the two glaziers elsewhere.

He swung around to face her. "Because I didn't want to—"

"Upset me?" She came up to him, nearly nose to nose with him, hands on her hips. "Well, I can assure you I'm damned upset now!"

He saw the stunned shock under the angry sparks spitting out of her white-fire eyes and the unnatural pallor of her face, which had come from seeing what that bastard who had been calling her had done to her house, and fought to hang on to his own temper. "I just didn't want you to have to see the worst of it, so I thought I'd—"

"Take care of it?"

His own temper ignited. "Damn it, Laurel, will you let me finish a sentence? I—"

"No!" She was shouting now. "I thought I'd made myself clear the last time this happened. *I*—" she slapped her chest with her hand "—take care of my house. *I* make the decisions. You have no right to try to control my life!"

"Good God, Laurel! I'm not trying to take over your life! I was just trying to pro—" This time, hearing himself yelling back at her, he interrupted himself. Dragging a hand through his hair, he spun away from her, the broken glass from the studio windows crunching under his feet. Regaining a thread of control, he turned back. "I was going to tell you tonight," he said in a more normal tone.

"And that's another thing!" she said furiously, stalking over the littered floor until she was toe-to-toe with him again. "I know a loud angry man is not automatically an abusive one, but you don't seem to think I do! You 'upset' me a hell of a lot more when you won't yell than when you do! I—" It was her turn to rake a hand through her hair and turn away. He watched her shoulders heaving raggedly as she fought for her own control. Finally she turned back to him. "Cleese, we both know that people who live together fight and yell occasionally. It's normal. When one of them is afraid to, for fear of upsetting the other one, they don't have a chance of staying together."

Her anger had disturbed him, but not nearly as much as the bleak look he saw in her eyes now. He hadn't lost her for good, he reassured himself. He'd caught her before; he could do it again. "What..." He cleared his throat. "What do you want to do?" he asked in a harsh rasp.

"I'm staying here tonight. We both have some thinking to do. The glaziers assure me they can cover the windows they can't replace today with plywood to make the house secure."

"I don't want you to be alone," he said tonelessly.

"I'll have Frank, and Ty says he'll increase patrols. Then, too—" her mouth tightened again with new anger "—there's the security man you've had watching my house, who you also didn't bother to tell me about."

He would have liked to blame the security man for this newest attack, but, in all fairness, he couldn't. The man had apparently come through the yard behind hers and over the back wall. If the security man hadn't heard the sound of breaking glass, the damage would have been a lot worse than just the smashed windows in her studio. "I still don't think you should stay here."

"I'll be all right."

Further argument at this point was useless, he knew. He nodded abruptly. "I'll call you tomorrow."

He found Ty Burnett out on the front sidewalk, talking to a uniformed patrol officer. Impatiently he waited until Ty finished with the officer and dismissed her. "What about the guy I gave you the private investigator's report on yesterday?" he asked without preamble.

"He didn't go in to work last night. He's not at his apartment, and nobody seems to know where he is. I've got a pickup order out on him." Ty glanced back at the house. "Is she staying here tonight?"

"Yeah."

Ty didn't have to ask if it was alone; the entire block knew the answer to that question, although it would be wiser not to mention it. "I'll let you know as soon as we find him, Cleese."

Cleese grimaced at the cold, bitter taste of the stuff the all-night convenience store a few blocks over was passing off as coffee. Arching his back, he tried to ease out the cramps and kinks that came from spending the night in his car. The security man had maintained surveillance on her street, and he had kept watch on the street behind her house, in case the man tried to attack from the back again. He could have had an extra man from the security firm assigned to do it, but he had taken the job on himself, because it gave him the illusion of closeness to her, and besides, he knew he wouldn't have slept anyway. He didn't think she had, either. He could see enough of her house through the trees to note that the light in the kitchen had not gone out until about four o'clock in the morning.

He blinked his scratchy eyes against the sun just coming over the treetops. Security was going to be twenty-four hours a day now, whether she liked it or not, until the man was caught. The front door of the house directly behind hers opened, and a man came out to get the morning paper. The people who lived in the house were obviously up. He yawned tiredly. It was safe for him to go find some breakfast, then change clothes and go on to the office.

Twenty minutes later he was sitting in a little café, enjoying real coffee, when his silent pager began vibrating. He pulled it off his belt and squinted, trying to read the message with his bleary eyes.

A couple of minutes later his breakfast arrived. Glancing back toward the bathrooms, the waitress started to put the plate of bacon, eggs and hash browns with a side order of a full stack on the table when the woman in the next booth volunteered helpfully, "He's not in the rest room, honey. He jumped up about a minute ago and just ran out."

"What a jerk!" the waitress muttered under her breath as she dumped the plates in the tub of dirty dishes waiting for the busboy. "Order a big breakfast like that, then take off without eating it, much less paying for it."

"It went up like a tinderbox, Cleese." Ty Burnett kept both hands on his cousin's arms, in case he tried again to run into the smoldering remains of Laurel Drew's garage. "He used some kind of accelerant, but the firemen put the fire out almost as fast as it got started. We're certain she's not in there. Her car's not here."

Cleese's head jerked around, and he glared at Ty. "When the hell did she leave?"

Ty relaxed one hand tentatively. "About twenty minutes or so before the fire, according to the security man. He was going to call you, but then he saw what he thought was maybe the guy climbing the fence of a house down the street, so he went to investigate. Turned out it was some high school kid trying to sneak back into his house after being out all night. He decided to take a look around anyway and was coming down the side by the garage when it went up. Scared the hell out of him. He ran back to his car and called 911, but didn't remember to call you until a couple of minutes ago."

"It must have gone up just seconds after I drove off," Cleese murmured starkly. "If I'd just—"

"Lieutenant!" One of the firemen checking the remains of the garage for hot spots was motioning Ty over. Ty let go of his arm, and Cleese got there ahead of him.

Silently the fireman pointed to what looked like the burned torso of a body under a section of collapsed roof.

Cleese wasn't even aware that he'd moved until he felt hands trying to wrestle him back. He threw them off, but they came back, and he was swinging his fist when Ty's voice finally got through. "Cleese! Cleese! It's not her! It's some kind of dummy!"

He let Ty lead him back out of the wreckage. Absently he beat out a smoldering patch on his pants cuff while he watched another of the firemen pull the dummy out from under the roof with a long, gafflike pole. "I think it's one of those sewing dummies, the kind women use for making clothes," the fireman said.

"Damn! What the hell is that?" the uniformed officer standing beside him breathed softly. He glanced toward the man, abstractedly noticing the red, raw patch near the patrolman's eye, as if he'd recently been in a fight, then looked in the direction he was pointing. An ash-covered apparition seemed to be rising from the left rear corner of the garage, the part that had suffered the least damage, mostly from smoke and the pressurized water from the fire hoses.

"Frank!" Cleese ran to the back corner of what had been the garage and picked his way through the debris. The dog was on his feet, but seemed too confused or too hurt to move. Bending, Cleese gathered the animal up in his arms, then staggered back to the lawn. Gently he laid Frank on the grass and carefully straightened his legs. Whimpering, Frank looked up at him from neon-yellow eyes, the pain in them obvious. Cleese ran his hand soothingly over the dog's head, carefully to avoid the singed spots on his neck and nose. His fingers found an egg-size lump behind the dog's right ear, as well. "It's all right, boy," he murmured soothingly. "It's all right. We'll get you all fixed up."

"Is that a dog? Hell! The damn thing must weigh two hundred pounds."

Ty silenced the garrulous patrolman with a look. "Get one of the paramedics over here," he snapped. He squatted down on the other side of the dog's body, examined him for a minute, then looked at Cleese. "He's got a lot of blood around his mouth. I don't think it's his."

Cleese agreed with a short nod. "I saw it, too, and I don't think so, either."

One of the firemen investigating the less damaged corner called out suddenly, "Hey, Lieutenant! Maybe you better come take a look at this. There's an awful lot of blood in here."

Cleese and Ty exchanged a look. "Garcia!" Ty yelled. "Have the emergency rooms and urgent-care clinics alerted to be on the lookout for a guy coming in with bad dog bites. White, about forty, six feet, one-eighty, brown hair, balding, brown eyes."

"What about a name?" Garcia yelled back.

"Byers, but he likely won't use it." Lowering his voice, he added to Cleese, "All animal bites have to be reported, so even if he goes to a private doctor, we'll find him."

Cleese stopped him with a hand on his arm as he started to rise. "He may try to patch himself up."

"You're right. Garcia!" he yelled again.

"Yo!"

"Go over to the pharmacy on Fifth and Collister and check to see if he's shown up there."

The paramedic arrived to check Frank, and both men stood up to get out of her way. As Ty started toward the garage, Cleese stopped him again. "There's still one problem, Ty. Where the hell is Laurel?"

"He hasn't got her, Cleese," Ty said, with an assurance he didn't entirely feel.

Chapter 13

Laurel released the bass and watched it swim away. Taking the key to the boathouse from the hiding place Cleese had shown her, she had borrowed his boat. She didn't think he would mind. The monotonous rhythm of cast and retrieve, cast and retrieve, always soothed and relaxed her, except when it was interrupted by a fish. It wasn't working quite so well today. Too many interruptions, she told herself, digging around in the tackle box for something that absolutely wouldn't catch anything. After drawing gibberish almost until dawn at the kitchen table, she had come out here to find some answers. All she had found out so far was that fishing alone was no longer any fun.

After glancing up at the gauzy sun, she looked across the lake. It must be close to ten o'clock, time to look for a little shade. Starting the engine, she frowned absently at the motor's rough idle. She shoved the boat in gear and aimed it toward the peek-hole rock across the lake. The huge rock jutting out from the shore with the fifty-foot hole in it marked the entrance to a small sheltered cover where, if she remembered right, the tall cliffs on either side blocked out all but the noon sun.

Fifteen minutes later she dropped the anchor over the side and picked up her fishing rod. Sitting down, she threw out her line, far away from any conceivable cover or fish.

She lurched awake suddenly to find herself on the bottom of the boat instead of the seat. Staring around, she saw immediately what had awakened her. The last thing she remembered was sitting on the seat, having given up even the pretense of fishing, and thinking that the slight swell in the green water rocked the boat like a cradle. The water wasn't green now, and the boat wasn't rocking like a cradle. The water was slate gray, with a stiff chop that was making the boat jerk on the anchor chain. It must have been one of those jerks, a little harder than the others, that had tumbled her off the seat.

After quickly stowing the rod and tackle box she had been using, she hauled up the anchor, then sat down in the middle seat behind the controls. Tugging her hat down more firmly, she looked uneasily up at the greenish-black clouds roiling overhead. One didn't have to grow up in tornado country to recognize the kind of clouds that spawned them. A jagged bolt of lightning suddenly stabbed downward, followed by a long and very loud roll of thunder. The breeze seemed to fall ten degrees in temperature as it picked up the same amount in speed, and she shivered inside her thin T-shirt. After several false starts, the cranky engine caught, and she swung the boat around toward the mouth of the cove.

As the boat entered the main body of the lake, the full violence of the storm slammed into it broadside. The wind snatched her breath and her control over the boat, while whitecaps broke over the transom, threatening to swamp it. The engine sputtered once, twice, and then cowardly drowned.

Grimly buckling on a life jacket she found under the seat, she looked around for something with which to bail. If she hadn't had other things on her mind, she would never have let herself get caught in such a dangerous situation. The cove she had just left would have been the safest place to wait out the storm, but even with the paddle she found stowed with a small plastic pail, she couldn't make any headway against the wind. She'd already been blown half a mile down the lake. Bailing rapidly—and watching water wash back in just as fast—she scanned the passing shoreline for any place she could try to reach and beach the boat. There wasn't one; sheer cliffs walled in the lake on both sides, without a break.

As if deciding that the wind wasn't enough, a particularly black cloud let loose an avalanche of hail that pummeled her exposed neck and arms and added to her general misery. When a blinding white light flashed simultaneously with an eardrum-shattering blast, followed by an almost overpowering stench of ozone, Laurel laughed blackly. It was a toss-up, apparently, whether she was going to drown or be electrocuted. She could be thankful for one small favor; Frank and small boats didn't mix, so she didn't have to worry about saving him, at least.

Those death threats eased somewhat as the thunderstorm passed over, but a new one—freezing—emerged. Pewter-gray clouds swollen with water settled heavily over the lake, and a cold rain began sluicing down, saturating her as quickly and effectively as a fire hose.

The only advantage to the rain was that the wind had lessened considerably, letting her quit bailing and start paddling. Gritting her teeth, she dug into the water, propelling the boat forward a pathetic foot or two. Her arm and shoulder and back muscles were soon screaming, but she ignored them, keeping up the endless stretch and pull while she peered through the watery gray curtain for any sign of safety and rest.

For several minutes the metallic buzzing rising above the sounds of the storm didn't register. Blinking through the water running steadily into her eyes, she saw a dark, cowled figure materialize out of the gray mist. Her chilled, exhausted brain allowed her imagination to take over, and she saw a boatman ferrying souls in the Stygian gloom. The boatman stood and called for her.

The stinging slap of a wet rope across her thigh was reality. She looked across the few yards of rain-pocked water into the dark, hard face and coldly furious eyes of her rescuer. She might be better off taking her chance with the storm, Laurel decided. As she stumbled across the boat seat, rope in hand, she wondered vaguely why she was surprised to see him. He had rescued her before, from illness, from paralyzing self-doubt, from a loneliness she hadn't even realized she felt, from the fear of loving and being loved. Why wouldn't he show up to rescue her one last time?

She tied the towrope to the bow of her boat, then stared stupidly at him as the slack rope tightened with a jerk. She didn't understand what he was doing until he had closed the distance between the two boats, then maneuvered his alongside hers. She was trying to time the rhythm of the choppy waves to jump into his when he leaned over and his big hands closed around her waist, jerking her off her feet. She sat down hard on the seat, and a canvas tarp smelling of long-dead fish and something else even longer dead was roughly wrapped around her. The metallic hum grew to a roar as, wretchedly cold, her teeth chattering like a set of those windup novelty ones, her body tried to match the frenetic beat with paroxysms of uncontrollable shivering.

She'd finally found the answers she was looking for; now she seriously questioned whether she would live long enough to give them to him.

Punishing the hull on the rocks, he ran the boat right up on the beach, then, wordlessly, slung her over his left shoulder. What happened to the other boat she couldn't see as she bounced like a soggy sack of flour over his rigid shoulder, his arm clamped ruthlessly around her knees. He strode up a faint trail, then she recognized the cabin at the boathouse.

"Oh, hell!" His hot curse blistered her ear. "I forgot the damned key is in the boat!" Since she couldn't see anything, she had to go by sounds. He shifted his weight to one foot while the other one sledgehammered the door, and she heard it swing open. It wouldn't have dared not to.

Kicking the door shut behind him, Cleese glanced around the bare-bones cabin. At least the woodbox was full. Setting his soaking-wet burden on her feet, he kept a hand on her until he was sure she would stay on them. She swayed and staggered back a step, then locked her knees. "Take your clothes off," he snarled, slinging his black poncho and then the tarp he'd wrapped around her into a corner. Kneeling on the stone hearth, he rapidly assembled old newspapers, kindling and a few chunks of pitchy wood in the fireplace and struck a match. Crossing the room, he yanked a blue-and-white ticked mattress from the built-in bunk and threw it onto the dusty plank floor in front of the fireplace. Flipping up the bottom of the bunk, he dragged out the one moth-eaten blanket and tossed it on the mattress.

Turning back to check on her progress, he cursed again. "I told you to get those wet clothes off."

Laurel managed to pull off her T-shirt, but the front clasp of her bra defeated her stiff, numb fingers. His fingers were working fine. He stripped her with silent efficiency, then, sacrificing his only dry clothing, he used his shirt as a towel to rub down her goose-pimpled body. His rough palms tugged on her bare hips, and gratefully she sank down onto the prickly mattress. Swiftly he swaddled her in the blanket; it was equally scratchy, but she didn't care. She was chilled merely to the teeth now, not the bone. She felt his fingers unraveling her dripping braid; then he folded his shirt over several times and wrapped it around her hair, twisting it to wring out as much water as possible. The rough tugging brought tears to her eyes, and when she blinked them clear, she saw that the fire was well caught now and his pants were beginning to steam.

Satisfied that her hair was as dry as he was going to get it, Cleese stripped down and arranged their wet clothes around the room to dry. Settling on the mattress behind her, he unwrapped the blanket, pulled her back against his chest, then rewrapped it around both of them.

"So help me, Laurel, if you ever take off without telling me where you're going again, I'll wring your damned neck," he growled.

He'd gotten over his fear of getting mad at her, Laurel thought sleepily, her eyes closing as his heat achieved what the fire hadn't. She was finally warm.

Laying them both down, Cleese turned her in his arms. Her legs tangled with his, her breasts, nipples still tight from the cold, flattened against his chest, while her belly nestled against his, and his body reacted automatically. He ignored it. Outside the rain tapped on the window, seeking admittance, while the wind whined around the sturdy door. For a long time, he lay awake, watching the firelight dance with the shadows on the wall. She might never admit it, but she needed him to watch out for her, to look after her. She needed him—as he needed her. They were supposed to be together because apart, as he'd learned today, the world was out of kilter somehow. He closed his eyes, wondering if it would ever be in balance again.

The damp chill woke him about midnight. He stoked the smoldering fire back to full strength, then looked out the window to see broken clouds scudding past the moon. He lay back down and pulled her unresisting naked body closer. Drifting from dream to reality to dream, he wasn't sure which he was in when she slowly rose over him on one elbow. Fireshine outlined her body in white gold and flamed her hair into a molten halo. "Laurel—" his tongue was oddly thick "—are you awake?"

"I'm awake." She bent lower, and rain-scented hair and even softer skin flowed over his body. The tip of her tongue delicately traced his lips, and they parted automatically. It flirted along his upper lip, then curled into the corners of his mouth, playing slowly inside, along the underside of his bottom lip, finally penetrating fully with a slow, deep stroking that brought him to full arousal so fast he temporarily lost the ability to breathe. Yet his body was strangely lethargic, and he wondered again if he was dreaming.

His hand came up heavily, winding itself in her hair, pulling her head back. "Laurel," he whispered hoarsely, "I think you're dreaming."

"Then don't wake me up."

Her hands slid over his belly and down his thighs, then leisurely smoothed back up as the breath hissed out of his lungs. Her ordeal today had roughened the skin on her fingertips, and they licked erotically over his skin like a cat's tongue, catching the fine hair with tiny pulling tugs. The sandpaper tips rasped over his nipples, followed by her velvet tongue, and his whole body jolted.

His forefinger traced the fire-limned shape of her breast. He brushed over the budding point, hardening it between his thumb and finger before urging it down to his thirsty mouth, waiting to taste the rain on her skin.

She moaned and moved over him, and he thrust unconsciously against her, every nerve ending excruciatingly alive. The feel of her stretched out on top of him, naked and fire-hot, while her cool hands slowly stroked and her eager mouth deepened the endless kiss, was an exquisite torment. He was desperate to take her now, before she drove him insane, and he was desperate to have her touching him, driving him insane.

A log exploded, showering sparks across the hearth. The sensual fog briefly lifted, and she felt him capture her wandering hands. "No," Laurel moaned in protest, opening her eyes.

His eyes had absorbed the fire and glowed into hers. That mouth that could give so much pleasure was tight with doubt and something else. Pain? "Laurel, we can't do this. It isn't right. There's too much unresolved between us."

Perhaps it was wrong ... but it felt so right, so necessary. She broke his hold on her wrists easily as her mouth moved on his, suddenly urgent. "I need this." Her hands beguiled his damp body. "I need you."

It would solve nothing, but, God help him, he needed this, her, too. His hand slipped down between their fire-burnished bodies into moist, welcoming heat. His low moan echoed hers as she slid down on his body, and they both melted into the dream.

Lying on his back, his hands deliberately locked behind his head, Cleese savored the feel of her sprawled over him, the flames of her hair licking over his chest and shoulder. The cool rose light coming through the dusty window gradually warmed to yellow. He knew the exact moment when she awoke; one second she was relaxed, snuggled into him, and the next her body was tense, easing away until they were no longer touching. Tossing aside the blanket, he gathered up his clothes and hers from around the room.

Laurel dressed rapidly, eyes on the floor, aware that he was openly watching her as he dressed unselfconsciously. She winced as she had to flex her achy shoulders to put on her bra, and he silently indicated that he would pull on her T-shirt for her. He did, and she started to speak. "Cleese, I—"

He turned away. "Laurel, I'm so damn hungry I could eat your Weedless Willard and like it. Let's go back to the ranch and eat, then talk."

They spoke only once on the way back to the ranch. "Where did you get the other boat?" Laurel asked, staring at the purple-and-silver-glitter bass boat on the beach.

''I 'borrowed' it. There's probably an Oklahoma tourist down at the sheriff's office right now, filling out a theft report.''

Breakfast was a loaf of bread, a dozen eggs, a pound of bacon and probably a gallon of coffee. To her surprise, Laurel ate her share. Finally they both pushed their plates away. Laurel watched him as he got up to bring a new pot of coffee to the table. Yesterday she had finally understood that flinch the morning she'd met him. She hadn't been subconsciously afraid of him; it had been herself she was afraid of.

She had accused him of trying to control her life, which was both unfair and untrue. It was true that he was a chauvinist, but the best kind of chauvinist; although—she smiled faintly into her coffee cup—some women would argue that there were no good kinds. She thought there was, one—his kind. He'd been raised to think that it was a man's responsibility to protect the woman he loved from all harm and difficulty, and he took his responsibility very seriously, just as he always took her hand when she was within reaching distance. Not as a male-of-the-species gesture to demonstrate ownership to other males and warn them away, because he did it no matter who was or wasn't around. Not because he thought she would get lost or stray, either. He did it because he simply wanted to touch her, to be connected to her. She knew, because that was why, when he reached for her hand, hers was already reaching for his. She loved the feel of his big, warm, hard, callused hand and the security of it. He wasn't asking her to change or to blindly do whatever he wanted. He had the strength and love to let her be herself and still keep her safe. He didn't demand capitulation for security, and she realized at last that it was perfectly fine to enjoy that security, even to want it. It was no betrayal of her self. He was totally masculine, yet he had a marvelous gift for nurturing, and she needed that gift. She needed him. Sometimes, she had finally understood, letting someone else take over was a sign not of weakness, but of strength.

For six years she had ignored that nasty little worm of doubt, ignored it so well that she had successfully forgotten it until Cleese Starrett came along. Now was the time to squash it once and for all and get on with life and what it offered. She suddenly felt a chill as nasty as any she'd felt yesterday in the storm. If the offer was still open.

He came back to the table and sat down, but, before she could begin, he spoke. "You had a fire at your house right after you left yesterday morning, Laurel."

She looked at him, stunned. "The caller?"

He nodded. Her voice was hardly more than a thread of sound. He'd debated how to tell her, and he'd finally decided on straight out, but now he wasn't sure that had been the right decision. Her eyes suddenly widened more, and she reached out to clutch his arm.

"Frank! Is he all right?"

"He's a little singed and probably has one hell of a headache from where the guy hit him with something, but he's fine. A lot better than the man is, in fact. Frank nailed him a few times. He needed seventy-eight stitches."

The news shocked her, especially that Frank had been hurt, yet oddly, aside from that, the identity of the caller and his capture did not have the urgent importance that they had once had. There were other, far more important, matters to deal with this morning. "Who was it?"

"Steven Byers."

After a few seconds she shook her head in bewilderment. "I don't know a Steven Byers." She frowned at him absently. "No...wait." She said the name again softly. "Steven Byers...he's the former husband of the owner of the pharmacy where I go." She frowned at him again. "Why did he come after me, and how did you figure out who it was?" Instinctively she knew it had been Cleese.

"I was convinced that it was somebody connected to the vet or the pharmacy. Ty checked out all the immediate employees and their families, but then I remembered you saying something about the pharmacy owner being divorced fairly recently. I had the security firm that was watching your house investigate him. It turns out the reason his wife divorced him was because he physically abused her. She got help at a clinic like Maxwell's.''

"So," Laurel said slowly, "he saw me doing the PSAs on TV, knew who I was, and suddenly he had somebody to blame." She was silent for a minute. "I don't understand how he kept getting my new phone number, though."

"When the Byerses were married, the prescription computers were linked so that customers could get refills at either pharmacy. After the divorce, they were never disconnected, so Byers had access to all your records, including your phone number."

"What happened when you found him?" Instinctively again, she knew Cleese had been on the scene when Byers was apprehended.

"He went to his pharmacy to try to patch himself up." For a moment, his eyes took on an intensity that almost frightened her; it wasn't the light that burned so hot for her, but one that was as cold as the last circle of hell. "I had planned to make sure he never touched another telephone, but Frank did enough damage to satisfy me," he said, then added as a seeming afterthought, "Ty has him in jail."

Finally it occurred to her that there was something else important she hadn't asked. "How much of the house is damaged?"

"Just the garage. He'd planned to do the whole house, but he hadn't planned on Frank being back."

"The garage?" Groaning, Laurel put her head in her hand. "Poor M.J. Most of the stuff in there was hers. I was storing it for her." She raised her head suddenly. "You thought I was caught in the fire."

"At first." Those were five minutes of his life that he didn't want to live over, even in memory. "After I knew you hadn't been caught in the fire, I thought maybe Byers had taken you with him."

Although his tone was matter-of-fact, Laurel saw the remnants of frantic worry and terror in his eyes. "I'm sorry, Cleese," she told him with quiet sincerity. "I was only going to be gone for the day. I never thought anyone would need to know where I was."

"Someone always needs to know where you are, Laurel," he said tonelessly.

Nodding, she dropped her eyes briefly to the table. "Someone." Not "I." "How did you know where to look for me?"

"Lonnie had been driving by the lake and saw you." His hand gestured vaguely as his eyes went to her head. "Your hair." She nodded again, and for a moment her hair caught the sun shining through the kitchen window. The memory of how her hair had looked last night in the firelight, as if it had been fire itself, how it had felt burning over him, how it had smelled, got away from him for a moment, and his next swallow of coffee was painful. He had known even then that last night might well be the last time he would ever know that feeling, that scent.

"Thank you for coming for me yesterday," she said softly. "I owe you a number of thank-yous lately, and I haven't been very gracious about saying them." Laurel started to reach her hand toward his, where it lay on the table, then pulled it back. His eyes hooded, his mouth in that grim, hard line it had been in since last night—except for a few timeless minutes—she had no clue to what he was thinking. She sensed he was still angry with her, and she didn't blame him. She'd been incredibly stupid, and, it could be argued, just as inconsiderate. Pushing her chair away from the table, she stood up. Because she wanted badly to touch him, she needed to put some distance between them.

She had been reaching for him, but something had stopped her. He would have given a great deal to know what. He watched her make an aimless tour of the kitchen until she stopped to lean against the counter, facing him.

Laurel took a deep breath. "I told you that I was planning to divorce my husband when he was killed. He died before the papers could be filed." She turned away, gripping the edge of the counter as she stared sightlessly out the window. "His death cheated me of making that final, necessary break, and ever since, I've had my doubts that I would have made it." Even if she couldn't touch him, she ought to at least be woman enough to face him, Laurel told herself, and turned around. "That's why I overreacted when I found out you hadn't told me about the second incident at my house. You should have told me," she reminded him firmly, "but to have accused you of trying to take control of my life was ridiculous, and I apologize. I was the one with control problems, afraid that I didn't have control of my life now, because I could never decide if I would have taken enough control to follow through on what I needed to do six years ago."

"And have you decided?" he asked quietly.

She met his shuttered eyes. "I decided it didn't matter. He and that life were six years ago. You're now." She smiled crookedly. "You're a very assertive man, Cleese. It's your nature and your need and, I know you think, your right, to protect what you considers yours." Her expression sobered. "But I can't be smothered in overprotection. I've worked too hard to get where I am."

He kept his expression neutral. Did she realize what she had just said? He rose slowly and approached her, stopping just within touching distance. "I do want to take care of you, Laurel, and protect you. And," he added softly, "it is my right." He saw her eyes widen, then narrow. "It's not easy for me when you don't wait for me to shake the trees and check the closets and under the bed because—" he smiled faintly "—I love you."

She nodded soberly, but he saw the wild happiness that flared briefly in her eyes. "As long as you understand it's my

right, too. There will be times when I need you to take care
of me, and times when you need me to take care of you.
That's how it should be.''

It was his turn to nod soberly as he moved imperceptibly
closer.

"Then I think we should go ahead with our plan to—"
the words stuck in her throat "—live together." Because
they weren't the ones she wanted to say. She hadn't found
the courage for them yet—but she would.

"I'm afraid living together isn't going to work out after
all, Laurel."

"It isn't?" She tried to keep the blank astonishment and
horrible disappointment out of her voice, with virtually no
success. All right. She took a huge mental breath. He had
caught her once. She was every bit as good as he was, she
assured herself. Now it was her turn. She would catch him.

He shook his head decisively. "No, it isn't. It's going to
have to be marriage or nothing."

"Marriage," she echoed hollowly. He did want marriage—before she'd prepared herself to accept, she realized
despairingly and with no small amount of self-disgust as
sudden panic blindsided her. My God, what was the *matter*
with her? He was offering her everything she wanted, and
the word that had almost come out of her mouth was *no?*

Marriage. He wouldn't walk out of her life if she said no,
but neither would they go on as they had. She would go
back to her house, alone, and they would go back to seeing
each other as their respective schedules permitted. That
wasn't what she wanted, but it seemed she hadn't con-
quered quite all her self-doubt after all. There were problems in any marriage simply from the fact of two people
trying to join their lives together, and she wouldn't kid herself that there wouldn't be more than the usual amount in
theirs. Cleese would try but he wasn't going to change ap-
preciably, and, if she was honest, she had to admit she didn't
want him to. That arrogant certainty that she was his to take
care of was part of what she had fallen in love with, but it

was going to take a strong woman to hold her own when he was at his most chauvinistic. She'd learned a few things about herself the past few months—out of bed, as well as in it—but had she learned enough? When she needed to stand up to him, could she? *Would* she? Could she finally silence that hateful but brutally honest worm of doubt forever?

She had to do it now, because if she didn't, she knew instinctively that she never would. No or yes? If she couldn't say "yes" with absolute certainty, then she would have to tell him no. His love and commitment to her deserved unequivocable commitment in return; she couldn't give him anything less.

Cleese waited in an agony of suspense. The stunned disbelief in her eyes became desperation, then dismay, then mutated into doubt before changing into something he couldn't read at all. Then, slowly...slowly, they changed again.

"Yes. Yes! *Yes!*"

He reached to take her in his arms, then found she was already there. Her mouth met his in a kiss that was frankly carnal yet oddly sanctified, too.

Minutes later, they climbed the stairs, arms around each other, tight. "You know, Texas is a community-property state," he mentioned, looking down at her. There was only one more thing he wanted, and he felt foolish and greedy for missing it when he'd just been given so much.

Her look of bafflement turned to a frown as understanding dawned. "Nooo...you might lose it."

"I won't lose it. I'll take good care of it."

She shook her head. "What if you ruin it? I only have the one."

"I won't ruin it. C'mon, just let me use it once," he wheedled.

"Welll..." She considered it. "No," she decided. "I'll make you one of your own."

He sighed deeply. "Well—okay."

They looked at each other, then burst out laughing, enjoying their ridiculousness.

Abruptly, she sobered. Her hand came up to cup his face gently. "Cleese," she said, "I love you."

He had everything.

*   *   *   *   *

Author's Note

Most of Laurel's and "L.J.'s" fishing experiences were my own. While the carp roundup was indeed hysterically funny at the time, L.J.'s experiences were funny only much, *much* later.

HE'S AN

AMERICAN HERO

He's a man's man, and every woman's dream. Strong, sensitive and so irresistible—he's an American Hero.

For April: KEEPER, by Patricia Gardner Evans: From the moment Cleese Starrett encountered Laurel Drew fishing in his river, he was hooked. But reeling in this lovely lady might prove harder than he thought.

For May: MICHAEL'S FATHER, by Dallas Schulze: Kel Bryan needed a housekeeper—fast. And Megan Roarke did more than fit the bill; she fit snugly into his open arms. Then she told him her news....

For June: SIMPLE GIFTS, by Kathleen Korbel: For too long Rock O'Connor had fought the good fight to no avail. Then Lee Kendall entered his jaded world, her zest for life rekindling his former passion—as well as a new one.

AMERICAN HEROES: Men who give all they've got for their country, their work—the women they love.

Only from

MILLION DOLLAR SWEEPSTAKES (III)
AND
EXTRA BONUS PRIZE DRAWING

No purchase necessary. To enter both prize offers and receive the Free Books and Surprise Gift, follow the directions published and complete and mail your "Match 3" Game Card. If not taking advantage of the book and gift offer or if the "Match 3" Game Card is missing, you may enter by hand-printing your name and address on a 3" X 5" card and mailing it (limit: one entry per envelope) via First Class Mail to: Million Dollar Sweepstakes (III) "Match 3" Game, P.O. Box 1867, Buffalo, NY 14269-1867, or Million Dollar Sweepstakes (III) "Match 3" Game, P.O. Box 609, Fort Erie, Ontario L2A 5X3. When your entry is received, you will be assigned Million Dollar Sweepstakes (III) numbers and be entered in the Extra Bonus Prize Drawing. To be eligible entries must be received no later than March 31, 1996. No liability is assumed for printing errors or lost, late or misdirected entries. Odds of winning are determined by the number of eligible entries distributed and received.

Sweepstakes open to residents of the U.S. (except Puerto Rico), Canada, Europe and Taiwan who are 18 years of age or older. All applicable laws and regulations apply. Sweepstakes offers void wherever prohibited by law. Values of all prizes are in U.S. currency. This sweepstakes is presented by Torstar Corp, its subsidiaries and affiliates, in conjunction with book, merchandise and/or product offerings. For a copy of the official rules of the Million Dollar Sweepstakes (III), send a self-addressed, stamped envelope (WA residents need not affix return postage) to: MILLION DOLLAR SWEEPSTAKES (III) Rules, P.O. Box 4573, Blair, NE 68009, USA; for a copy of the Extra Bonus Prize Drawing rules, send a self-addressed, stamped envelope (WA residents need not affix return postage) to: Extra Bonus Prize Drawing Rules, P.O. Box 4590, Blair, NE 68009, USA.

SWP-S494

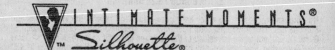

CONARD COUNTY

continues...

Once again Rachel Lee invites readers to explore the wild Western terrain of Conard County, Wyoming, to meet the men and women whose lives unfold on the land they hold dear—and whose loves touch our hearts with their searing intensity. Join this award-winning author as she reaches the POINT OF NO RETURN, IM #566, coming to you in May.

For years, Marge Tate had safeguarded her painful secret from her husband, Nate. Then the past caught up with her in the guise of a youthful stranger, signaling an end to her silence—and perhaps the end to her fairy-tale marriage.... Look for their story, only from Silhouette Intimate Moments.

ROMANTIC TRADITIONS continues in April with Carla Cassidy's sexy spin on the amnesia plot line in TRY TO REMEMBER (IM #560).

"Jane Smith's" memory had vanished, so when Frank Longford offered her a safe haven and a strong shoulder, she accepted. Then the nightmares began, with memory proving scarier than amnesia, as Jane began to fear losing the one man she truly loved.

As always, **ROMANTIC TRADITIONS** doesn't stop there! July will feature Barbara Faith's DESERT MAN, which spotlights the sheikh story line. And future months hold more exciting twists on classic plot lines from some of your favorite authors, so don't miss them—only in

IT'S OUR 1000TH SILHOUETTE ROMANCE, AND WE'RE CELEBRATING!

JOIN US FOR A SPECIAL COLLECTION OF LOVE STORIES
BY AUTHORS YOU'VE LOVED FOR YEARS, AND
NEW FAVORITES YOU'VE JUST DISCOVERED.
JOIN THE CELEBRATION...

April
REGAN'S PRIDE by **Diana Palmer**
MARRY ME AGAIN by **Suzanne Carey**

May
THE BEST IS YET TO BE by **Tracy Sinclair**
CAUTION: BABY AHEAD by **Marie Ferrarella**

June
THE BACHELOR PRINCE by **Debbie Macomber**
A ROGUE'S HEART by **Laurie Paige**

July
IMPROMPTU BRIDE by **Annette Broadrick**
THE FORGOTTEN HUSBAND by **Elizabeth August**

SILHOUETTE ROMANCE...VIBRANT, FUN AND EMOTIONALLY
RICH! TAKE ANOTHER LOOK AT US! AND AS PART OF THE
CELEBRATION, READERS CAN RECEIVE A FREE GIFT!

YOU'LL FALL IN LOVE ALL OVER
AGAIN WITH
SILHOUETTE ROMANCE!

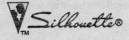

CEL1000

SILHOUETTE... Where Passion Lives

Don't miss these Silhouette favorites by some of our most distinguished authors! And now, you can receive a discount by ordering two or more titles!

D#05706	HOMETOWN MAN by Jo Ann Algermissen	$2.89 ☐
D#05795	DEREK by Leslie Davis Guccione	$2.99 ☐
D#05802	THE SEDUCER by Linda Turner	$2.99 ☐
D#05804	ESCAPADES by Cathie Linz	$2.99 ☐
IM#07478	DEEP IN THE HEART by Elley Crain	$3.39 ☐
IM#07507	STANDOFF by Lee Magner	$3.50 ☐
IM#07537	DAUGHTER OF THE DAWN by Christine Flynn	$3.50 ☐
IM#07539	A GENTLEMAN AND A SCHOLAR by Alexandra Sellers	$3.50 ☐
SE#09829	MORE THAN HE BARGAINED FOR by Carole Halston	$3.50 ☐
SE#09833	BORN INNOCENT by Christine Rimmer	$3.50 ☐
SE#09840	A LOVE LIKE ROMEO AND JULIET by Natalie Bishop	$3.50 ☐
SE#09844	RETURN ENGAGEMENT by Elizabeth Bevarly	$3.50 ☐
RS#08952	INSTANT FATHER by Lucy Gordon	$2.75 ☐
RS#08957	THE PRODIGAL HUSBAND by Pamela Dalton	$2.75 ☐
RS#08960	DARK PRINCE by Elizabeth Krueger	$2.75 ☐
RS#08972	POOR LITTLE RICH GIRL by Joan Smith	$2.75 ☐
SS#27003	STRANGER IN THE MIST by Lee Karr	$3.50 ☐
SS#27009	BREAK THE NIGHT by Anne Stuart	$3.50 ☐
SS#27016	WHAT WAITS BELOW by Jane Toombs	$3.50 ☐
SS#27020	DREAM A DEADLY DREAM by Allie Harrison	$3.50 ☐

(limited quantities available on certain titles)

	AMOUNT	$_____
DEDUCT:	**10% DISCOUNT FOR 2+ BOOKS**	$_____
	POSTAGE & HANDLING	$_____
	($1.00 for one book, 50¢ for each additional)	
	APPLICABLE TAXES*	$_____
	TOTAL PAYABLE	$_____
	(check or money order—please do not send cash)	

To order, complete this form and send it, along with a check or money order for the total above, payable to Silhouette Books, to: **In the U.S.:** 3010 Walden Avenue, P.O. Box 9077, Buffalo, NY 14269-9077; **In Canada:** P.O. Box 636, Fort Erie, Ontario, L2A 5X3.

Name: _____

Address: _____ City: _____

State/Prov.: _____ Zip/Postal Code: _____

*New York residents remit applicable sales taxes.
Canadian residents remit applicable GST and provincial taxes.

Silhouette®

SBACK-AJ